For Nom
Best wishes

Romance Language

a novel by

Alan Elsner

Portals Press

Cover Photo by Charles Platiau, Reuters News Service

Published by Portals Press
New Orleans, LA USA
www.portalspress.com

ISBN 978-0-916620-90-5

Library of Congress Cataloging-in-Publication Data

Elsner, Alan.
Romance Language : a novel / by Alan Elsner. -- Limited ed.
p. cm.
ISBN 978-0-916620-90-5
1. Young women--Fiction. 2. Americans--Romania--Fiction.
3. Romania--History--Revolution, 1989--Fiction. 4. Romania--Fiction. I. Title.
PS3605.L76R66 2009
813'.6--dc22

2009034083

Romance Language

For my students at "The Bullet"

Part I: Old Letters

"You take old letters from a crumpled heap,
And in one hour have lived your life again."
- Mihai Eminescu: Sonnet 1

1 – Bucharest, Romania: October 2007

"Purpose of visit?"

Petra hesitated.

"The reason for your visit. Why are you here?" the passport officer asked again.

Petra had been asking herself the same question for the past 24 hours. She'd left home the previous afternoon, still unsure whether she would have the courage to go through with her plan. Even while changing planes in Paris that morning, she could still have backed out. She could have spent a couple of days wandering through the art galleries, visiting the Eiffel Tower and Notre Dame, and then returned to college before anyone noticed her absence. It was only after she boarded her final connection that she was truly committed. It was by far the bravest, and probably the stupidest thing she'd ever done.

That last leg, on an airline she'd never heard of, was bumpy, making her even more anxious. After one jolt, the young man in the next seat took off his headphones, leaned over, flashed a brilliant smile and said something European. Her confusion must have shown because he instantly switched to almost perfectly accented American.

"Don't worry, the turbulence is pretty normal as we fly over the mountains."

"I'm not worried." Not about that.

"And our national airline has an excellent safety record."

"Good to know."

"So what brings you to my country?" He was wearing a black T-shirt emblazoned with the words *"Spawn of Dracula"* in large silver letters. Petra had been aware of him from the minute he sat down, carefully stowing a violin case under the seat.

"Studies," she muttered, looking away, twisting a lock of lank brown hair around her index finger. Petra figured he was maybe 22 or 23, five or six years older than her, with pale blue eyes and curly black hair. Guys like that—hunky, self-confident ones—always rendered her tongue-tied if they deigned to notice her at all. Her own red and black T-shirt read, *"Marblehead High School Mathletes, 2004."* Underneath in smaller letters it declared, *"Math Rocks The World."*

"I'm Mihai," he said, zapping her with another dazzling smile. "I know, it sounds strange to Americans. Call me Mike if it's easier."

"Petra," she said, reluctantly taking his outstretched hand.

"So what do you do?"

"Student." Petra tried to reclaim her hand; he was hanging on to it way too long, his fingers long and brown and strong. Perhaps this was a custom in his country. Still, it made her edgy.

"Wonderful. Me, I'm a graduate of musicology. Where do you study?"

"Brown University in Providence." He looked blank so she felt obliged to add, "It's in Rhode Island, south of Boston."

His face cleared. "Fantastic! I did a year at Indiana in Bloomington. So already we have something in common. What's your major?" He'd finally released her hand but now he was leaning even closer, giving her a close-up of his stubble. She could smell aftershave even though he certainly hadn't shaved for a day or two. She squashed herself back against the window.

"Literature, maybe creative writing. I'm not sure yet."

"Not mathematics?" he said, looking at her sweatshirt.

"No."

"And this is what—a semester abroad? Will you learn Romanian?"

What did he want from her? She was way too strung out to talk, too busy wondering what she'd do once they landed. How would she get to the city? Where would she sleep? She'd need to find a cheap hotel, hopefully not too skanky. She figured she had enough in her bank account for three or four weeks, but that should be ample time.

"Call me Mike" was still talking. "My country is very beautiful; you'll love it. And Romanian is what linguists call a Romance language, derived from Latin. The grammar is just like Latin, totally logical."

"Really?" Petra said, interested against her will. This wasn't among the half dozen random historical and geographical facts about Romania she'd memorized for high school general knowledge competitions.

"So where will you be staying?"

Petra was silent.

He laughed. "I know, I know. I'm asking too many questions. Bad habit."

She offered a flimsy smile. "I have a lot on my mind." Like, how long before they realize at college that I'm gone? And what's Mom going to do once she finds out? For a second, Petra felt a stab of guilt. Her mother would be frantic. Then she suppressed the feeling. If her mother had only told the truth, none of this would have happened.

He shrugged his shoulders, clearly hurt by her lack of response. "I can see you're wrapped up in your own thoughts. I'll let you rest. Sorry for the interruption."

"OK."

Petra closed her eyes. Now the conversation was over, she found herself half hoping he would talk to her again. But when she sneaked a peek, he'd put his earphones back on and was absorbed in his iPod. She felt really dorky. Why had she come off so rude and hostile? She could definitely have used a friend in Bucharest, someone who knew his way around, someone with a gorgeous smile. He ignored her until they landed, only offering a curt nod as they filed off the plane.

And now she was at passport control. The official looked up, comparing the pale, nervous creature before him to the mugshot taken three years ago when she still had braces and wore those horrible, thick glasses that made her look like she was about to go snorkeling.

"Purpose of visit?" the passport official asked again. "Business? Vacation? Study?"

What should she answer? That she was here to find her father? That she was here to find herself? Or perhaps, that she was just running away. The official's pen tapped impatiently on his desk.

"It's a family visit," she said at last.

"You have family here?"

"Yes."

"How long will you stay?"

"Two weeks, maybe three."

"Your relatives, they are Romanian?"

"He's a poet."

"What is his name? We are a nation of poets."

"Stefan Petrescu."

The officer looked surprised for a second; then he smiled broadly and declaimed a few lines in his language. Goodness, Petra hadn't realized her father was famous. The officer finished his recitation, stamped the passport and handed it to her with a flourish.

"Welcome to Romania."

2 - Massachusetts: October 2007

Dear Petra,

This letter is a peace offering. I know you're still angry with me—and perhaps you have a right to be. But I'm your mother, the only one you'll ever have. We need to find a way to get along.

I've been composing this letter on and off ever since you left for college. Of course, as a journalist, I'm used to sitting down behind the word processor, but this has been harder than any professional assignment I ever had. I hope you'll excuse its length and the fact that I'm sending it by what your generation so quaintly calls "snail mail." I know you're used to communicating through instant messages, or texting, everything rat-tat-tat to the point. Compared to you, I'm a technological dinosaur. Still, some things are too complicated to express through text messages.

When I dropped you at Brown, I'd been bracing for a bittersweet moment. We were both still mourning, still in pain. How proud your father would have been to see his little girl all grown up. The years of piano lessons, the spelling bees and geography quizzes, the debating competitions—they all paid off. Tom should have been there to help you move into your dorm. Instead it was just you and me. The silence between us that day really hurt.

Since then it's been more than a month and I've hardly heard a word. The few times we've talked on the phone, you've answered in monosyllables. You won't tell me about the friends you're making, your classes, your professors, which clubs you've joined or how you're spending your spare hours. I was willing to give you some time and space to get over your anger—but enough is enough. Petra, you're not a child any more so stop behaving like one.

Before we parted, you told me you believe your whole life was built on a lie. That simply isn't so.

Tom may not have been your biological father but he was in every other sense your real dad. He was there when you were born, the first to take you in his arms, and he tried to be there for you every day for 17 years. Why he wrote that final letter, I'll never know. We'd agreed years ago never to speak about your birth. He should have at least consulted me first before ripping open those old wounds.

For a while, I was furious—but what's the point being angry at a dead man? In any case, Tom didn't know the whole story. There were things I never told him, memories too precious to share.

I can see now it was a mistake to keep those secrets from you. You deserve to know exactly how you came into this world. This letter is the beginning of an attempt to tell you. I promise to leave out nothing, no matter how painful.

Let me start with the most important thing: Despite what you may think, Petra, you were conceived in love. My affair with Stefan Petrescu was not a casual fling. If it were, I would not have named you after him. Our story unfolded in desperate times and became entwined with the fate of an entire nation. I know that sounds pretentious, but as you read on, you'll see that it's true.

All summer, since Tom's funeral, it was easy to decipher your thoughts whenever you looked at me: "Slut, adulteress, cheat, liar, deceiver, seducer…" You could probably add other words as well—you have such a rich vocabulary. I'm not making excuses; the truth is, I was swept away by a force I couldn't have resisted even if I'd wanted to—and I didn't want to.

How can I make you understand the kind of rapture I had with Stefan? We burned with it. It was dangerous but we didn't care. In the end we paid a heavy price. The Bible says, "Greater love hath no man than a man lay down his life for his friend." For Stefan, that became the literal truth. He sacrificed himself to save my life—and yours.

That's what this letter is about. I want you to know how I met Stefan Petrescu and how and why it ended so badly. I'm going to take you back in time to 1989.

I started writing this a few days ago. Here's the first installment. More will follow soon.

Petra, please read this material carefully. When you've learned the whole story, you may still be angry at me. But at least you'll have the facts.

Love,

Mom

3 – Massachusetts: January 1989

Let me begin on the day Ralph Eskew made the telephone call that changed my life. It was a miserable winter afternoon and everything was going wrong. The washing machine was broken, the car was acting up and the twins would soon be arriving home, ravenous as usual. I was trying to finish a magazine article but it was impossible to concentrate. Tom was in a foul mood, as he'd been so often recently, snapping at whatever I said. He'd been working hard on his latest novel but it hadn't been going so well. It was he who answered the phone.

"Lizzie, it's that asshole editor of yours on the phone," he yelled from his study.

"OK, I got it. You can hang up."

"Tell the arrogant, fat-ass to get lost. Can't a man get a moment's peace and quiet, for the love of Christ? If it's not one fucking thing it's….."

I shut the door. "Hello Mr. Eskew."

"My word, Thomas sounds testy today."

"You heard that?" I was deeply embarrassed. Eskew was one of the most influential editors in America, but more than that, he was a valued mentor and friend. "I'm sorry, I don't know what to say. Tom hates being interrupted while he's writing."

"Relax Elizabeth, after a lifetime of dealing with writers, I have the hide of a rhinoceros," he said. "And of course, one must always defer to genius. But tell me, how is the 'Great American Novel' coming? One hears so many rumors. Shall it soon see the light after all these years of labor?"

I said nothing. It was a sensitive subject.

"Still blocked? Regrettable. That must be hard for you. I've always said, a blocked writer is like a blocked toilet, if you'll excuse the crudity. The waste words tend to bubble up into the living quarters."

I imagined him leaning back behind his desk in Harvard Square, chuckling at his own witticism, his gut straining the buttons of his tweed waistcoat, his bow tie slightly askew below his sagging, old man's neck.

"Thanks for returning my call," I said, anxious to get the subject away from Tom.

"Not at all, I was glad to hear from you. It's been too long. I think about you often. As you know, I've always hoped you'd find your way back to me, although I was sure by now you'd be settled deep into suburban bliss with an infant or two at your breast."

Ralph Eskew allowed himself to speak this way because he thought of himself as a living legend, which in some narrow circles—the only ones he cared about—he was. Now pushing 70, he had edited *The Brahmin*, the brightest, snootiest, wordiest weekly in America for the past 35 years. On first name terms with presidents, physicists and philosophers, he had published the works of almost every author of international note or notoriety since the Second World War.

"No, no babies so far, although I have my hands full looking after Tom's kids," I sighed, looking out the window at the falling snow. "I try to keep busy with freelance assignments here and there."

"Indeed, I saw your story in *The Globe* a few weeks ago about the proposed reconstruction of the major roadways of our fair city. An admirable piece of work, Elizabeth. You made it sound like a real scandal in the making. You've lost none of your ability. What else have you been doing lately?"

"That was the most challenging assignment I've had in a while. To be honest, you wouldn't be interested in most of my recent stuff. I've been doing a lot of work for women's magazines, writing about menopause and face lifts and diets."

"Your enthusiasm underwhelms me. But remember, this was your choice. Nobody forced you to leave *The Brahmin*. In fact I distinctly recall doing my best to persuade you to stay."

Eskew was notoriously tough on his reporters but his stony heart had always concealed a soft spot for me. He had hired me as a young reporter and gradually given me more and more opportunities. Under his guidance, I'd developed a particular interest in foreign policy and traveled all over Europe and Asia. Then, I'd given it all up to become wife of novelist Tom O'Neill and step-mother to his 12-year-old twin boys.

"At the time, leaving seemed like the right thing to do. I was newly married and expecting to become a mother. I thought family should come first."

"So what's changed?"

I forced myself to answer. "Tom isn't ready for more kids right now. He says his novel has to come first. After the last one flopped, this next one has to be brilliant. His career is riding on it. That's all he thinks about, all he does, all he is."

I sighed. "I guess great artists have always been self-absorbed but it's tough on the people who have to live with them. I did want to be a mother—I still do—but if that's not going to happen any time soon, perhaps it's time to go back to serious journalism."

"So your marriage is all about Tom, Tom, Tom."

"That's a bit unfair. He's having a rough time of it right now, as you guessed. He demands complete silence which is pretty tough with two young boys around. You have no idea how hard it is dealing with them. Do you know how much laundry two young tykes generate? No, of course you don't, how could you? And if it's not that, it's the shopping, or the cooking, or the cleaning or waiting for a man to come, because there's always something in the house that's broken or leaking or falling apart." I realized I was coming off self-pitying and pathetic, the last thing Eskew needed to hear.

"So you called me."

"I miss writing the big, in-depth stories, the kind I used to do for you. I was hoping …" I paused.

"You were hoping for an assignment."

"Yes."

"And what would you be willing to do?"

"How do you mean?"

"Would you, for instance, be willing to travel?"

I thought about it. "Sure, if it was a short trip, a few days or a week maybe."

"I see."

We were both silent for a moment, before Eskew spoke again. "Excuse me saying this, Elizabeth, but I can't help wondering why you put yourself in this spot. I warned you it wouldn't make you happy. You're a professional journalist for heaven's sake and a damn fine one, not a domestic drudge."

"I guess I was bewitched by Tom. The novelist and the journalist—we were a perfect match, that's what they all told us, a marriage made in heaven."

"You make it sound like a merger of two overlapping interests."

"What's wrong with two people sharing a love of language and literature?"

"You don't have to convince me of the power of language. Words have been my life. It's just, what you describe doesn't sound much like love. You know, you remind me a little of Martha Gelhorn, whom I had the honor to publish many years ago. She, like you, was a brilliant journalist who decided to tie her fate to that egotistical prick Ernest Hemingway, although it's doubtful she ever loved him. Unlike you, she did not abandon her career to cater to the great man's every need. Wherever there was a war or a conflict, Martha was there. While she was off reporting battles and revolutions, Hemingway would send her pathetic notes asking, 'If you're my wife, why aren't you here in my bed?' Martha once told me he was a rotten lover, all flag and no pole, despite the macho image. But here I am rattling on about things that happened 50 years ago while you wait for an answer."

"Not at all, this is interesting. So you think I should be more like Martha?"

"Martha's absence didn't seem to hurt Hemingway. While she was off in Finland covering the Soviet invasion, he was writing *'For Whom the Bell Tolls'*. Probably the best thing he ever wrote."

"I wonder who looked after his kids."

"I assume their mothers." Eskew paused for a second, wheezing. "The fact is, Elizabeth, I do have an assignment which might suit your talents—but I hesitate. From what you just told me, it may not fit your needs. It would involve more than a few days of travel."

"How many?"

"Perhaps a month or six weeks, perhaps longer."

My heart sank. Who would drive the twins around to soccer and boy scouts? Still, I had to know more.

"Where is it?"

"Romania."

"You've got to be kidding. Why Romania?"

"Romania has always been a tortured country but things have never been as bad as they are now. People are virtually starving because of the delusions of a petty, cruel, vindictive, tin-pot tyrant and his megalomaniac wife. I had occasion to spend time there when I was young, during my clandestine period. I still feel affection for its unfortunate people. I'm looking for a reporter with the talent, the determination and most of all the compassion to write a definitive exposé of the worst dictatorship the world has seen since the death of Chairman Mao."

It was widely rumored that Eskew had spent part of the Second World War as an undercover agent somewhere in Europe. This was the first time I'd heard him allude to it in person.

"And you think that person might be me? Of course, I've been to Eastern Europe before but never to Romania. I don't know much about it and I obviously don't speak the language."

"You have some French and Spanish, I believe."

"Yes."

"Then you'll manage. Romanian is a Romance Language, close to both of them as well as Italian. The problem will be finding people willing to risk talking to you in any language. It's a crime, severely punished, for Romanians to have any contact with foreigners. I'll be honest with you Elizabeth, you are not my first choice. But as it turns out, you may be my best hope. As you said, you've been to the Eastern bloc so you know how these communist societies operate. I've been trying to send a correspondent there for a couple of years without success. The two writers I put forward both had their visa applications rejected."

"What makes you think they won't reject me?'

"A new opportunity has arisen. I'll explain if you accept the assignment. It also helps that you have a relatively clean record. Unlike the men they rejected, you've been out of foreign policy for a while. You aren't on their radar screens. There's no reason for them to reject you."

"Haven't you got an assignment closer to home?"

"Sadly, not. It's Romania or nothing. Of course, that may change if you're willing to wait six months. But this is a real opportunity. If you do well, you'll instantly restore your professional standing. Other assignments would definitely follow."

"And you really think I could do it?"

"I do, Eliza. You have the rare ability to get inside other peoples' skins—to feel their pain, as it were. And I also believe you're tough enough to withstand whatever pressures the authorities may exert on you."

"I'd have to think about it." Even as I spoke, I was mentally listing all the many reasons I couldn't go. But I didn't want to turn Eskew down point blank.

"Of course," he was saying. "If you're really interested, we should sit down together. Shall we say Thursday at noon, here in my office? If it would help entice you, I can also offer lunch at Jaspers, where the scallops this time of year are truly heavenly."

"The twins have hockey after school on Thursdays."

"Ah. That is indeed a weighty consideration. I'd neglected to consider the transportation needs of the twins. But wait, a thought occurs! Could not Thomas be prevailed upon to drive them?"

He waited, knowing I would not refuse.

"Mr. Eskew, you're right," I said. "Let Tom drive for a change. I'll see you Thursday."

4: Bucharest: October 2007

Petra reclaimed her backpack, cleared customs and walked into the terminal concourse. The place was bustling with people holding up signs with names on them. Everyone seemed to be talking on cell phones, some with one in each ear. Of course, there was no-one waiting for her. No-one in the entire world knew she was here.

A runty-looking man stinking of cheap aftershave tried to grab her elbow. "Taxi? You need taxi?" She shook her head but he persisted. "Where you go? I cheap, very cheap." Petra started to feel uncomfortable; the guy was grossing her out. "Please, just leave me alone," she said. Finally, spotting a more promising victim, he let her go. She sighed in relief.

Now what? Get money. She saw a bank machine and inserted her ATM card. To her relief, it worked. The machine asked how much she wanted and she requested 400 *lei*, around $160 according to the signs posted at the money exchange booths. Eight 50 lei bills slid out, each bearing the picture of an ominous looking bird of prey on one side and a mournful guy with dark hair and a bushy mustache on the other. She put them carefully in her purse.

Next, she needed a bus to the city. Walking out of the building, she was greeted with a blast of hot, humid air and blinding afternoon light. She started walking up and down the sidewalk, but it was confusing. There were mini-vans, lots of them, lined up, all bearing different signs, none of which said "City Center" or anything similar. Petra started sweating, pushing her hair out of her eyes. She was terribly thirsty. Maybe she should go back to the terminal, find a bathroom, clean up a bit and then ask for help. Was it safe to drink the water here or were you supposed to buy bottled? Perhaps there was a desk where they could find her a cheap hotel or direct her to a youth hostel.

She was about to go back inside when a battered old car blaring foreign rap music pulled up. Petra saw two girls sitting up front, both speaking into cell phones, and turned away, assuming mistaken identity. Then, the rear door opened and a face stuck out.

"Need a ride?" It was Mihai, the guy from the plane. "Come on, get in, you can't just stand there. You'll be kidnapped by sex traffickers."

"Where are you going?" Petra asked.

"Downtown. These are my roommates. We'll take you to your dorm or wherever you like. Come on." He patted the seat beside him.

Petra handed him her backpack and got it, sinking into the broken upholstery while she tried to untangle a seat belt that looked as though it hadn't been used in years.

"You don't need that here. This is Romania, not Rhode Island," Mihai said.

The girl in the passenger seat up front closed her cell phone and turned around, smiling. "Hi, I'm Angela," she shouted above the music. She had alarming, purple hair, black lipstick and an almost perfect American accent. "This is Cristina," she said, indicating the driver who stuck a hand in the air without looking back.

"Petra."

"Great. Sit back, enjoy the ride. Where are you going?" the first girl asked.

"I need a cheap room for the night."

"What?"

"A hotel or a hostel, somewhere cheap," Petra yelled.

"You don't have a reservation?"

"No."

"OK, we'll figure something out."

They were driving down a four-lane highway lined with car dealerships and hoardings advertising cigarettes, computers, cars and casinos and others bearing slogans she couldn't translate.

Petra turned to Mihai. "Did you mean it about the sex traffickers?"

He flashed his widest smile yet. "It was a joke. Although for a sexy woman like you…"

She looked away feeling like an idiot. Meanwhile, the car had become stuck in a traffic jam and was barely moving. Angela and Christina were conversing in their language, the radio was still blasting Balkan pop, the air smelled of vehicle fumes and Mihai's cell phone was ringing. Petra yawned and looked at her watch which she hadn't yet adjusted to local time. Back home, it was only seven in the morning and she'd still be in bed. Three hours from now, she was supposed to be at her *Introduction to Modern Poetry* class. Petra realized she'd been up for over 36 hours straight. She felt like she was sitting in a puddle of her own sweat. She yawned again and closed her eyes.

5 - Massachusetts: January 1989

I dressed carefully for my lunch with Eskew, choosing a black sheath dress under a fitted grey jacket with lightly padded shoulders. I'd worn it once before for an interview with the head of a local Chamber of Commerce, which had proven to be a mistake. The poor man had been quite intimidated. But I felt instinctively the dress was perfect for a battle of wits with my esteemed editor.

Recalling our phone conversation, I wasn't sure how well I'd handled it. Had I come across whiny and self-absorbed? I needed to erase that impression. Even if I didn't take this assignment, I was convinced there would be others, closer to home. The main thing was to get back in Eskew's good books. I strung a white gold necklace around my neck and chose a deep, crimson shade of lipstick. Silver, dangly earrings completed the ensemble.

I examined myself critically in the mirror. Under close scrutiny, there were the inevitable small signs of aging, but thank heaven I'd been blessed with good bone structure. Perhaps another dab of mascara? No, not necessary, I wanted to come across as professional rather than seductive.

I left a note on the kitchen table. "Tom, I've gone to Cambridge for a meeting. The boys have hockey practice after school. Make sure you take their pads and skates when you pick them up. Practice should be over around five. I'll be back for dinner."

I thought of asking him not to drink before driving but decided not to. It would only encourage him.

As soon as I entered the venerable quarters of *The Brahmin*, I wondered why I'd stayed away so long. I slipped quietly into the newsroom and stood unnoticed by the door for a moment, taking in the familiar, comforting sounds of murmured telephone conversations and the muffled clicking of keyboards. I still missed the clattering typewriters I'd grown up with, but they'd been phased out a few years before.

Then, someone looked up and called out my name, provoking a stampede in my direction. Eskew issued forth from his office chomping on his trademark cigar.

"Ah, there you are Elizabeth. Welcome back," he growled.

"You're back?" a colleague asked.

"We hope so," Eskew said putting a possessive arm around me. "Eliza, step this way, if you please. You can catch up with your colleagues later."

Seated behind his desk, he handed me a manila folder.

"What's this?" I asked.

"I wanted you to see why this story is important. Take a few minutes to glance through it," he said, puffing a noxious cloud in my direction.

The first paper was a press release from Amnesty International headlined, *"Treatment of Women Under Nicolae Ceaușescu."* It described how the Romanian dictator had banned abortion for all women under 45 even if the woman was sick or the pregnancy dangerous. "The fetus is the property of society," Ceaușescu had declared. I read how women were forced to undergo annual compulsory gynecological exams, with the results reported to the state. Some 25,000 women had died risking illegal abortions. Thousands of others simply abandoned their unwanted babies shortly after birth. Most wound up in horrific orphanages, subjected to all kinds of abuses. In Romanian hospitals, premature babies had died during government-ordered power cuts.

"This is barbaric," I said, giving Eskew the response I thought he expected. Of course, I knew I was being manipulated. Eskew had given me this document first hoping to get me riled up. I told myself to keep my wits about me and not make any commitments I might regret later.

"We're just getting started," Eskew replied grimly. I felt myself shrinking inside. But I had to at least pretend to take it seriously. The trick would be to convince him that I was gung-ho for the job but that it really wasn't suitable for my particular talents.

The next paper dealt with Ceauşescu's plan to destroy more than half of Romania's villages. Rural life was obsolete, he had decreed, and should no longer be tolerated. He'd also ordered scores of churches and tens of thousands of homes in one of Bucharest's most historic quarters razed to make way for a massive presidential palace, intended to be the largest building in the world.

"What do you think?" Eskew asked.

"It's awful, of course," I said. But the more I read the more determined I was not to subject myself to several weeks in this awful place.

"Elizabeth, my sources tell me people are almost starving to death over there. They spend their nights huddled in cold, dark apartments and their days scrabbling for black market supplies. And none of this is necessary. The Romania I remember was green and fertile, perfect for agriculture and rich in natural resources. Sure, they were backward but they were never starving. They had plenty of coal and oil. That was the main reason we were so interested in them during the war. They were supplying the Nazis with vital raw materials. Now, Ceauşescu sends almost everything they produce overseas and uses the proceeds to line his own pockets."

I was surprised at Eskew's passion. He really cared.

"What kind of piece are you looking for?" I asked. Having come all this way, I owed it to him to hear the full pitch.

"I want to expose the whole evil system. I admit I have a personal interest. When I was younger than you are now, I fell in love with the country and its people—one person in particular who is no longer alive—but this has much wider implications.

It's a universal story about how far a society can go to crush freedom and individuality and whether ordinary people have the courage to resist."

As Eskew paused for breath, I remained silent, trying to picture him as a young man head over heels with an exotic young Romanian woman. It was hard to picture.

"We'll give it the full treatment," Eskew resumed. "It will be a cover story and take up much of the magazine. I'm looking for someone who can describe these horrors in a way that people over here and around the world will understand. It will take time and patience. It's become very difficult for foreign correspondents to work there. Half the country is in the pay of the secret police and Ceauşescu has made it a crime for ordinary Romanians just to speak to foreigners. But I still think it could be done."

"How would I even get into the country?"

"Ah, I have a plan for that. But first, Jasper's scallops await."

It felt crass to eat so lavishly after hearing about the starving Romanians but Eskew had no such qualms. He started with a dozen oysters, slurping them with gusto, washing them down with a bottle of Chablis, which he pronounced "acceptable." I stuck with iced tea.

"The thing is," Eskew said, ripping off a chunk of bread, spreading it with a thick dollop of butter and cramming it into his mouth, "...The thing is, Elizabeth, something is stirring behind the Iron Curtain. Something very big indeed, I feel it in my gut." He patted himself affectionately on the stomach. "Things are opening up in the Soviet Union under this Gorbachev fellow and once people get a taste of freedom, they're not going to be satisfied with just a taste..." He ingested a scallop, chewing with relish. "They're going to want more and more. Eventually, I predict, the Soviets will face a choice. Do they crush reform, as they did in Hungary and Czechoslovakia in the fifties and sixties, or do they relax their grip? And if they relax their grip, what then?"

"What?"

"The whole monstrous system could come crashing down."

To me, this seemed preposterous. I'd grown up in the shadow of Soviet power and the Cold War and couldn't imagine a world without them. But I also knew Eskew was savvy and well-connected and I'd learned to respect his instincts.

"You look doubtful," he said, as if reading my thoughts.

"I guess I am. But even if what you say is true, how would that affect Romania? From what you told me, the country is in a category of its own."

"Romania is still part of Europe. What happens across their borders will affect them profoundly. Could an isolated Ceauşescu survive without Soviet support? The point is that Romania represents the most extreme form of tyranny left in Europe. That's what makes it a compelling subject. Eat up your scallops, my dear. We still have work to do but we can't leave without sampling Jasper's heavenly Grand Marnier soufflé, which I took the liberty of ordering in advance. And then, perhaps a brandy to finish."

Back in his book-lined office, Eskew loosened his belt, leaned back in his chair and sighed. I wished I could have done the same. My head was spinning from cigar smoke, rich food and wild talk. I told myself once again to keep a firm grip; otherwise I might find myself agreeing to the nutty venture before the afternoon was over.

"Take a look at this," Eskew said, shoving another folder across the desk. I pulled out a black and white photo of a young man scowling vehemently at the camera. It's hard after all these years to recall exactly what I felt at that moment. Of course, I've thought about it countless times. I do know there was an undeniable physical response—a sudden flush, an unnerving rush of blood that caught me by surprise.

"Who is this?"

"Stefan Petrescu, a Romanian poet. I published two of his poems back in '84."

I tried to collect myself, aware of Eskew's gaze across the desk. "Why does he look so peeved?"

"He has every reason to be peeved, as you so inadequately put it, Elizabeth. After I published his poems, he lost his teaching job and was arrested and beaten up by the *Securitate*—that's their secret police. When they released him, he was placed under house arrest for several months. He hasn't been allowed to publish a single a word since, although I'm sure his poems continue to circulate illegally underground. Eliza, you've been a journalist for quite a few years and you've interviewed hundreds, if not thousands of people. Let me ask you, have you ever met a real, genuine hero?'

"I guess that depends on what you mean by hero."

"Don't be cute with me, young lady. You know very well what I mean—a man who stands up for his principles and is prepared to suffer and even die for them?"

"I once met Solzhenitsyn."

"Then you know what I mean. I think this man, Petrescu, is cast in a similar mold. I feel partially responsible for what happened to him, even though it was his own decision and he knew what he was doing. I want you to find out how he's keeping body and soul together. Perhaps we can help—with money, or cigarettes..."

"Cigarettes?"

"Yes, apparently Kent cigarettes have become the most accepted medium of exchange in Romania. Their local currency isn't worth the paper it's printed on."

"You have to be kidding. Cigarettes are money?"

"They say a carton of Kents is worth $100 on the street— an absolute fortune for most Romanians. I'd also like you to tell Petrescu that he always has an open invitation from me to publish again in the pages of *The Brahmin*, whenever he feels able to do so."

I took another, closer look at this picture, noting the square jaw, long dark hair flopping over his forehead and thin, straight lips. And again, those burning recessed eyes under thick black eyebrows.

"Why would he do that after what happened last time?"

"Because, as the songster put it, fish gotta swim, birds gotta fly and true poets, my dear—they gotta write and publish. They can't help themselves. That's even truer in times of tyranny, when only the bravest souls have the courage to speak out. In Stalin's Soviet Union, poets like Anna Akhmatova were the conscience of the nation."

"I've read Akhmatova—she's heartrending. You're not saying Petrescu is in her class, are you?"

"Probably not, but we're not conducting a seminar in comparative literary analysis. We're talking about moral courage—the courage to stand up and speak out. Romania needs whatever free voices it can get. Why don't you read one of his poems and see what you think? I think there are a couple in the folder."

I pulled out a sheet of paper and read the poem to myself.

The Horse

My father was a lean, taciturn man
and his horse, Bogdan, was the same.
Sometimes, on autumn evenings, I'd see them
plodding home together,
a slow, silent walk,
old comrades,
stumbling and nodding together.

Summers, my brothers and I
would sneak into the orchard
to plunder luscious clusters
peaches, apricots, plums...
Remember!
We'd pelt each other with wormy, windfall apples.
Sometimes, we'd feed him some.
How sweet to be kissed on the hand by the gentle breath
of an old horse.

Almost despite myself, I was strangely moved, although I could not have said quite why. The poem was certainly not deep or profound. Still, it exuded a haunting melancholy. I said, "Well, it's kind of sweet but I don't see why anyone would lose their job over this."

"That's because you're reading as an American, not a Romanian. Here, almost nobody reads poetry at all and it has little cultural or political importance. Over there, every single word not approved by the state takes on immense significance. Words really matter. A poem like this is deeply subversive."

"How so?"

"First, it tells of a time where apples are so numerous that children throw them at each other and feed them to horses. Today, apples in Romania have become a rarely-seen, much longed-for treat, only available to most city dwellers on the black market. The orchard in the poem drips with peaches, plums and apricots—likewise, all unimaginable luxuries today. Then, there's the use of the word 'comrades' to describe the relationship between the man and his horse—which of course points out the fake comradeship of communism. The poem also alludes to the fact that not so long ago the communists were proudly proclaiming that the horse was obsolete, having been replaced by machines. They actually ordered all their horses slaughtered."

"They killed all the horses?"

"Fortunately, the order was not carried out. Ironically, today people are so short of gasoline that the country has returned to the age of the horse and cart. But getting back to the poem, Eliza, you yourself picked up on its most important feature which is its sweetness and innocence. It evokes a simpler, better time—a time before Ceauşescu. The key word is *'remember!'*—by which the poet means, remember when life was different, better. That word alone is an unendurable rebuke to the regime. You told me on the phone the other day how much you loved literature. You said your shared love of words is what brought you and Tom together. If that's the case, you ought to appreciate a man like Petrescu who really lives by that credo. He knew exactly what he was doing when he wrote those lines—and the personal price he might pay for them."

"And you think a poem like this can make a difference?"

"Who knows what really makes a difference? Some day, when this nightmare is over and Ceauşescu is nothing but a bad memory, perhaps people will step forward and say that poetry made a difference, the way it did in the Soviet Union. I certainly pray that will be so."

There was silence while I absorbed this and sneaked another peak at the poet, who now seemed to radiate intensity and moral strength. What would I say to such a man, me with my $120 hair-dos, my manicures, my designer dresses and jewelry? What would he say to me? I felt something inside shifting almost imperceptibly. This was madness. I had a life, responsibilities—Tom, the twins. But I found myself wondering what color his eyes were.

"I'm not saying I'm going," I said. "But just out of interest, what is your grand plan for getting me into this hellhole?"

"Excellent," said Eskew, rubbing his pudgy hands together. "I knew I could count on you."

6 – Bucharest: October 2007

Petra awoke to a cacophony of dogs growling and barking outside her window. She opened her eyes and found herself in a double bed. In the pale light, she could see another girl lying next to her, dark hair spread out on the pillow like a fan. Petra jerked upright, fumbling for her glasses, finding them on a bedside table. Someone had removed her jeans and bra; she was wearing only a T-shirt and panties. She glanced at her watch—just past one o'clock. Then she remembered, she was in Romania, seven hours ahead of the United States. Here, it was already eight in the morning. She must have slept all night next to this girl whose hair she now saw was purple, the one with the black lips. What was her name? Angela? Now, it was coming back. She remembered Mihai trying to rouse her as the car pulled up outside a house on a cobbled street. She was so exhausted she could hardly move. One of the girls had led her like a sleepwalker up some steps and through the front door.

"Why not just stay here tonight? We'll help you find where you need to go tomorrow," she'd said. Petra had just nodded thankfully, allowed herself to be taken into a bedroom and put to bed like a child. How humiliating!

She got out of bed, needing to find a bathroom, and padded

barefoot out of the room, polished wooden floorboards creaking beneath her. She found herself in a corridor with closed doors on either side. The house was silent. Now what? The last thing she wanted was to burst into a stranger's bedroom. The corridor opened into a large, rectangular living room with a picture window at the far end that looked out over a garden where washing hung on a long line strung between two trees. Inside, one wall was covered by a massive mirror. Petra glanced at herself, then turned away miserably. She looked like a little lost girl.

Now she heard the sound of a violin playing Bach from one of the rooms and remembered that Mihai had been carrying an instrument with him on the plane. She could tell after just a few seconds that he played really well. Knocking on the door, she opened it a crack. He was sitting on a chair facing her, violin tucked under his chin, hair in glorious disarray, a look of intense concentration on his face. Petra was so captivated by his face it was a few seconds before she realized he was stark naked. She slammed the door shut, and stood trembling. It had just been a fleeting image but she knew she would remember it forever.

"Hey there, wait a second, I'll be right out," he called, as if nothing out of the ordinary had occurred. Petra was about to cry; she thought about retreating to the bedroom but before she could move, Mihai came out wearing jeans and a T-shirt bearing the legend, *"Experience Preferred."* Well, that certainly ruled her out. Her own shirt read, *"Quizmaster Classic, January 2005."* Couldn't get much dorkier than that.

"Good morning," he said, smiling like butter wouldn't melt in his mouth.

"Hello." She could tell her face was as red as a tomato. Damn him, even his eyelashes were longer than hers.

"What is this *Quizmaster*?"

"It's a high school general knowledge contest," she said, suddenly unsure whether he was interested in the T-shirt or what was under the T-shirt. This was all new and strange; she'd never been leered at before.

"You mean, where you are asked all sorts of problematical questions and you have to hit a buzzer before the other contestants? Like *Jeopardy*?"

"Yes, that's it."

"I saw this on TV in America. So strange! We do not have it here. So you are a kind of young genius."

"I just like collecting random facts."

He smiled. "So, tell me young genius, what is the capital of … of Azerbaijan?"

"Baku. And I'm not a genius, not really. I just remember stuff."

"And what was I playing on the violin when you burst into my room?"

She blushed again, lowering her eyes. "Bach," she whispered.

"And do you also know anything about our country? Who was the first king of modern Romania?"

"I don't know."

"You are cute when you blush. To save you the trouble of finding out, it was Carol I." He put his hands on her shoulders as if he were about to pull her to him, then let her go when he felt her flinch. "OK, never mind. So which would you like to do first? Shower? Get dressed? Eat some breakfast?"

"Um, bathroom."

"Of course, this way."

Mihai was waiting patiently when she emerged. "Would you like to call your family to let them know you've arrived? You could use the phone as long as you keep it short."

"What? I guess so. I mean, maybe not. Maybe I could email."

"Of course." He shoved a pile of magazines to the side and sat her down on a sofa in front of a coffee table, clearing a space between half-empty wine glasses, candles, magazines and ash-trays full of cigarette butts. It looked like she'd slept through quite a party.

"You can use my laptop," he said, tapping the keys to set her up.

Petra logged on to the Brown network. Ignoring emails from professors and friends, she thought for a minute before typing:

"mom, hope you're ok. i'm doing fine, having lots of new experiences. classes have been getting pretty interesting. in poetry,

we're studying whitman, ultimate cool stuff. i actually want to start reading some modern european poets. i also might start learning a new language." She backed up and deleted those last two sentences before continuing. *"my calculus class is pretty easy. i already did it all last year in school. boooring! i joined the choir. they will be doing handel's messiah for christmas which ought to be ultra cool."*

She paused again. Petra felt bad about lying. Actually everything she'd written was factually true, yet it was all meaningless since she was here in Bucharest, not Providence. But there was no way to come clean without endangering the entire purpose of her trip. She continued: *"mom, there's something wrong with my cell phone. it stopped working. i'm trying to get it fixed but it might take a while. so don't worry if you always get voicemail when you call me. the best way to reach me is by email. say hello to everyone back home, love, petra."*

She hit send and then began composing a message to her roommate, to whom she'd hardly spoken all semester, taking care over the wording.

"andie, i had to go away for a few days. major drag but shit happens, right? don't worry if you don't see me for a while. if anyone asks, say i'm dealing with a family situation and i'll be back soon, petra."

7 – Massachusetts: February 1989

"What are you reading?" Tom asked.

"A poem," I said, relieved we were finally speaking again.

"Who's it by?"

"Stefan Petrescu. A Romanian."

"Never heard of him. Shove it over, let's have a look."

We were lying side by side in bed, not touching. For the past four days, I'd been wrestling with my decision. I'd left Eskew's office still intending to turn him down but hadn't been able to pick up the phone to tell him. There was something intoxicating in the thought of getting on a plane and flying far, far away, leaving all my troubles behind. It was a fantasy of course; I knew I had my life, my marriage, my daily routine. I hadn't mentioned the possibility to Tom, who'd been furious that I'd skipped out even for a day.

"Don't you ever disappear on me again like that?" he'd yelled. "I need you here. Don't you understand I'm at a particularly crucial point in the book right now? I can't have any distractions." For the next three days, he'd given me the silent treatment, closing himself in his study in the mornings, leaving each evening to meet his buddies at an Irish tavern, returning after midnight well stewed.

I spent those evenings alone, wondering how he could have changed so much from the witty, debonair man who'd introduced me to all his artistic friends and charmed me with red roses, gourmet meals, scintillating conversation and weekend getaways to romantic country inns. Of course, I knew how much the novel was weighing on him. Tom was desperate to redeem himself after the critical panning his last book had received. But why take it out on me and the boys? Miserable though I was, I knew in my heart this wasn't the time to run away. I still fully intended to stand by my man. On the other hand, a little voice inside my head kept whispering that perhaps a time out would be good for us.

Tom scrabbled for his reading glasses. Glancing at him, I was newly aware of the 15-year gap between us. Tom didn't look good. His eyes were puffy and bloodshot, his nose red and bulbous, his neck wrinkled like parchment as he hunched over to read. In his striped pajamas, I thought he looked faintly ridiculous. How long was it since we had made love? Six weeks? Two months? Somehow I knew he was going to absolutely hate Petrescu's poem.

The Poet's Silence

I am exiled from my body,
I've broken relations with my mind
— like strangers on stairs we nod in passing.

I've piled high a dike,
Finger in mouth, holding back words
— I feel them lapping against my throat

In naked nights, a still small voice,
Above wind and earthquake and fire
— Sometimes, I swear I hear it.

A flick of the mighty finger
pulverizes streets, squares, churches
— but words like weeds push through cracks in concrete.

"What do you think?" I asked, wanting him to like it.

"Pretentious bullshit," Tom said, disdainfully tossing the poem aside. "I wish I could get away with crap like that. Words forcing themselves out indeed! He probably tossed it off in quarter of an hour. I tell you, real literature is a lot harder work than that." With distaste, I noticed his Adam's apple bobbing up and down in his throat like a cork in water.

"Perhaps he experiences creativity differently from you?" I said mildly.

"You betcha he does. He scribbles down a few random thoughts and calls it poetry, while I'm trying to do justice to the vast, panoramic tapestry of life, with all its joy and heartbreak, triumph and sorrow. You think that's easy? You think the words just flow, just push themselves out of me? I have to squeeze them out, every single one, and sometimes they don't want to be squeezed." He was shouting.

"He says he hears a still, small voice. Is that what you hear?"

"What am I, an Old Testament prophet? Gimme a break. I hear a whole cavalcade of voices, all jostling to be heard, none of them small and quiet."

"Maybe you're trying to do too much in this one book."

"Well that's fucking grand. How can an artist try to do too much? You think I ought to be able to churn out a couple of thousand words a day on demand like you do for your magazine articles. But I'm not writing about lipstick and lingerie. Literature doesn't work like that, creativity doesn't respect deadlines. Making art is not like making sausages."

I tried to keep my temper. "I never knew you felt that way about my journalism. I don't mean the women's magazine stuff I'm doing now, although it pays the bills, but what about the investigative reporting I used to do for *The Brahmin* before we were married? Some of that was pretty good."

Tom didn't reply.

I tried again, hoping to keep the conversation going. As belligerent as he was, I still preferred his words to his silence. "Anyway, aren't there different ways for artists to express themselves? You can be a Charles Dickens or an Emily Dickinson. Some people write hundreds of pages like you; others a few eloquent lines like Petrescu."

"Are you comparing my work to his? I don't fucking believe this."

"I'm not comparing them directly. I'm just saying great art can be deceptively simple, like Cezanne painting a plain pile of peaches on a white table cloth—so spare and understated yet it says so much."

"Bullshit. You obviously don't understand anything about what I'm trying to do in this book—the magnificent enormity of it."

"Is that my fault? You won't show me a word. I see page after page crumpled up in the trash every day but how much have you actually written? You have other responsibilities as well, you know—to be a good father, a good husband, a decent human being. Just because you think you're a genius doesn't excuse you from your obligations. I know you think you're America's answer to Tolstoy— but what if you're not? How long are you going to keep trying?"

The conversation had suddenly taken on an ugly edge but I was not about to back down. We had instinctively moved apart and were glaring at each other from opposite edges of the bed.

"Here we go. You think I don't hear you and my agent and my publisher and all the critics and the press looking at me every single day, asking, 'When will it be done, when will it finally be done'?" Tom said heatedly. "Well here's the answer, Missy Journalist, and you can quote me on it: It will be done when I say it's done, when I'm good and ready for it to be done. It might be three years, it might be five—whatever it takes to realize my vision. In the meantime, you can all eat me, like a plate of Cezanne's fucking peaches."

"And what am I supposed to do for five years?" I knew I was upping the ante but I couldn't help myself. I was aware of a large, painful lump in my throat.

"Do? Your job is to support me, to be there for me, to get food in the fridge and meals on the table, even though you can't cook for shit. Your job is to keep the kids out of my way so I can write. I thought you understood when you signed up for this."

"No I didn't," I hissed. "That wasn't the deal at all. I thought you wanted a partner, a soul mate, a lover—not a maid." I snatched a Kleenex from the box on my bedside table and angrily dabbed my eyes.

Tom shook his head, apparently surprised to see me so upset. "I do, Lizzie. And once the book is a success, we'll get back to that. I just need time and space to finish. Just two or three more years."

At that moment, I decided. I didn't want to put my life on hold for two or three more years.

"Tom, I've been offered an assignment," I said, not quite believing I was actually saying it. "Mr. Eskew wants me to go overseas for a month, maybe longer. And I've decided to go."

"Overseas? Where?"

"Romania. He wants me to write an exposé of the regime. I'll be leaving as soon as I can get a visa. I think we could both use a break from each other."

Even as I spoke, I think I was half-hoping Tom would persuade me to change my mind. Just a few, tender words might have done the trick. But that was not his reaction.

For a second, as his face reddened, I thought he was about to hit me. I lifted my arm to stave off the blow. Instead, I felt his big, brawny arms pushing me—not particularly violently but firmly—and then I was tumbling out of bed. I landed, more shocked than hurt, in an undignified heap on the carpet.

Tom leaned over. "Romania? You think you're going to fucking Romania?" he shouted, his lips flecked with spittle. "No you're not. Not if you value your marriage. Not if you want a place in my bed."

From my position on the floor, the room looked different—the blond wood furniture, my silk scarf flung carelessly over the chaise, the sleek, Danish audio system, the Escher lithograph above the bed, all the empty symbols of my life. I caught sight of myself in the mirror over the dresser, shaken and vulnerable like a little girl who just fell off a bike. Summoning all the dignity I could muster, I hauled myself into a sitting position, readjusting the straps of my nightgown.

"It's not your bed, it's our bed. At least, it was. But you can have it. It's obviously not big enough for both of us. I'll sleep in the living room tonight and I'll be out of here tomorrow. Please don't try to stop me." I stood up and reached to take a spare blanket out of the closet.

"Don't count on coming back. If you walk out of this house, you'll be walking out of this marriage as far as I'm concerned," he yelled.

"What marriage?" I asked bitterly, closing the door behind me.

8 – Massachusetts: October 2007

Dear Petra,

Here is the second installment of my memoir. I've been working on it for the past few days. It describes my arrival in Romania and what I found there.

I've had a lot of time recently, sitting in this empty house. It's hard to get used to being so alone. I've been thinking of selling it. It's too big now that you've left. How would you feel about that? I know it could be a big wrench, first losing your father and then losing the home you grew up in. But it could also be a new beginning. I could get an apartment in Boston, right in the heart of the city. You'd have your own room for weekends and vacations and we could go to the ballet or the symphony or the Museum of Fine Arts whenever we liked. Let me know what you think. I won't do anything until I've heard from you.

Sometimes, when I come home, I forget you're not there and call out to you. Often, I think about getting in the car and driving down to Providence just to see your face. Don't worry, I won't actually come. I'm not one of those clinging parents who can't let go. You deserve the chance to enjoy your independence. We'll see each other at Thanksgiving and that will be soon enough.

Still, I'd like to hear more from you—not just those brief, non-descript emails you've been sending. You don't respond to my phone calls, though I've left several messages. I received your email saying your cell phone was broken, but why is it taking so long to fix?

I was especially anxious to hear your reaction to the first part of my story. Haven't you had time to read it yet? Your last message didn't mention it at all. Perhaps you were upset about the harsh way I described the argument I had with Tom before I left. You have to realize that he was at a low point then, struggling with a book he was destined never to finish. That novel was like a cancer, devouring him from within. It had eaten away at our marriage. Who could have imagined that you would come along to save him?

The book he wrote in the first year of your life—that slim, funny, modest, charming book—became his true legacy. Wherever he went, people would introduce themselves and thank him for writing it. Life is strange. Tom wanted to write an American '*Brothers Karamazov*' or '*Great Expectations*'—but he wound up writing about the miracle of becoming a middle-aged father. It was so sweet and honest and wise that no-one could resist it. Thousands of people wrote to him over the years to say how it had touched them. That meant the world to him. And it still sells like crazy. It's paying your college fees.

Petra, I'm not just writing this to explain how you came to be conceived. I also want you to understand on a deeper level what happened to me in Romania. It was the decisive experience of my life. Looking back, I see that my fate was sealed the moment Eskew gave me that black and white photo of Stefan Petrescu. I still carry it around with me to this day, together with a poem he wrote for me which I've never shown anyone.

What was the *real* reason I accepted the Romania assignment? Was it to meet the man in the photograph, or to escape from Tom, or to revive my journalistic career? Probably there were elements of all three. I do know I was seeing Petrescu's face in my dreams long before I actually met him in person. Can you fall in love with a photograph? The idea seems childish, absurd—but I still remember what I felt. It was like a shaft of light penetrating my heart. I know that must sound ridiculous to you. After all, I hear you saying, the heart is only a muscle, not an organ that feels emotion. But there is such an emotion and science cannot fully explain it. The Italians have a phrase for it— *il colpo di fulmine*. It means, 'the thunderbolt of love.' Once struck, you never forget.

I once had a discussion with Petrescu about memory. He said he would never regret our time together and that remembering it would always inspire him, no matter what happened to us. I hope it did but I seriously doubt it. For me, these memories are almost insupportable. Whatever happiness we experienced was far outweighed by all the suffering later.

Almost 18 years have passed since the last time I saw him. Our final hours together were on December 22, 1989, the day on which the Romanian people rose up against the dictator. That evening, with Bucharest in flames, amid the chaos of the fighting and the dying, disaster struck. I'll never see him again, not in this world. But I dream about him still. Did I do the right thing, abandoning him in his hour of need? For years, I was racked by guilt. But what was I to do? I had you, my unborn child, to think of. I needed someone to look after me. Tom stepped forward.

Petra, I see now how wrong we were, Tom and I, to keep this from you. You deserve the truth. You need to know everything,

Love,

Mom

9 – Massachusetts/Timişoara, Romania: Feb. 1989

I had to admit, Eskew's plan for getting me into Romania was crafty.

"I have a great-nephew, 13 years old, who happens to be a formidable chess player, one of the best in the country for his age," he explained when we met again in his office two days after my argument with Tom.

"Why doesn't that surprise me?"

"It so happens that the world championship for players 13 and under will take place later this month in Romania, in the city of Timişoara, in the west of the country near the Hungarian border. William has qualified but sadly, neither of his parents can get away from their jobs to accompany him and obviously he cannot go alone."

"Wouldn't you like to go with him?"

"Don't be silly, Eliza, I'm far too old to go traipsing around Eastern Europe with a teenage boy and I have an important weekly magazine to manage. You, on the other hand, would make the perfect chaperone. You'll remain in Timişoara with young Will for the 10 days of the tournament. Then, you'll simply see him safely on to the plane back home, after which you'll be free to remain and begin your investigative work."

"And you think I'd get a visa for this?"

"It's our great opportunity. The Romanians are anxious for the tournament to be a success. William is one of only three invited competitors from the United States and I know for a fact that the other two are not going. I shall inform the embassy that if your application is rejected, William will also be unable to make the trip. I don't think they'll make any trouble; they're desperate for American participation. If all goes well, you'll receive a standard three-month visa—more than enough time to get the job done."

"But wouldn't I be going under false pretenses?"

"Not at all. We'll state on the application that you are a journalist and that you intend to stay after the tournament. You'll need to present yourself to the Information Ministry in Bucharest once

Will has left and follow their tiresome regulations. The rest will be up to you. Did you bring your passport today, as I requested?"

"Yes."

"Excellent. My assistant has the paperwork. You can fill out the forms right now and we'll courier them straight down to the embassy. You can meet William and his parents this evening. If everyone gets along, we'll have you on the plane in a couple of weeks. My only request is that you not try to do any journalism while the tournament is underway to avoid jeopardizing William's participation. Just wait until he's safely out of the country."

The Soviet-made plane belonging to the Romanian state airline Tarom did not inspire confidence. It boarded two hours late and sat on the runway in Germany for another 90 minutes before takeoff without a word of explanation from the crew, during which time I became increasingly nervous. One half of my seatbelt was orange, the other blue. If they were cobbling together the seatbelts from spare parts, I thought, God knows what they were doing with the engines. There was a weird silence on the half-empty aircraft—the passengers all seemed sunk in their own private gloom. There was no food or drink service.

William was a singularly self-possessed young man, small for his age with round spectacles and tousled hair. He had spent much of the previous flight from Boston to Frankfurt fiddling with a magnetic chess set, apparently playing against himself. He didn't talk much; I wasn't sure if he was shy or just naturally quiet.

"What are you doing?" I asked at one point.

"I'm just reviewing the Sicilian Defense," he said. "Mainly the dragon and poisoned pawn variations." This was the most he'd said since I'd met him.

"Why is it called Sicilian? It sounds quite romantic."

"Romantic?" The term plainly baffled him.

"Evocative—blue skies, fortified medieval villages, terraced hillsides, olive trees, vineyards…"

"It's a chess opening. It doesn't have anything to do with

olives. It's one of the most common openings. I like playing it when I'm black but I have trouble against it when I'm white. There are too many different variations to learn. You don't play chess, do you?"

"My father taught me the moves when I was a girl but I haven't played for years. I was never much good anyway—not even good enough to know the difference between the Sicilian Defense and the Sardinian Defense."

He snorted impatiently. "There's no such thing."

"Maybe you could invent it."

"That's dumb. Chess doesn't work like that. Kids don't invent new openings."

"Why do you have to study so hard?"

"The thing is, some of the people I'll be playing against have their own coaches to practice with and teach them openings, especially the Russians. So they have a big advantage. They can play lines I've never seen and they know the analysis."

"Is that important?"

William gave me a pitying look. He obviously thought I was simple-minded.

"It means almost every move I make, they've seen before," he said patiently. "So I'm not just playing against them. I'm playing against their coaches too."

"That doesn't seem fair."

He looked me straight in the eye. "Life's not fair is it?"

Duly rebuked by the child, I left him to his studies.

The countryside out the window as we descended toward Timişoara looked flat and barren with large snow-covered fields interspersed with forests. We taxied to a halt, disembarked and were immediately surrounded by soldiers carrying submachine guns who herded us into the terminal, swiftly separating the Romanians from the few foreigners. One man took a camera out of his carry-on. The guards rushed forward shouting for him to put it away. Thinking of the comfortable life I'd left behind and the next few weeks facing me, I wondered if I'd made a huge mistake.

Even when we identified ourselves as participants in the

chess tournament, it took another couple of hours to fill out the paperwork and collect our luggage and another hour to get to the city, by which time we were both exhausted. The border officials were particularly interested in my battery-operated word processor, the likes of which they had evidently never seen before. It was a little technological wonder for those days, with about 12 lines of text on the small screen. You could transmit text over a phone line, although it later became clear that it didn't work in Romania where all the lines were monitored by the secret police. After much muttered conversation, the officers decided to let it go.

The hotel room we shared, which I assumed was the best Timişoara had to offer, could be described as basic—and that was being generous. The sheets were wrinkled and threadbare, the carpet frayed, the wallpaper discolored with little burn marks where previous guests had put out their cigarettes and there was an abiding stink of stale smoke. The decorative motif was brown—brown walls, brown carpets, brown bedding and brown rings around the drains in the bath tub and toilet.

I was glad I'd thought to bring two rolls of American toilet paper, as well as a thick, flannel nightgown that buttoned up to the neck to spare either William or myself embarrassment. At least, there was enough hot water for a bath that first night and the room was adequately heated.

The hotel that evening offered a formal banquet for the foreign delegations attending the tournament. There were long speeches in unfamiliar languages without benefit of translation. William and I were seated at a table with British and Canadians participants, all equally bewildered by this strange world we had entered. The menu featured an uninviting form of "mystery meat" and very little else. It was served by elderly waiters wearing old-fashioned blue uniforms with frayed gold piping. A tinny sound system played wailing violin music. All the Eastern Europeans were smoking.

The shop in the foyer sold Romanian Pepsi, which according to William tasted "really weird—kind of bitter and sweet at the same time." I bought half a dozen bottles of water that first evening and told William to use them even when brushing his teeth. All purchases had to be made in dollars. Fortunately, I'd stuffed my suitcase with canned tuna, crackers, peanut butter, apple sauce and cookies. We wouldn't starve, at least not for a few days.

Next morning, the tournament began. I watched for a while, but not understanding what was going on, soon wandered off down a broken escalator, which looked as if it hadn't functioned in years. Both sides of the street were piled with heaps of snow several feet high. People, most in thick woolen overcoats down to their knees and heavy work boots, trudged in single file down narrow, icy pathways on the sidewalk. Romanians, it seemed, did not believe in snow removal. They had a curious way of half-walking, half-sliding, shoulders hunched, feet close to the ground. I observed them for a few moments, breathing the heavy, smoggy air, shivering as the cold tried to find a way inside my jacket. After a couple of minutes, my hands were freezing inside my gloves and the tips of my ears were numb. I was struck by the lack of color. No reds, no yellows or greens—everybody wore the same dark brown or black.

I ducked into a store and waited for my eyes to adjust to the gloom. The city was evidently having one of its regular power cuts. A few salespeople hung around in the shadows talking to each other in low voices—they all froze when I entered but no-one approached. Anyway, there was almost nothing for them to sell. I didn't stay long before stumbling back out the doorway, almost slipping on a frozen puddle. In the stairwell leading back to the street were two posters lettered in bright red. I took off my gloves and wrote down the slogans in my notebook; later I had one of the tournament organizers translate them.

One said, *"Long Live Our Heroic Working Class Under The Leadership of Comrade Nicolae Ceauşescu."* The other, *"We will not rest until we have stamped out the last vestiges of formalism and superficiality."*

I started walking aimlessly, glad I'd brought my American ski parka and a sensible pair of boots. Some people stared, obviously registering me as a foreigner, before averting their eyes and hustling on their way. There were a few beggars on the streets—wizened old men and women with rheumy eyes and no teeth, flaunting ghastly disabilities.

I went into a fruit shop. It had nothing to offer except a few heads of cabbage and what looked like plastic bags full of nettles; a milk store next door displayed only empty shelves and cobwebs. There was a long line waiting in a butcher shop for the chance to buy chicken feet, the only item for sale. But at a street corner, a crowd suddenly gathered around a man who had opened up a canvas bag. I drew closer and saw he was selling apples, which reminded me of Stefan Petrescu and his poem about the horse. Within minutes, the produce was gone.

As the days passed, I was to see this scene repeated again and again. Sometimes, a truck would pull up and someone would start selling cigarettes or other black market goods from the back. Scores of people would instantly materialize for the chance to buy food, or Western items they could later barter for food, and disperse just as quickly before the police could arrive. My own two cartons of Kent cigarettes remained safely stowed in my suitcase.

When I returned to the hotel, I discovered William had won his first match against a French player. He and some of the other competitors spent the afternoon playing what they called "blitz games," where each player had only a couple of minutes to complete all their moves. The Soviet and Romanian players, who did not mix with the Westerners, had disappeared to huddle with their coaches.

I watched for a while. William was a different kid surrounded by his peers—he slammed his hand down on the chess clock whenever he made a move; at one point, both he and his opponent dissolved in laughter. They were from different countries but clearly shared a common language in chess.

"What's going on?" I asked during a break in the action.

"Suicide."

"What's that?" I asked, a little concerned.

"It's when you try to lose a chess game on purpose," William said. "Could we get a hamburger for dinner? I think I deserve one."

"I doubt it," I replied. "I'm not going to that restaurant again if I can help it. God knows where that meat came from. We'll eat in the room. You can have tuna on crackers, or any of the other stuff I brought, and there's chocolate for dessert. Don't look at me like that; compared to the people who have to live here, we're lucky. But first we should call your parents to tell them about your victory."

It took almost an hour for the hotel switchboard to patch the call through and there was a lot of clicking on the line.

I thought about calling Tom but decided not to. I found, somewhat to my surprise, that I didn't miss him at all—and that made me sad. Had I ever really loved him, or did I just talk myself into thinking I did? Who was the real Tom anyway—the sweet-talker who had wooed me, or the self-centered blowhard he'd turned into? In any case, I had no intention of allowing the Romanian secret police to listen in on my personal affairs.

We settled into a routine. William played chess all morning and messed around with his new friends most of the afternoon while I got dressed in several layers of clothes and walked purposelessly around the gray, drab city, watching my breath dissolve in the air, waiting for the tournament to be over, impatient to start work.

Walking around, I kept my eyes open to see if I was being followed, but I never spotted anyone. I tried to avoid the many wild street dogs scavenging for food. Here, I reflected, dogs and people shared a similar predicament. There were few cars, mostly little sedans and two-seaters that looked like sardine cans on wheels spewing leaded gasoline fumes; instead, I saw people riding bikes, slipping and sliding on the rutty ice, and many horse-drawn carts and wagons. It was a weird feeling—as if time was stuck in neutral. In the rest of Europe it was 1989, but this place was a world apart.

Many of the city's modern concrete and cinderblock structures, jerrybuilt by the communists, were crumbling. Conditions were better in the historic center which boasted elegant, Baroque buildings, spacious squares and two monumental cathedrals. The orthodox basilica was crowned with a massive onion dome rising from a lovely roof of yellow and blue tiles arranged in a geometrical pattern, a reminder of a more gracious era.

I was struck by how unnaturally dark and quiet the city seemed. At home, Boston was always alive with people eating, chatting, shopping, pushing baby carriages, listening to boom boxes, generally having a good time. Here, people shuffled around like zombies and conversed in low voices. The streetlights mostly didn't work or were deliberately switched off; the shops were dark, there was no neon or advertising placards. Practically the only splash of color came from the jowly, thick-lipped portraits of Ceauşescu—*"The Genius of the Carpathians, The Great Leader"*—which plastered the city. Often he was portrayed as a young man with black wavy hair and thick, almost swollen lips. Usually he stood with one arm raised to bless the masses, against a background of red, gold and blue Romanian tricolors. A bookshop down the road from the hotel seemed to be stocked exclusively with books by him and his wife, Elena, who lived under the illusion that she was a world-famous chemist, even though she had no actual scientific education or knowledge.

One day, I went inside the orthodox cathedral hoping for some spiritual uplift. The place was as cold and gloomy as everything else, its icons and artwork obscured under a thick layer of grime, its few worshipers mumbling softly to themselves. An old woman entered the sanctuary, crossed herself three times and painfully lowered herself to kiss an icon that had no doubt been kissed a hundred thousand times before. Candles flickered near one of the shrines but their faint light was swallowed in the black immensity of the basilica, its roof towering high overhead. I sat on a bench for a few minutes, searching for a sense of the divine, not feeling anything.

As I emerged, two men in blue uniforms started following me. I turned into an adjoining street hoping to lose them but they stuck behind me and came closer. Seeing they were not about to let me escape, I turned to face them, telling myself not to panic. They backed me up against a wall. Now I was scared. One held out his hand and demanded "passport"; the other brandished a pistol.

"I'm American," I said, voice shaking. I could smell liquor on their breath. What did they want? Was this some kind of a warning? Should I try to offer them a bribe, or might that get me into deeper trouble? When one soldier nodded, I took my U.S. passport out of my bag with trembling hands. He gave it a cursory examination, then grabbed the bag itself and started rummaging through my things.

"Hey, that's mine, leave it alone," I protested when he pulled out my small, pocket camera. The man ignored me, opened the back and ripped out the film. Fortunately, I'd only taken a few snapshots which were no great loss. He looked suspiciously at my vitamin pills, makeup and the small notebook I always carried with me. Finally, his companion muttered something, glancing at his watch.

"Hotel," the first officer said, pointing the way back the way I'd come. "Here no good. Hotel good. Stay hotel. Here, bad." He handed back the passport and bag and gestured with his arm. I was amazed by his effrontery, his absolute confidence that he had the right to poke around my personal effects and destroy my property. If this is how they behaved with foreigners, what might they do to their own citizens? I quickly made myself scarce, shaking with anger and relief, looking behind every few seconds to see if they were still following and almost breaking into a run when I finally saw the hotel, which now seemed like a welcome refuge.

I had been consciously avoiding contact with ordinary Romanians. A leading critic of the regime, a pastor named Lazlo Tokes, had his church in Timişoara across the river from the cathedral, but mindful of Eskew's instructions, I did not contact him. I'd wait until arriving in Bucharest before trying to meet dissidents. A couple of times I took Stefan Petrescu's picture out, imagining conversations we might have. The thought made me feel foolish and excited all at once.

Evenings, I usually read and William analyzed chess games. We had tried watching TV but there was only one channel which broadcast for a just couple of hours each evening and seemed to consist exclusively of footage of Ceauşescu and his wife touring factories, reviewing military parades and making long speeches, frequently interrupted by rapturous applause. They were often seen entering stores packed with food supplies, which seemed like a particularly cruel joke. The broadcast began every night with a martial-sounding hymn sung by a full choir. We couldn't understand most of the words but we eventually figured out the chorus, which seemed to be:

The people, Ceauşescu, Romania,
The party, Ceauşescu, Romania.

"How do they stand it here?" William asked one evening.

"Nothing to do, nothing to watch, nothing good to eat, nothing to drink except that nasty stuff...."

"They have no choice.'

"Why don't they leave?"

"Some try, but they risk getting shot crossing the border."

I tried to pay attention to the language, which sounded a little like Portuguese with a Russian accent. Despite my knowledge of French and Spanish, I couldn't understand much, just an odd word here and there.

By now, the tournament was approaching its climax. William had won five games, drawn three more and lost three. He was challenging for a top-ten finish in the field of 50.

"I think you're doing fantastically," I told him.

"Better than I expected. Some of these kids are really good. One of them will probably be world champion in 10 years."

"What about you?"

"Oh no, not me," he said solemnly. "I'm going to be a doctor, probably a heart transplant surgeon or a brain surgeon. This is just for now. I won't have time for it when I'm older." I tousled his head. I'd grown fond of the kid.

On the final day, I went to the airline office to confirm William's ticket out of Timişoara and arrange his exit visa. While waiting for the paperwork to be done, I started talking to the father of one of the other players, a gruff man who said he came from Scotland.

"I'll be glad to be out of this hole," he said in a low voice.

"Can't leave soon enough."

"Yeah, things are difficult here," I said.

"You're not kidding. My laddie, Andrew, had a bad asthma attack the other day, probably from all the mold and rot in the rooms and the polluted air. We had to call an ambulance. You've never seen a place like that hospital. My goodness."

"That's awful. Is he OK?"

"Yes, he's fine; brave little lad he is."

"What was the hospital like?"

"Paint peeling from the walls, almost no light, cold as hell with all kinds of creepy-crawlies scampering around."

"Creepy-crawlies?"

"Spiders, cockroaches, even inside the emergency room. They probably have rats as well. The doctors and nurses were kind though. They do their best, even though they're obviously very short of medicine." He lowered his voice even more to a whisper. "The scariest thing was the ancient glass syringes—they use them again and again. I can only imagine the AIDS problem they have here."

I shuddered. "I hope I never see the inside of a Romanian hospital."

That evening, there was a celebration dinner for the players and their families. As a special treat, our hosts had come up with a menu of fried chicken, boiled potatoes and stewed fruit for dessert. Again there were long speeches punctuated by toasts with vile, Romanian plum brandy that tasted like cleaning fluid. William had lost his final game and wound up tied for 15th place but seemed pleased enough with his result and dug into his meal with gusto. Next morning, I took him to the airport.

"Now you know what to do when you get to Frankfurt," I said. "An American flight attendant should be waiting for you at the gate."

"I'm going to have the biggest hamburger in the world when I get home. And a proper Coke."

I reached down to give him a hug. "You'll make a great brain surgeon one day. Say hello to your uncle for me and please give him this." I handed him an envelope with preliminary observations and another addressed to Tom.

The flight was called and the passengers walked away, surrounded by armed guards. Now, I was on my own.

10 – Bucharest: October 2007

Petra trudged back to the apartment after another day of trekking around the city. She'd been here for more than a week and accomplished almost nothing. Worse was the feeling that she was accepting the kindness of Mihai and his friends and repaying them with an elaborate deception.

It had started promisingly. That first morning, Mihai had given her a map and pointed out their location. "We're here, *Strada Latina*, Latina Street. This place belongs to Cristina's father—he's a property speculator, filthy rich. But I shouldn't complain. He allows us to live here for cheap, otherwise I could never afford such a place. Look here, this is the main building of the university. Do you know if that's where your course is?"

"I think so," Petra said.

"Because there are many other faculty buildings spread around the city. And there are other institutes that offer language classes. I assume you have all the details written down."

"I had a whole bunch of papers but … but I think I may have accidentally forgotten them. I'll have to email my professor back at Brown. He has all the details." Petra wasn't ready to tell him the real reason she was here. It sounded overly melodramatic even to her.

"When do the classes start?"

"I think next week."

"You think? Hmm. Anyway, it shouldn't take you more than 20 minutes to get there and you can ask in the faculty office. I'll walk part way with you. But I'm surprised your school sent you here all alone without any backup. They don't seem very organized."

"I guess it's because Romanian isn't a popular language for American students to study."

"That's true. So tell me, Petra, what made you interested to learn it?"

"Um, because … I guess, maybe because … because I took Latin in high school."

"It will be easy for you then. Grammatically, they are very close."

"So that's why, I guess."

"Great." He smiled again, making her knees a little weak. "Well, let's go."

They started walking. The cobbled street was lined with gracious homes which had seen better days. Several had mock Roman columns and intricate carved motifs around their windows and doors. The outside walls were all smeared with graffiti. They passed a yard strewn with heaps of garbage.

"Be careful of the dogs," Mihai said, pointing to one sniffing a pile of trash. "There are still thousands of strays in the city. Most are harmless but you never know."

"Are you sure? They make me nervous. You don't see wild dogs where I come from."

"These are only half wild. They don't belong to anyone but neighbors feed them so they're not usually aggressive. There used to be a lot more a few years ago. The authorities have been catching them," he said as they reached a main road. "This is Carol I Boulevard, named after…"

"Romania's first king."

"Excellent. Five points to you."

They walked on past the Bucharest stock exchange, a couple of sex clubs and casinos and a building site where a large glass-covered building was going up. The boulevard was choked with traffic hardly moving.

"It's the new Bucharest," Mihai said. "Construction everywhere you look, new towers appearing all the time. Sometimes I walk down a street I've known all my life and I hardly recognize it. Soon, it will be a completely different city."

"Why are there so many cars parked on the sidewalk? At home, they'd all be ticketed," Petra asked, as they squeezed between them, occasionally forced to step out into the traffic to get by.

"Nowhere else to park. There are almost no parking garages in Bucharest. Remember, you're not in America now."

They arrived at a large traffic junction.

"Now we are entering University Square," Mihai told her. "This was one of the main places of the revolution in '89. A lot of people died here, students like us. My parents were here, facing the tanks. Hard to imagine, isn't it when you see all the traffic? Now, kids don't even know who Ceauşescu was. Show them a picture and half of them can't identify him."

"My mom was also here," Petra murmured, suddenly moved by the idea of her pregnant mother standing on this very spot all those years ago.

"She was? Then you do have a connection to us. What was she doing here?"

"She was a writer for an American magazine, *The Brahmin*."

"Wow! I'm impressed. She must have told you fantastic stories."

"No, she never spoke of it. It was a complete taboo in our house. Something happened to her here but I don't know what. If I ever brought it up, both my parents totally clammed up."

"OK, here is where we part company. You cross the street through this underpass and the main university building is right in front of you. I'd come with you but I have some meetings. And here, write down my cell phone. If you need anything, just call." He kissed her on both cheeks and was gone before she could react.

Petra reached the colonnaded building of the university and stood outside by a row of second-hand book sellers, looking at the students milling around, smoking and talking on cell phones. The building, like many in Bucharest, was grungy, its grey walls disfigured by graffiti and old posters for rock concerts, half scraped off. She walked around to the back and found a small square, *Piața (Piazza) December 21, 1989*, obviously named to commemorate the revolution. Avoiding the pigeons, she sat down by a fountain to gather her thoughts.

Could her father really be inside this building, today, right now? The thought was almost paralyzing. Petra hadn't really thought through what she'd do once she arrived at this moment. All her planning had gone into just getting here. Of course, she'd imagined what might happen but her fantasies had unfolded like scenes from a soap opera, with cries of amazement and tears of joy. Now, her imaginary dialogues seemed childish. What was she supposed to say? *"Hi, my name is Petra. I'm your long, lost daughter."* Or maybe, *"Professor Petrescu, I have a surprise for you. Me!"* Or maybe just, *"Hi Dad. I'm here!"*

What if he was married and had kids of his own? She might be an unwelcome embarrassment. She'd looked him up on the University of Bucharest website but all she'd found was a long list of publications and literary awards. No photograph, no personal touches at all. Maybe she should phone first; better yet, email. But she'd come all this way; she couldn't wait any longer. She'd go in and say whatever came into her head.

Petra entered the building and asked for the literature department. She was directed to the fourth floor where she found herself walking along a narrow corridor, checking the names on the doors. Suddenly, she stopped, heart beating. There it was— Professor Stefan Petrescu. Summoning up her courage, she knocked.

No answer.

Again.

Still nothing.

A student came by and said something. She must have looked blank because he immediately switched to English. "He's not here, the professor. He's at a conference in Belgium."

"Do you know when he'll be back?"

"Next week maybe, or the week after. I'm in his Shakespeare class but it doesn't begin until October 17. So he could be away until then."

Numb with disappointment, Petra wandered back into the street. Had she come all this way for nothing? What should she do? The one thing she wouldn't do was give in. She needed a plan, not useless tears. So she'd walked on, wandering around the city until it was time to return to the apartment. There, she'd asked Angela if she could stay a few days, until the Romanian course began. "I could give you some money, maybe help pay for groceries," she'd said.

"Sure, why not?" Angela replied. "Cristina is going out of town today for a week. You can have her bed until she gets back."

Next afternoon, it suddenly got cold and the sky turned dark. Petra was three or four miles away from the apartment, near Ceauşescu's grotesque *Palace of the People*, when the rain began. She wasn't wearing a coat and didn't have an umbrella. She tried to hail a taxi but they all ignored her so she started walking toward *Unirii (Unity) Square*, a huge traffic circle surrounded by stores and restaurants plastered with advertisement placards. By now the rain was torrential. She ducked into a McDonald's and bought a cup of coffee, waiting for the weather to clear. The place was crowded with young Romanians devouring Big Macs and yacking into their cell phones.

After a few minutes, with the rain slightly slackening, Petra started walking again, trying to avoid puddle splashes from the endless traffic. An enormous thunderclap signaled the return of the storm with new ferocity. Drenched and discouraged, Petra looked for somewhere else to shelter and saw the Hilton Hotel logo. This particular Hilton was called the Athénée Palace. Petra entered through the revolving doors and found herself in a resplendent, marble-floored lobby populated by business people in fancy suits. She tried to make herself inconspicuous but the desk clerks glared at her as if to say, *"What are you doing here?"* After only a couple of minutes, she went back into the downpour and trudged the rest of the way back to the apartment.

"Poor you, just look at you," Angela greeted her. "Here, let's get these wet clothes off and you can warm up in a bath."

"Thanks," Petra stammered through chattering teeth.

When she got out of the bath, Angela had laid out some of her own clothes. Petra slipped on a red top made out of a spandex-like material that hung down over one shoulder, clinging to her body, leaving half her neck and her other arm completely bare. She'd never worn anything remotely like it before. "It looks good on you. We're the same size," Angela said, coming into the bathroom.

"I don't think I can wear this," Petra said.

"Why not? You have a nice body. Why not show it off?" Angela herself always seemed to wear low slung jeans that stopped several inches below her waist and shirts that ended several inches above her navel, revealing a diamond-shaped tattoo in the gap in between.

"I just never have. It's not me." Inside Petra was thrilled. She was used to people praising her mind—that had happened all her life—but nobody had ever paid much attention to her body.

"Who is you? You can be whoever you want. When I feel a little blue, I change my hair color, or buy a new outfit. Now you, all you need is a touch of makeup, some perfume, do something with your hair which is a total disaster, lose the glasses, you'd be totally hot. Don't you have contact lenses?"

"I mostly can't be bothered with them. It's a pain having to buy the solution and do the rinsing and the soaking every night."

"You should. You'd be a new person. People would start reacting to you completely differently."

"Maybe," Petra said doubtfully. But the thought was intoxicating. Angela was right. Not a single person from her real life knew her here. She could experiment with different identities, try things out. Nobody would care.

"Tomorrow we'll go to the mall. You can't keep on wearing this stuff. I mean, give me a break. Look at yours and look at mine," Angela said pointing with disdain at Petra's white cotton underwear, which hung forlornly on a clothes line, next to a row of her own frilly black bras and bikini pants. "Not exactly *Victoria's Secret* is it?"

"I guess not. But what would I do with those?" Petra asked, half fascinated, half appalled. "What does it matter what you wear under your jeans anyway?"

"What does it matter? Jeez, of course, it matters. How will you feel when you take a guy to bed and you're wearing things only a nun or an old lady would wear?"

"But I'm not going to bed with any guys."

"Why not? What about Mihai? He likes you. I can see it from

the way he is around you. Don't you like him?"

Petra blushed furiously to the roots of her hair, her neck and beyond. "He's nice I guess. Doesn't he have a girlfriend?"

"He's had a few, but nobody permanent. You should fuck him if you like him."

Petra was speechless.

"Well, why not? He's fuckable, isn't he?"

"Did you and he …?" Petra asked, looking down.

Angela laughed. "No, Mihai is like a brother to me. We've known each other since kindergarten. I have a boyfriend — Andrei. You'll meet him sooner or later if you hang around here. You'll probably hear us in bed together. The others always complain that I make too much noise. Tough luck, they're just jealous. If I shout too loud, put a pillow over your head."

Again, Petra was flabbergasted. No-one had ever spoken to her like that before. But Angela wasn't finished. "I've got to say, you're not Mihai's usual type. He likes his women more, you know, more … more…"

"Sexy?"

"Don't be upset; I just mean sexier on the outside. You could be sexy if you tried. I think it's sweet he likes a serious girl like you. Maybe he's growing up."

Petra's blush grew even deeper, if that were possible. She needed urgently to change the subject.

"Your English is amazing—how did you learn to speak like that?"

"I've been watching American TV since I was little. It started with cartoons. Lately, my favorite is *Sex in the City*. Don't you just love that show?"

Petra was too embarrassed to admit she'd never seen it. Her parents disapproved of TV on principle, with the possible exception of PBS.

Petra had already noted that there seemed to be a lot of sex in the city in Bucharest. It was gross—but also a bit thrilling. Walking through the Cişmigiu Public Gardens the previous day, she'd been surprised how many kids her own age were shamelessly making out on the benches. She had a sudden image of herself and Mihai kissing passionately in the park, his violinist's fingers making inroads under her sweater, under her bra, and found the idea perversely arousing. God, her nipples were stiff. She forced herself back to the present. If she ever did get it on with Mihai, which would totally never happen, she'd want to be in the privacy of a bedroom where nobody could see or hear them and not in public which was way too … public.

Angela gave her a sardonic look, as if she was a mind-reader.

"What do you do? Are you a student?" Petra asked abruptly, hoping to change the subject to something safer.

"Fourth year, languages. I have good English and German and I'm learning Turkish. I want to be an interpreter at the European Commission in Brussels or maybe the European Parliament in Strasbourg. Since Romania joined the EU last January, all Europe is open to us for jobs. And maybe someday I'll move to New York and work at the U.N."

Next day Angela took her to a mall. "You see, we have everything here you have in the States," she said proudly. "DNKY, La Perla, Max Mara, Versace, Victoria's Secret, Dolce e Gabbana. It's like *Beverly Hills, 90210* right here in Bucharest."

They went into La Perla. Petra blanched at the prices and even more at the merchandise. "I'm not buying anything here," she insisted. "I can't afford it, and anyway, it's too over the top for me."

"OK, we'll try Zara," Angela said. Prices there were slightly more reasonable, though most of the merchandise was still outrageous in Petra's eyes. After half an hour of rejecting Angela's suggestions, she settled for a few, not too offensive bras and panties—mauve with adorable little flowers on them —and a seashell pink camisole.

"This is fun. I love the mall, don't you?" Angela said.

"I don't know. I don't go much at home."

"You mean your mom doesn't take you shopping?"

"Not much."

"Wow. What else are moms for? I go with mine all the time. It's how we bond. Never mind, let's try in here," she said, dragging Petra into a shoe store.

After trying on several pairs of pumps and ankle boots while Petra watched, Angela left reluctantly without buying anything. "One day, when I'm rich, I'll have 500 pairs of shoes. Next, we need to get you waxed," she told Petra. "And maybe a little tattoo, like mine."

Petra drew the line at that. But when they got home, she did agree to paint her nails, both fingers and toes. Angela had a dozen shades to choose from, from bright orange to silver. Petra finally opted for a dark red embedded with iridescent particles of some glittery substance. She had to admit, the changes did make her feel different, kind of slutty but in a good way. She couldn't stop looking at her sparkling fingers, wiggling them like a pianist warming up, wondering if they really belonged to her. She'd never painted them before. And the bikini briefs—even if nobody else could see them, she was aware of them the whole time.

Still, for the next two days she'd kept out of Mihai's way, retreating to her room whenever she heard his voice. She could hear him playing his violin every evening. He was practicing a Beethoven quartet, apparently preparing for an upcoming recital, but occasionally he'd break into his own jazz riffs. Sometimes she heard other, more dissonant, sounds as well. He had some kind of electronic synthesizer in there which he would occasionally play.

It seemed Mihai scraped together a living by filling in spots in orchestras and chamber groups and giving kids violin lessons. Almost every afternoon, he would take buses or the Metro to the suburbs. He used the money to pay for his own lessons from a prominent professor.

"He wants to be a composer. He's writing an electronic symphony or something," Angela told Petra. "It's awful in my opinion but it keeps him off the streets."

While she waited for Professor Petrescu's return, Petra spent her days walking around the city, people watching. Romanians were weird, she decided. Even girls like Angela, who probably only went to services once or twice a year for Christmas or Easter, crossed themselves three times whenever they walked by a church, of which the city had many hundreds, some dating back four or five centuries.

Bucharest was an odd mixture of old and new. There were cellular phone stores and kiosks on almost every block. The first thing anyone did when they sat down in a café or restaurant was take two or three cell phones from their pockets and place them on the table, like poker sharks laying down their cards. Phones were always going off in the apartment, sparking a scramble to find which one was ringing and whose it was. There always seemed to be five or six lying around.

Another thing Petra noticed was that Romanians, men and women alike, favored strong perfume. She often smelled them as they passed on the street several feet away, reeking like walking air freshener dispensers. Not Mihai, though. He wore aftershave most days, but it was discreet and somehow refreshing. It was nice to be near him. To her shame, that kissing-in-the-park fantasy wouldn't go away. In fact, it was getting more and more detailed.

Petra had gotten into a sort of routine but she knew it could not last. Her mother was sure to discover her absence eventually and Cristina would be returning to claim her bed in a couple of days. If she really wanted to meet her father, she had to act.

She decided to email him. After discarding several drafts, she settled for a few bland words that gave nothing away:

"Dear Professor Petrescu, I am the daughter of Elizabeth Graham. I think you may have crossed paths with her in 1989. I'm in Bucharest right now and I'd love to meet you. Please email me when and where we could meet. Sincerely, Petra O'Neill."

Next afternoon, she let herself in the apartment anxious to check for a reply and almost bumped into Mihai standing by the door.

"There you are, haven't seen you for days" he said, bending to kiss her on both cheeks in the Romanian manner. She knew it meant nothing and he would do the same to every woman he met, but she still felt herself redden each time it happened.

"So what's the capital of Turkmenistan?" he asked, grinning broadly.

"Ashgabat."

"Bravo. Ten bonus points. And who was the second king of Romania?"

"Ferdinand. See, I've been studying."

"I'm impressed." He stepped back and examined her. "But Petra, something about you seems different."

"It's the contact lenses."

"And the hair and the nails, especially the nails. Wow!" She noticed his dark chest hair through the open buttons of his shirt and wondered what it would be like to run her fingers through it.

"So when do your classes start?" he asked.

"Soon. Next week."

He frowned. "Which school did you end up at? Will you be studying in the *Pantofi Institute*?"

She hesitated. "Yeah, that's right."

Unexpectedly, Mihai grabbed her shoulders and walked her backwards into the living room, sitting her down on the sofa. Petra was too surprised to resist. For a thrilling second, she thought he might be about to kiss her but that idea died when she saw his face turn serious.

"Petra, when are you going to stop lying?" he asked.

"What … What do you mean?" Flustered and ashamed, she felt tears gathering and turned away.

"You're not here to learn Romanian. There is no *Pantofi Institute*. I just made it up. *'Pantofi'* is the Romanian word for 'shoes.'"

"Oh."

"I was a little suspicious from the start. You show up with one backpack, not knowing where to go. You say you forgot your papers; you have no contacts, not even a phone number—it doesn't add up. Petra, what's really going on? You are obviously extremely bright but I also am not totally stupid. Are you in some kind of trouble?"

"No."

"I don't believe you. Are you running away from something? Are you really a student at Brown? What's the story? Tell me, I'm your friend; I want to help. No matter what, you can trust me."

Petra sighed. Could she really? What would he think of her when she told? Maybe she should just gather her stuff and go. But she couldn't face being alone in the strange city. And she didn't want to say goodbye to him. She lifted her head to meet his gaze.

"OK, I'll tell you."

11 – Bucharest: March 1989

I phoned Eskew as soon as I'd checked into my hotel in Bucharest. It took the operator 45 minutes to put the call through.

"Where are you staying?" he asked, his voice tinny over the connection.

"The Athénée Palace Hotel, opposite the concert hall with the big dome."

"I stayed there myself in '38. Or was it '39? I remember the wonderful marble pillars and floors in the lobby. It was opulent. Do they still have the English Bar there at the back of the hotel? That was quite a place, full of reporters, intellectuals and spies. There was a time when Athénée Palace was the most notorious den of spies in all Europe. The Germans spied on the British, the French on the Germans, the Poles on the Russians, the White Russians on the Reds and vice versa; there were émigrés from every country in Europe and most of the Romanians you met worked for one secret service or another and probably two or three all at once."

"They still have a bar; I haven't tried it yet," I said, trying to wrench him away from his youthful memories. "But this is definitely the most elegant place I've seen so far in Romania. The doormen and bellhops are very polite, and they all wear charming old world uniforms. Anyway, I wanted to let you know I'm finally here and ready to start work."

"And the city, how does it look to you? In my day, it was known as the *'little Paris'* you know, elegant mansions, lovely architecture."

"It's nothing like Paris now, I can assure you. It's spooky. I saw anti-aircraft batteries at the airport, although I can't imagine who they think is going to attack them."

"This is a regime that doesn't take chances."

"That's for sure. As soon as you get off the plane, the place is swarming with police and militiamen with submachine guns. They herd you around like prisoners of war and you have to fill out a dozen different forms before they allow you to leave. Driving to the city, the streets were almost empty and totally dark. There are no lights anywhere. As for the people, they look utterly defeated—cowed, afraid, brainwashed. They hardly talk in public. It's a nation of whisperers. They won't meet your eyes. They trudge around looking at the ground. It's the strangest feeling being here. It really is Orwellian. I keep expecting the clocks to chime 13."

"That's why I sent you, for details like those. I trust you to bring it all to life when you start writing. By the way, I assume this conversation is being monitored so a degree of circumspection may be indicated. And before I forget, Eliza, I received a call from your husband. He sounded quite contrite and earnestly beseeches you to call him."

"OK, noted."

"Lastly, don't forget our friend, the one who feeds apples to his horse. I assume you'll be reaching out to him." Just the mention made my heart beat a little faster.

"I haven't forgotten. But I think I should get an idea of how things work here first," I said.

"I'll leave it in your capable hands. By the way, our young grandmaster arrived home safe and sound. His parents wanted me to thank you for looking after him so well and I too am in your debt. He was not overly impressed with either the food or the accommodation."

"He's a nice kid. Tell him 'hello' from me." I rang off.

I unlaced my boots and lay down on the bed. I didn't want to deal with Tom right now. What I really wanted was a hot bath and a double whisky at the bar. But it had to be faced sooner or later. I sat back up and called the hotel operator to request the call. Half an hour later, it came through. He picked up on the first ring.

"Lizzie, is that you? Where are you? Thank God you called. I've been frantic, worried sick."

"No reason to worry, everything's fine. I'm in Bucharest."

"It's not fine, not fine at all. Lizzie, you've got to come home. I can't deal with it any more. The twins—they're driving me crazy. I can't focus. I haven't written two words worth a damn since you left. Liz, I'm sorry for what I said. I didn't mean it. Only please come home."

I thought, *That's the way he is, the way he always will be. Why did I never see it before?*

"Tom, I'm on assignment, you know that. I'm a professional. I can't just drop it and rush back 5,000 miles because you're having a tough time with the boys."

"We're eating junk food every night and the laundry's piling up. For Christ's sake …"

"So that's why you want me home? To be your housekeeper?"

"No, that came out all wrong. I want you back because I love you and I miss you and the kids miss you too. I was hasty; I know I said some terrible things. And I've been selfish, I see that now. But I'll do better, I'll be different."

"Right!"

"Look Liz, I know you've been unhappy. But we can try again, start over, make it like it was before. Just, please come back."

"Tom, get a grip. You're a capable guy. You can work the washing machine, it isn't rocket science. The manual is on the top shelf in the laundry room; it explains everything. My assignment will be over soon enough. Then we'll talk some more. Look after yourself, Tom, and tell the twins hello."

I hung up and lay down, exhausted. Five minutes later, there was a quiet knock on the door. I opened it warily. A small, middle-aged woman dressed all in black stood outside.

"I am your hotel telephone operator. May I speak to you a minute?" she whispered in heavily-accented English, looking down the corridor in both directions.

"What about?"

"I have a proposal to your advantage." Intrigued, I ushered her inside. The woman immediately grabbed my arm, pulled me into the bathroom and turned on the shower. She turned back to me.

"You made two calls that lasted nearly 30 minutes."

"Yes?"

"I want to tell you I have charged you only for 20 minutes."

"You did?" I felt like I was in a scene out of a John le Carré novel.

"So I have saved you much money. Also, you not pay hotel tax, 15 percent, on the other 10 minutes. Perhaps you are grateful." The woman glared at me with intense, glittering eyes.

"I guess so," I said, still not quite understanding.

"And I can make your calls go through quick, without waiting, whenever you want."

"That would be good."

"So you must to be grateful. Perhaps you have cigarette for me, Kent, Marlboro—Kent better—or maybe some dollars, also good."

Ah, now it was becoming clearer. Intrigued, I took a 10 dollar bill from my purse. Quick as a cricket, she'd grabbed it, folded it into a tiny square, tucked it into one of her socks and was gone without another word.

Next morning, my first stop was the Government Press Office. I soon found myself sitting across a desk from a Mr. Bărbulescu, a skinny man with sharp, pinched features and sallow, unhealthy skin. His narrow eyes kept darting around the room as he spoke. I noticed a yellow brown stain on the wall opposite that seemed to be creeping slowly downwards from the ceiling toward the giant, plump-faced portrait of Ceauşescu hanging behind the desk.

"I think we can accommodate some of your requests Madam Graham. I can arrange a briefing with the Ministry of Foreign Affairs, another with the Finance and Trade Ministry; this will be no problem," he said.

I shivered and pulled my coat tighter. The office was frigid, even colder than the street outside, and the light provided by the room's single bulb was dim.

Bărbulescu was wearing a shiny suit made of some polyester substance that glinted in the half-light and a ratty, pencil thin black tie. He seemed impervious to the cold. Perhaps he was wearing several layers of long underwear.

"Your request to visit one of our factories will take longer," he continued. "I must seek approval and arrange an escort. It is not regular. How long will you be staying with us?"

"Two or three weeks, a month perhaps."

"Ah, then we have time. Do you have any other requests? Perhaps you need a translator to accompany you. I can arrange one."

"That won't be necessary, thank you," I replied, anxious to avoid having a government spy with me at all times.

"As you wish," he said coldly. He stubbed out one foul-smelling cigarette and immediately lit another, taking a long drag. "Perhaps you have an American cigarette?"

"Sure," I replied, taking a packet of Kent from my pocket-book. He grabbed it without thanking me. Suddenly, a TV jingle from my youth came into my head: *"Happiness is the taste of Kent. More taste, fine tobacco."*

"Are American cigarettes better than Romanian?" I asked innocently.

Bărbulescu looked shocked. "No, not at all, how can you say so? We have *Carpaþi* if you like them without filters, or *Snagov*, both very nice brands. Only, it is good sometimes to have a change."

"Actually, there is something you could help me with," I said. "I'm interested in Romanian culture and the arts, especially poetry. I'd like to see some recent publications if you have some."

For the first time he smiled, revealing a wolfish set of yellow teeth. "Ah, there I can certainly help you. Romania is famous for its poets. I have several volumes here, including one just published last year of poems written by children. I even have a version in English. I'm sure you'll find it inspiring and even heart-warming, the way our young citizens express their talent." He rummaged through his desk and extracted a slim pamphlet entitled, *"Our Ardent Love for the President of the Country."*

I turned to the first poem and read a stanza:

"Comrade Nicolae Ceauşescu ,
The loving father of all children,
He shows us the road toward communism,
Built with heroism under the tricolor."

The second poem began:

"Comrade Nicolae Ceauşescu , all children
Are bringing you burning love from their souls."

"This is indeed inspiring," I said, without even a trace of irony. "Could I take it with me?"

"Certainly, honored Madam." He stood up and walked around the desk. "Let me accompany you back to the street." We walked silently down dank stairs. I had to clutch the banister every step of the way to avoid slipping and falling. I'd noticed there was an elevator. Either Bărbulescu considered it more patriotic to walk or it was out of order. At the bottom of the stairs, I hesitated before stepping back into the slushy street. Bărbulescu glanced down at my leather boots. "American?"

"Italian."

"Ah yes, *bella Italia*. Your feet will be warm." Looking furtively in both directions, before meeting my eyes, he whispered, "You can have no idea, Madam what it is like to go through an entire winter and never have dry feet." As soon as he disappeared, I wrote down the comment in my notebook. It was the closest thing to an opinion I'd yet heard.

At the American embassy, the press officer seemed laughably glad to see me. He unraveled himself from behind his desk and leaned over, offering a hand as big as a baseball mitt.

"Clinton Aldrich, ma'am. Call me Clint." He was at least six foot five with long, blond hair flopping over his forehead and a wide, American smile his orthodontist would have been proud of.

"They make them big at the State Department nowadays," I said, taking my coat off. At least here, it was warm. We both sat down. "Are you a basketball player?"

"Ah, you have me pegged. Starting center, University of Richmond, went to the Tournament in '84, eliminated in the second round one step away from the sweet sixteen. I missed a jump shot just before the buzzer and I've been cursing it ever since."

"And this is your first foreign assignment?"

"Yeah, and it sucks." He gave a cartoon-like grimace and looked around the room as if he too were being monitored. "I never could have imagined such a crap hole—excuse my French—if I hadn't seen it with my own eyes. Where are you staying?"

"The Athénée Palace."

"It's nice there but be careful. It's notorious. Every single employee, from the manager to the cleaning women, works for the *Securitate*. Every room is bugged, every phone is tapped, and that includes every pay phone on the streets within a mile of the place. The taxis waiting outside—all *Securitate*. Leave a document in your room, they'll photograph it. The tables in the restaurants and the nightclub are miked so they can listen in. The so-called intellectuals you meet at the bar—the writers and artists wearing berets and discussing Jean-Paul Satre and the meaning of life—don't talk to them; they're *Securitate*. So are the whores in the lobby and half the guests. Also, don't let them shine your shoes overnight—they'll put bugs in them quick as a flash."

"My goodness. How do you know all this?"

"Guy named Ion Pacepa, used to be Ceauşescu 's right-hand man, defected to us in the late seventies. Wrote a book. You should read it."

"I will."

Clint hesitated before continuing, "You might as well hear this from me before someone else tells you. There are some embarrassing details about our embassy as well."

"Like what?"

Clint lowered his voice another notch. "According to Pacepa, one of their agents managed to seduce the wife of our ex-ambassador. So they were getting real inside information."

"You mean the embassy was literally penetrated by a

Romanian?"

Clint laughed. "Good one. But seriously, I gotta tell you, Ms. Graham, I've had dozens of gorgeous women coming on to me since I've been here, even more than when I was a ball player. I don't think it's all because of my pretty face. It's tough 'cause you get lonely here but I don't touch 'em. I assume they all work for Ceauşescu. I've learned not to trust anyone here. Ma'am, it's a terrible thing when you don't even trust your own secretary, when you're sure your cleaning lady is a spy."

I told him about my visit from the telephone operator the night before.

"Yes, I've heard about that scam," he said. "What she probably does is, she overcharges guests for their calls—half a minute here, a minute there. That way she builds up her own block of time that people have already paid for on their hotel bills. Before you know it, she's collected 20 minutes that the hotel doesn't know about. Then she comes to you and sells you the time for cigarettes or money."

"So she's a thief."

"Everyone has to live. If you don't have an angle, you'll starve. She probably has kids at home. Your 10 bucks will make the difference between them eating pigs' feet and cabbage all the time or occasionally getting an apple and a candy bar for Christmas."

"Could it be a government trap to embarrass me?"

"It's possible but I doubt it. It sounds more like good, old-fashioned private enterprise to me. Still, it's risky, more for her than for you. They watch everything that happens in that hotel. She won't get away with it forever. Eventually, they'll bust her."

"So what do you do here for fun?"

"Catch a plane to West Germany or London for a long weekend every couple of months. That's about it. Ma'am, would you do me the honor of having dinner with me tomorrow night? We could go to the Hotel Bucureşti. The food isn't as good as at the Athénée—but you don't feel as much like you're on *'Candid Camera'* all the time. They have a gypsy band there that isn't too awful if you like that kind of thing."

"Why Clint, you make it sound so appealing," I said, flattered at the attention. He was kind of cute, in a buttoned-down, Southern sort of way, and I was lonely after more than two weeks without adult company. "Sure, why not. Pick me up at eight. I'll wear my best dress."

We exchanged coy smiles. "But let me ask you, what about dissidents? Is anyone speaking out against Ceauşescu?" I asked.

"Hardly at all. It's not like Poland or Czechoslovakia where there's a real, organized opposition. God, I wish I was in one of those countries instead of here. That's where it's all happening. They're reforming in Hungary, heck even the Soviets have opened themselves up under Gorbachev. Here, politically, it's deader than dead. Half the people are jailers and the other half are prisoners and you don't always know which are which. Not even they know. They say one in four Romanians works for the *Securitate* in some way or another. Everybody is watching everybody else. Every apartment block, every school, every factory has its informers and spies. If anyone says even half a word against the regime, they get harassed and fired from their jobs or they're arrested or the government just kicks 'em out. A lot of intellectuals have left; if anyone becomes too prominent, the government gives 'em an exit visa and tells 'em never to come back. They mostly get jobs in U.S. or European colleges."

"So there's no opposition stirring here at all?"

"Just tiny stuff that you wouldn't even bother reporting anywhere else. Like a year ago, a poet wrote something taking a poke at Ceauşescu. That was a big deal here."

"A poet? Was is Stefan Petrescu by any chance?"

Clint scrunched up his features. "No, that name doesn't spring to mind. Actually, I think it was a woman." He rummaged through his desk and extracted a file. "Ana Blandiana: her poem was called *'Tom Cat Onion.'* I'll get you a translation if you like."

"Yes please. What happened to her?"

"The usual. We understand she's under house arrest with her mail and telephone cut off. At least, they didn't throw her in prison or torture her."

"Clint, could you do me a favor. I need to make a sensitive

phone call and I want a secure line."

"Sure, use mine. I'll leave you in privacy. But remember, they're probably listening at the other end. There is no truly secure line in this country. Would you like some coffee or soda? We have the real stuff here, not that dreadful Romanian cola made from toxic waste."

"Coffee would be great. Black, no sugar."

As soon as he left, I pulled my *filofax* out, turned to the page where I'd written down the number and picked up the phone. It rang a dozen times; I was about to quit when someone picked up.

"*Da?*" The voice sounded tired and cautious.

"Mr. Petrescu, you don't know me. I'm Elizabeth Graham, a writer for *The Brahmin* ..."

I heard the dial tone; he'd hung up on me.

12 – Bucharest: March 1989

There was a big crowd in the lobby of the Athénée Palace when Clint appeared to pick me up. Women in heavy makeup and low-cut dresses strutted around dripping jewelry, accompanied by older men with thick-rimmed glasses and comb-over haircuts.

"Must be a big Party bash," Clint said, taking my arm and steering me out into the cold. "Come back at one or two in the morning, you'll see them reeling through the lobby, groping and slobbering over their mistresses' tits. Oops, did it again; please excuse the language." He looked genuinely contrite, like a huge little boy.

"I'm not an infant, Clint. I've heard the word 'tits' before. And please call me Liz."

Standing on the sidewalk, Clint whistled under his breath. "Holy moly, there are some real bigshots here tonight. Take a look at their wheels."

It was the largest number of cars I'd seen all in one place since arriving in Romania but most were tinny little Dacias, the Romanian knock-off of the French Renault. No true-blooded

American would ever be seen dead in such a vehicle.

"How can you tell?" I asked.

"You've got to look at the colors," Clint explained. "The darker the color, the more important the owner. White is for the junior party honchos, pastel colors for the middle ranks. Black is reserved for real heavy-hitters. If you see a foreign car like an Audi or a Volvo, like the one over there, it's got to belong to a minister at least. Ceauşescu's playboy son, Nicu, tools around in an Audi. Of course, his parents have a fleet of Rolls-Royce limos. If you're really lucky, you might catch one of their motorcades. They flood the streets along his route with security agents disguised as ordinary people. And then, there's his dog, of course."

"His dog?"

"His dog, Corbu, sometimes gets his own motorcade. The animal was a gift from a British member of parliament. Now, it's officially a colonel in the Romanian army. The Romanian ambassador in London has to personally buy dog food every week from a *Marks and Spencer* department store. They ship it back in the diplomatic pouch."

"What do you make of the relationship between the Ceauşescus? Is it true love?"

"It's a pretty twisted kind of love, if that's what you want to call it. You know they have half of Bucharest miked up. According to the defector Pacepa, Elena likes listening to cabinet members screwing their girlfriends. That's not love. It's all about power."

We reached the Hotel Bucureşti, which was obviously a step down the social scale from the Athénée Palace, and went into the restaurant. As promised, there was a four-piece gypsy band, all dressed in embroidered peasant blouses and baggy, white pants. The star was the violinist who twiddled away with tremendous enthusiasm on an electrically-amplified instrument.

"Cool hey?" Clint said. I smiled wanly. The music, screeching and demonic, was giving me a headache and we'd only just arrived.

"What's he playing?" I asked, pointing at one of the musicians who was striking a stringed instrument with small mallets in each hand. "Is it a zither?"

"I think it's called a hammered dulcimer." It gave the music a percussive, out-of-tune quality.

After a while, a surly waiter brought leather-bound menus, each the thickness of a substantial book. "Quite a choice," I commented, quite surprised, as I turned from one page to the next, scanning the almost endless variations of *ciorbă* , the sour soup Romanians love so much.

"It's deceptive. Most items they won't have," Clint said. "You want to stay clear of the *ciorbă da burta*. That's tripe soup, made with milk or sour cream. Awful stuff. The national dish is called *mammaliga*—it's like Italian polenta or grits back home. I recommend the beef *ciorbă* if they have it. I had it here once before and it wasn't too bad. At least you know the meat probably comes from a cow."

"What do you mean?"

"You know this is a land of wild rumors and gossip because nobody trusts anything the government says. Last year, a story suddenly went round that the meat on sale in some shops – course most shops never have any meat on sale at all—was actually human flesh. I didn't believe it, though I didn't eat any for a while either."

"Are you kidding me?" His face told me he wasn't.

The waiter returned and Clint asked for the beef.

"Sorry, no beef tonight."

"Then the pork. That's not too terrible either."

"Sorry monsieur, no pork."

Eventually, we both wound up with roast chicken and cabbage which arrived lukewarm in puddles of congealed fat. I thought about sending it back but decided it would be pointless. Clint was working his way through a bottle of vinegary Romanian red wine and talking earnestly about the NCAA basketball tournament about to begin at home. I picked at my food without enthusiasm, occasionally tuning into Clint over the wailing instruments, wondering how I had let myself be talked into this.

"What do you think of the entertainment?" he asked, during a gap between numbers.

"It's not exactly my type of music. Is this what Romanians like?"

"Older people love the peasant culture. Our generation prefers Euro pop, Abba, that kind of crap. Hey, if you think this is cheesy, you should be here when they stage one of their massive public pageants. I've never seen anything like it—thousands of young girls and boys marching around in formation like mechanical dolls, waving flags, all glorifying the great leader. It's like the halftime show at the Super Bowl, only a thousand times bigger." He lowered his voice. "There's an old Romanian joke: why does Ceauşescu always hold a huge parade on May 1?"

"Why?"

"To see how many people survived the winter."

By now, the violinist had begun circulating, trailing his long electrical cord behind him, to serenade the diners. The other players thankfully did not follow him on his trip around the room. With fascination, I watched the cord become entangled with one leg of the dessert trolley. The violinist arrived at our table, flashing gold teeth, playing at his instrument at its highest, most piercing register. Unaware he was now dragging the trolley several feet behind him, he launched into a *czardas* an inch from my ear. I leaned away but he refused to take the hint and bent even closer.

He finished the piece with a deafening flourish and bowed. Clint applauded enthusiastically and gave him a few banknotes. "Damn good," he said.

As the gypsy moved off, a waiter pushed the dessert cart in the other direction. The cord tightened, the violinist struggled to maintain his balance, there was brief tug of war and the dessert cart toppled sending a heap of plates and a mountain of cakes and whipped cream crashing to the ground. Everyone looked up, the room fell silent. The manager appeared, yelling curses at the unfortunate fiddler, who was dragged off in disgrace. The rest of the quartet struck up another dance as a squad of waiters rushed in to clear up the mess.

Clint looked embarrassed. "Shucks ma'am, this ought to never have happened," he said, as if it were his fault. I was trying not to giggle, although I felt a little guilty. I'd seen the cord become entangled with the cart but had kept my mouth shut instead of preventing the catastrophe. As the philosopher said, *"All that is needed for evil to triumph is for good men to keep silent."* On the other hand, the violinist had insisted on continuing his caterwauling right down my ear canal after I'd made it clear his musical attentions were unwelcome.

Back at the Athénée Palace, Clint insisted on accompanying me to my room. I should have declined his advances right then but I didn't want to say goodnight. Despite the rotten food and entertainment, I'd enjoyed spending time with a fellow American. As we stepped inside, he took me in his arms. I leaned into him for a moment, nestling my head against his shoulder. But it felt wrong. I was a woman of 38, not a high school kid, and this was not the man I wanted to be with. As he tilted my head, I turned away. "I'm sorry Clint, I can't do this. You're a sweet guy but I'm a married woman."

Instantly, he stepped back. "Jeez Liz, I didn't know. I'm sorry."

"It's OK, how could you have known? I didn't tell you. And in fact, I'm not even sure what the state of my marriage is at this point. That's why I'm so confused."

There was a tense silence while he stood shuffling his huge feet, obviously deeply mortified. "I thought you wanted this," he said at last, not meeting my eyes. For the second time that night, I felt a little guilty, but not enough to change my mind.

"Maybe part of me did. But I can't. Let's just forget it happened and remember our nice evening. Come on Clint, don't look so despondent. This can't be the first time a woman has turned you down."

"I guess not ma'am. But they generally say yes." He grinned sheepishly.

"Sure they do. A great, strapping guy like you. Don't worry, we're still friends. I'll call you tomorrow."

Next morning, I resolved to find Petrescu's apartment. Eskew had given me his last known address but I didn't dare ask anyone at the hotel for directions, knowing my inquiry would instantly be reported to the secret police. Stepping out of the hotel, I was intrigued to see a long line of people in front of the Romanian Athenaeum, the domed building across the street —dozens of men and women stamping their feet in the snow.

"What are they all waiting for?" I asked the concierge.

"Philharmonic tickets. The season goes on sale today at noon. People have been waiting since three in the morning."

As I watched, a young woman approached one of the men waiting in line. The two embraced briefly; then the man stomped off, the woman taking his place in the queue. I was impressed. Despite all their troubles, these people were still willing to wait seven hours in the freezing cold to hear classical music. That would never happen at home.

Not knowing exactly what to do, I headed for the art gallery across the square. At the ticket office, I showed a woman a piece of paper with Petrescu's address. The woman looked frightened and shook her head. She pointed back outside the door.

I began walking, threading my way between mountains of ice piled by the side of the road. I found myself adopting the same sliding shuffle as the rest of the people, trying my best to stay upright on the pitted, uneven surface, wondering once again why on earth the Romanians didn't put down salt or gravel.

When I'd gone a mile and was safely out of range of the *Securitate* taxis surrounding the hotel, I hailed a cab and told the driver the name of the Petrescu's street, *Calea Plevnei* (Plevnei Rd), but not the number. I had to assume this trip also would be reported and did not want to link myself to Petrescu. It turned out to be a long street. The driver kept asking exactly where I wanted. Finally, I told him to stop and paid with a pack of Kents. I began walking, checking the numbers, until I found Petrescu's building, a four or five-story block with shops on the ground floor, all shuttered. The upper floors had circular balconies with rusty wrought iron railings and there were crumbling stucco designs under the roof. Once, it had been elegant. Now, like most of Bucharest, it was sad.

I'd thought that once I'd found the place, I'd simply go up and knock at his door but now I was here, I realized this was a bad idea. Every building had its informer reporting on comings and goings and I obviously stood out as a foreigner. Just by standing outside the building, I could be putting the poet in danger.

I walked a couple of hundred yards up the street and back, thinking perhaps he might emerge. A couple of people passed by, staring at me, obviously wondering who I was and what I was doing there. This wasn't going to work. I decided to return to the hotel to reconsider my options.

That afternoon, I had a meeting at the Trade Ministry with a Mr. Daescu, who explained how well the Romanian economy was doing. I began by handing over the obligatory pack of cigarettes which disappeared into his pocket without a word of thanks. I noticed a line of books on a shelf behind him.

"Those are your economic year books?" I asked. They began in about 1965 with a rather thick volume and got progressively thinner as each year passed.

"Yes. Is there some data I can provide for you?"

"May I see the latest edition?" He handed over the volume for 1987. It was only about 60 pages long. "I see your books are getting shorter every year," I commented.

The official had the grace to look embarrassed. "Well, we are becoming more efficient in every way," he mumbled. "As you know, we have eliminated our foreign debt, a magnificent achievement."

Something about his evasive manner made me want to probe deeper.

"But hasn't that just increased shortages of vital supplies at home and encouraged black market speculation?" I asked.

"Nonsense." He blew an angry cloud of fumes in my direction.

"Just yesterday as I was walking in the city, a van pulled up in front of me and immediately 50 or 60 people had gathered and were pushing and shoving for the chance to buy some food. He was selling chicken parts. I've seen such scenes often. How do you account for that?"

He smiled condescendingly. "Ah, Madam Graham, it is the Romanian mentality. You do not know the Romanian mentality."

He leaned forward, speaking slowly, as if to a child. "The Romanian is at his heart still a peasant. These people, they hoard food, they are all hoarders, even though hoarding is socially irresponsible and should be stamped out. I suppose if you went to their homes, you would find they each have five or six chickens hidden away in their freezers."

"How do they run the freezers when the electricity goes off every night?"

"The food stays cold, don't worry about that." That was probably true, I reflected. With no heat, the temperature in most homes stayed several degrees below zero most of the winter.

"If they have so much, tell me why they stand in line for five or six hours to get one kilogram of meat a month," I asked.

"Nobody stands in line so long. I wonder to whom you have been speaking, Madam Graham. People arrive in line in good time, that is true, but then they simply leave their bag there to reserve their place and return when it is time to buy the meat."

Afterwards, I regretted my outburst. These officials were not free to speak their minds. They had to survive just like everyone else. In Romania, it was best to assume that someone was always listening. One false word could cost them their jobs. I was beginning to understand that everyone in this country wore masks to hide their true opinions and feelings. Opinions and feelings were far too dangerous to share with strangers.

Next morning, I returned to Calea Plevnei on foot, even though I knew it was foolish and probably futile. But some force I didn't fully understand drew me back, almost against my will. For half an hour, I walked up and down feeling terribly exposed. A nasty wind whipped down the street; my nose was dripping and my ears numb. I was about to give up when a man emerged from the building. Trembling in excitement, I forgot the cold. It was him! I'd only caught a brief glimpse of his face—but it was enough. He was bundled up in a thick black coat and wore a black, knitted hat. His eyes flickered in all directions—part of the Romanian routine to see who was watching—then he set off purposefully through the slush. I also looked both ways before following 20 yards behind. I didn't know whether he'd seen me.

He reached the corner and turned left on Boulevard Republicii, a main street that led back in the direction of my hotel. A couple of hundred yards later, he arrived at the Cişmigiu Gardens. He went in, tramping through the snow around a frozen pond under bare trees, before sitting down on a bench.

By this time, I was fairly sure he'd spotted me—I'd made no attempt to hide my presence—but he gave no sign. As I watched from under a tree, he took a small notebook out of his pocket and began writing. I knew I had to approach him. There might not be another chance.

Just let him be a real man among these automatons, I remember thinking. *Please, just let him be for real.*

Cautiously I sat down at the other end of the bench. He continued writing, ignoring me, then ripped a page out of his notebook and crumpled it up. I sat for a moment, intensely aware of his physical presence. I could hear his breathing. His face looked wan and drawn and he sported several days of stubble but his eyes were bright blue.

"Mr. Petrescu, please don't be alarmed. I am Elizabeth Graham, the American reporter who called you on the telephone," I said softly.

Without looking at me, he stood up and walked away leaving a trail of footprints in the snow. I felt so crushed I could hardly think. Had I come all this way to be rebuffed without a single word? Then I noticed the piece of paper Petrescu had ripped from his book lying on the bench. Hands shaking, I took off my gloves and carefully smoothed it out.

It said, "Next Tuesday, 11 o'clock. *Domnita Balasa.* Wear a hat."

When I looked up, I was alone in the park.

13 – Massachusetts, October 2007

Dear Petra,

I was up for much of last night writing the latest installment of my story which I'm sending to you with this letter. I'd hoped for a reply by now, but I guess you need more time to digest it all.

It's curious, I hadn't thought of those events for so long and now I find the more I write, the more I remember. I've also been referring to my old reporter's notebooks which I'd stuffed in the back of a wardrobe, all neatly dated. They help bring back the details—the names of those dreadful Romanian officials I interviewed; the strange phone lady in the hotel, and of course my old friend Clint, with whom I've kept in touch all these years. He was recently appointed Deputy Chief of Mission to our embassy in Turkey.

I told you I'd be completely honest, but that's turning out to be harder than I imagined. After a career spent writing about other people, I'm not used to baring my own soul. And now I find myself hesitating for another reason. I don't want to embarrass either one of us with descriptions of private, intimate moments—but I can't totally ignore them either. It's a difficult balance.

I looked at myself in the mirror today—really *looked*. Gravity is starting to have its way with me. Everything is beginning to sag—my neck, my eyelids, the skin around my mouth. Ah Petra, you should have seen me then, especially after I met Stefan. When you're in love, there's a spark that lights you up from within so that you positively glow.

Petra, I worry about the personal side of your life, your capacity to make friends and form relationships. I was never concerned about your academic success. It was obvious almost as soon as you were born that you were exceptionally bright. You started talking at nine months. I recall when you were very little, you used to get car sick every time we went even on short trips. (Thank God, you grew out of that.) One day, when you couldn't have been much more than a year old, I put you in your car seat—we were going to the zoo I believe—and you looked up at me with your big eyes, very grave and serious, and said, *"Not going to throw up; going to grow up."* It was like a news flash from heaven, an instinctive little poem from a tot who didn't even know what a rhyme was. Tom heard. He didn't say anything, but I could tell from his face he was upset. They say biology is destiny. Tom knew in some deep, profound way you would always be Stefan's child, even if Stefan didn't know that you existed. That's why I insisted on naming you Petra. I wanted you to have something that linked you to him.

From an early age you were eager to learn; you devoured books. You skipped the second grade and graduated high school a year early. How many times did you make the state finals of the spelling bee? How many weekends did we watch you competing in geography quizzes? We weren't like other families. While most parents cheered on their kids playing soccer or T-ball, we were at the *Math Olympics* or *It's Academic*. Perhaps we should have tried to be more *normal*—but I never saw you going out for the cheerleading squad.

It's not easy being the smartest kid in the class. I know it hurt when classmates called you a nerd. I saw how you've tried to fit in, how you try to talk like them and be like them—but it never quite worked. In some ways, you know much more than most girls your age. In others, you know much less.

That leaves me with a problem. How can I describe the overwhelming attraction Stefan and I felt for one another in a way you can understand?

There's another reason why writing this has become so difficult. Reliving these memories—reconstructing the details in my mind and committing them to paper—it's like ripping a scab off a wound I thought had healed and feeling the pain all over again.

I don't approve of self-pity and I'm not about to succumb to it now. But sometimes, I can't help myself asking what life has left in store for me. Here I am, in my mid-fifties. With any luck, I might live another 30 years or more. Am I capable of loving again? Physically, I'm not quite a dried up prune yet, despite what the mirror tells me. But emotionally, after so many years, I'm not sure I'd know how.

I read that Romania has joined the European Union. The

country must finally be developing. It's about time. After you were born, the idea of going back seemed unthinkable. It was too unstable, too unpredictable, too dangerous. But maybe everything would have turned out OK after all. If I had gone back, you might be attending the University of Bucharest today instead of Brown. Stefan Petrescu and not Tom O'Neill would have been your father.

There's no point in recriminating. You only get to live one life. You make your bed and you lie in it, and if it turns out to be colder than you ever imagined, you just add another blanket on top and turn the central heating up a notch.

Love,
Mom

14 – Bucharest, October 2007

"Your father's Stefan Petrescu? I can't believe it," Mihai said. "Hey Angela, come here. You're not going to believe this."

"You've heard of him?" Petra asked.

"Are you kidding? Petrescu's like a national icon because he's one of the few who stood up to Ceauşescu. We learned his poems in high school."

"Wow."

"What's the big deal?" Angela asked, coming into the room, hair all spiky, wearing only a flimsy nightgown, though she did have her usual thick layer of makeup on.

"Stefan Petrescu. The poet! He's Petra's father, at least her biological father. She only found out a few months ago when the man she thought was her dad all her life got sick and died. He left a letter for her to read after his funeral. Petra just showed me. This is amazing, no?"

Angela looked amused as she sat down next to them and stretched like a cat, then tucked her legs under her. At least she was wearing panties. "So that's why you're here. I couldn't figure out what you were doing in a backwater like Bucharest."

"I came to meet him," Petra said.

"It's like a soap opera story. Wait till our TV gets hold of it. You'll be a star."

Petra was aghast. "No, please don't tell anyone. Oh God, that would be awful. He doesn't even know I exist."

"Just kidding. So how did your mother happen to meet a hero of the Romanian resistance?"

"I guess they had an affair," Petra said. "She's a magazine reporter. She covered the revolution in 1989."

"You guess she had an affair? You don't know? What kind of affair?"

"She's never spoken about it. For all I know, it could have been a one-night stand at the Athénée Palace. That's one of the problems. Maybe this Petrescu doesn't want to be reminded. Maybe he's the kind of guy who slept with hundreds of women and doesn't even remember her, or he'll deny knowing her. Maybe she had a good reason for never speaking about him."

Mihai said, "I think he'll remember if your mother is anything like you."

"She's the total opposite of me. She's beautiful and confident and glamorous."

There was an uncomfortable silence; Mihai seemed about to say something but decided not to.

"So why the delay?" Angela asked, chewing her lip. "Why haven't you met him yet? You've been here more than a week already."

"He's abroad at a conference and he won't be back for another eight or nine days. So I've been hanging out, killing time, trying to make my money last. I feel terrible about lying to you guys after all you've done for me, but I also felt too dorky to tell you the truth. And I know I'll have to move out when Cristina gets back tomorrow."

"Don't worry about that," Angela said. "You'll share my room. Or I can sleep at Andrei's place. And we're all going up to Sinaia in the mountains this weekend to hear Mihai's recital so you have to come to that."

Petra looked at him. "You didn't tell me you were in a recital. I'd love to come."

"It's no big deal; just a small recital in a church. But of course, you're welcome. Sinaia's a couple of hours north of here by train. It's very beautiful. You should definitely see it." Now, it was his turn to look embarrassed.

"Can I read your father's letter?" Angela asked.

Petra handed it over. Turning to Mihai, she asked, "Do you have one of his poems you could show me?"

"Maybe, but only in Romanian. Wait a minute." He disappeared into his room. Meanwhile Angela finished the letter. Putting it down, she leaned over impulsively and hugged Petra. "That must have been intense, reading that. Spooky."

"It was. I read it the day after his funeral. I was devastated. It knocked me off kilter. I was so angry with my mother, with both of them. How could they have lied to me like that all my life? Nothing seemed real any more. It's weird, six months have gone by but I still don't feel like I'm the same Petra. I can't look at my life the old way. I keep asking myself, 'Who am I really?'"

Angela put her arm around Petra, stroking her hair.

"She didn't actually lie to you, your mother. She just didn't tell you everything."

"That's lying by omission, the same as I've been doing to you the past week. It's still lying, believe me. It totally felt like lying to me."

"But Petra, who you are doesn't depend on someone else. I can see you wanting to meet your long, lost father, but I would not hang my whole identity on it."

"I can't help it. If I could only see him and maybe get to know him, I could figure out how everything fits together. Maybe I'm like him in ways I don't realize. I don't know anything about him, if he's married or has kids or what."

"That shouldn't be difficult to find out."

"What do you know about him?"

"Not much. Sure, the Shakespeare course he gives every year is legendary in the faculty. I think Cristina tried to sign up for it last semester but it was already full."

Mihai returned with a dog-eared paperback. "There are a couple of poems by him in here," he said. "Maybe we can translate one into English, but of course it won't be the same. You'll need to learn Romanian to really appreciate it. I hear they still have places open at the *Pantofi Institute*."

"The what?" Angela exclaimed.

"Private joke," Petra said. "Not funny. Yes please, could you translate it?"

For the next 10 minutes, Mihai and Angela huddled by the desk, whispering to each other, occasionally arguing fiercely over a particular word or phrase. At one point, Angela disappeared into her bedroom and emerged with a Romanian-English dictionary. Petra tried waiting patiently but she couldn't keep still. She tried to look over their shoulders but they shooed her away. So she paced the room, waiting for them to finish.

"Hey, chill out," Mihai said. "This is important. We want to get it absolutely right."

"How often do we get to translate a famous poem for the poet's own daughter?" Angela added.

Finally, Mihai said, "OK, we're done. It's called, *'When all this has passed'*. It was written in the fall of 1989, when he was under house arrest, just a couple of months before the revolution. That's why it's so famous. It helps to know that Ceaușescu used to call himself *'The Genius of the Carpathians'* and this poem refers to that."

He began reading in a soft, slow, serious tone, completely unlike his usual voice.

When all this has passed
and it will pass,
how will men remember us?
I hope they do not remember us at all.

Perhaps, in two thousand years,
an archaeologist will stumble on our lost civilization,
examine our artifacts
and decide we are of little interest,
a dead end in the story of human progress.

Perhaps, they will set aside for us a tiny alcove,
a small corner in their Museum of Human Folly
dusty, inaccessible, virtually unvisited.

As for me, I gladly choose oblivion.
A culture whose only genius is evil
Does not deserve memory.

15 – Bucharest, October 2007

That night, when the apartment was quiet, Petra took out Tom O'Neill's final letter and read it once again. It was dated January 1, only 10 months ago. And now the man who had written it was lying in his grave and she was thousands of miles from home, trying to make sense of her life.

My darling daughter.

Well, that was quite a New Year's Eve—it's been many years since I allowed myself to get hammered like that. Back in the day, before you were born, it used to happen more often—too often. Anyway, your father is truly sorry he embarrassed his girl by slurring the words of Auld Lang Syne—not that it matters because nobody understands them anyway. Also, I take comfort in the thought that by the time you read this, you'll have forgiven my social indiscretion. You're obliged to forgive the dead their sins, or at least most of them—including what I'm about to write in this letter.

It's strange sitting here with the mother of all hangovers, thinking that this is almost certainly my last New Year's Day. I still don't quite believe it. I feel fine but the quacks tell me I won't last until Labor Day, maybe not even Memorial Day. Screw them! I'm going to fight this disease with everything I've got. If you're reading this letter, you'll know I lost the battle.

At the hospital, they gave me a booklet which is supposed to help me cope with my own forthcoming demise. Reading it, I learned that I'm in the psychological state officially known as denial, stage one of the five stages of grief that affect all terminal patients. Next come anger, bargaining, depression and finally acceptance. And then the one they never mention—oblivion.

The book suggests seeking help from a pastor or a priest. Ha! I've been an atheist all my life and I'm not about to go wobbly now. It would be nice to believe in life after death but it's not going to happen. The only way I'll live after my death is in the memories of the people who loved me, most of all I hope in yours.

So I'm officially terminal. Strange word, isn't it? It means the end of the line, or the place where you change for the next destination. In my case, to quote the bard, that would be, 'The undiscovered country from whose bourn no traveler returns.' I imagine a kind of O'Hare Airport for the nearly dead. But I'm becoming banal, always a fatal weakness of mine.

Honey, to get serious, there are a couple of things you need to know and I want to write them quickly before I chicken out. First is, I love you more than life itself. That's the most important thing—but I hope you already know it and will always remember it. You are my sweet, beloved daughter.

The other thing I need to say is going to come as a shock but I don't know how to sugarcoat it. So here goes: Petra, I'm not your real father. Your real father—that is to say your 'biological' father— is a guy in Romania called Stefan Petrescu, a poet no less! Until recently, I thought I'd take that secret to my grave, the way your mother and I agreed before you were born. But I find I can't.

This next bit is important: I don't want you to blame your mom. I was the one who insisted on secrecy. We made a deal. She needed me badly at the time and her unborn child needed a father. I insisted she banish Petrescu from her life, completely and forever. It sounds petty but I felt threatened by him. I wanted to be your father in every way. I didn't want anyone else claiming even a small part of your love. I was jealous of what he had with your mother. He took her heart and never gave it back. If I couldn't have her, at least I'd have you all to myself. But circumstances have changed and now that I find myself staring at the abyss, it seems to me you have a right to know who you are and where you come from.

And to my surprise, I feel I owe it to Petrescu as much as to you. I actually feel sorry for the guy. He's been cheated out of something amazing and he doesn't even know it. Stefan Petrescu should know he has a daughter, a wonderful, brilliant, special girl. He deserves a chance to know you—and maybe it's not too late. I always dreamed of walking you down the aisle on your wedding day, but if it can't be me, let it be him.

Petra, I leave it up to you what to do with this information. You may decide to ignore it or deny it and continue on with your life. But if I were you, I would act on it. Let Petrescu know you exist; try to meet him and when you do, tell him I am truly sorry.

Honey, I'm going to sign off now. One thing I've learned is to say what you have to say and then shut the hell up. So this is farewell. I love you. I'll always love you,

Your Dad,
Thomas O'Neill

Petra had lost count of the number of times she'd read it, but it always brought tears to her eyes. This time was no exception.

Part II: Trembling Fingers

Years have trailed past like clouds over a country,
And they'll never return, for they're gone forever.
These trembling fingers touch the strings in vain
To find the rights notes from the fading memory
Of youth, so that my soul can vibrate again.
- Mihai Eminescu

1 – Massachusetts/Bucharest/Brussels: October 2007

To: Poneill@brown.edu

Fm: Lizgraham@tmail.com

Petra, it's been a while since I received any word so I'm emailing you. Feeling especially maternal, I baked you brownies. Check your mailbox, they should be there after tomorrow.

I spoke to your godfather, Ralph Eskew, today. He sends his love. Incredible to think he's 87 but he still stays interested in everything that's going on and would appreciate it very much if you dropped him a line. He'll be with us for Thanksgiving. I'm counting the days.

Your brothers have both said they're coming with their kids so we'll have a full house. We'll cook the turkey and all the trimmings together the way we always do. Of course, it will be tough, our first Thanksgiving without Tom, but it will also be wonderful to be together.

Love,

Mom

To: Lizgraham@tmail.com

Fm: Poneill@brown.edu

mom, tks for yr note and tks for the brownies. please don't send me any more, i'll get fat. i'm not sure what my plans are for thanksgiving, may decide to spend it with friends. not much else to report here except i'm hoping to start a new shakespeare class with a really neat professor, quite charismatic according to what i've heard. the course specializes in shakespeare's sonnets. i'm sure you'd appreciate him, love petra

Stefan Petrescu sat in his hotel room in Brussels hunched over his laptop. He'd delayed responding for two days, trying to figure out what to say. He told himself to stay calm. Soon he'd be home and could meet the girl and everything would become clearer. Meantime, he owed her an answer.

To: Poneill@brown.edu

Fm: Stefan.Petrescu@univbucharest.ro

Ms. O'Neill,

Thank you for your note *which came as quite a shock to me.* (He backed up and deleted the last eight words.) I do of course remember your mother—*how could I forget her? (Again he hit the delete button, and kept hitting it periodically as he wrote).* I hope she and your father are well. I don't know what she told you about our relationship; however I'd be *more than* happy *and very curious* to meet with you on my return to Bucharest next week. *How interesting that she named you, I presume, after me, yet never saw fit to inform me. (He deleted that entire sentence.)* Please feel free to call my personal assistant in the literature department to make an appointment. Or come in to my class on Shakespeare's sonnets which will be held in room 311 of the main university building on Tuesday Oct. 24 at 11 am. We can talk afterwards.

Petrescu stopped typing to think for a second, then started writing very fast without stopping to consider. This was how he used to write his poems, allowing them to pour out of somewhere deep in his brain. The polishing and editing always came later.

I assume you are in Bucharest because your mother told you about me. I wonder, did she ever tell you why she never answered the many letters I sent her? Did she explain why she sent them back unopened, even those I wrote from the hospital at the darkest moments of my life? Did she say why she went back to a man she never loved? How old are you anyway? When exactly were you born? And how is she, your mother? Is she still as beautiful? Do you look like her? You know, sometimes I still dream about her.

He read over what he'd written, staring at the words for a few seconds. Suddenly, he felt old and tired. Then, he deleted the entire final paragraph before pressing the send button.

2 – Bucharest: March 1989

Domnita Balasa, I discovered, was a church, located about a mile-and-a-half from my hotel, near the Unirii Square. According to the guide book, it was the unluckiest church in Bucharest, having been repeatedly destroyed by fire and earthquake, only to rise again. On the other hand, unlike so many others destroyed by Ceauşescu, at least it had survived. Gazing at its orange-striped brickwork and three domes, I wondered if Petrescu had chosen it for symbolic reasons. I was 10 minutes early but I decided to go in. With a biting wind, it was too cold to linger outside where I would draw unwelcome attention.

Like most Romanian churches, the interior was dank and murky, the air full of the scent of melted candle wax and incense. As my eyes adjusted to the gloom, I took in the rich, silver and gold ornaments hanging over the altar. The central area of the sanctuary was empty but there were a couple of rows of pews lined up against the side walls. A few worshippers sat, heads bent in prayer. I took a seat and waited.

It was almost as cold inside as out, even though the dim lights cast a glow. I couldn't relax. My gloved hands were trembling; every nerve end seemed to twitch. I looked at my watch. It was already five past the hour. One worshipper crossed herself and left. Another slipped into a seat behind me.

"Take off your coat and hat and give them to me," she whispered in accented English.

I was taken aback. I'd expected to meet Petrescu here, not a go-between. "Don't look around," the woman hissed, as I began to turn. "Quickly, quickly, before someone else comes."

I hurried to obey. The woman handed me her own coat and a scarf. "Put these on. Hide all your hair, quickly." With some difficulty, I got myself into the coat—a black, sack-like garment which smelled of cigarette smoke—and tied the scarf around my head making sure to tuck in all my hair.

"Give me your gloves."

I fumbled to take off my merino wool-lined goatskin gloves and handed them over, receiving in return a ragged pair of gray wool mitts. "Now, your hotel key, give it to me," the woman whispered. For the first time, I hesitated. Then, I fumbled in my purse and gave it to her. I had to go along with this crazy adventure no matter where it led. If I wanted Petrescu to trust me, I must trust him in return.

"Where is your bag?"

I lifted my leather pocketbook.

"Take your things, put them in here. Be quick." The woman gave me a plastic shopping bag. Self-consciously, I transferred my purse, two packets of Kent cigarettes, an umbrella and my personal organizer which contained all my contacts. The rest I left in the handbag which I handed to the woman.

Someone came into the church, crossed himself, kissed an icon near the entrance and approached the altar. I felt the woman behind me freeze. She started muttering some prayers. I bowed my head and half closed my eyes, as if in deep communion with the Almighty. The worshipper mumbled a few words, crossed himself again and left.

The woman spoke. "I'm leaving now. Wait five minutes. When you arrive at the street, turn left and then left again. When you meet him, do not show surprise." There was a rustle as she stood up and she was gone.

I waited in an agony of suspense and then quietly left. Reaching the street, I turned left as instructed and then left again. In my new coat and headscarf, I felt acutely different. For the first time since I'd been here, nobody paid me any attention, either by looking at me or averting their eyes. One of my fingers stuck through a hole in the left glove; I retracted it bending it back into my palm. The meager lining of the coat was ripped in a couple of places. I felt the cold begin to seep into my body and wondered if spring would ever come to this country. The scarf was completely inadequate; already the tips of my ears were frozen. Thank God, my feet were warm; the woman had not demanded my beautiful Italian boots. They were pretty much hidden beneath the coat which came all the way down to my ankles.

A man carrying a battered satchel over one shoulder came out of a shop and stood in front of me.

"Elisabeta," he called, adding something in Romanian. He was wearing a black woolen cap pulled down over his forehead, almost to his eyebrows. I was confused for a second, not recognizing him even after he grasped me by both elbows and leaned in for a kiss. Awkwardly, belatedly, I responded. I was a couple of inches taller than him. Our faces searched clumsily for each other. Finally, we got it right. His lips brushed one cheek, then the other—soft, soft lips. Mine touched his unshaven skin, lingering a second too long. A mild shock tingled through me, making its way down my neck and through my body. I shuddered involuntarily and saw him react with surprise. Had he felt something too? I looked for an instant into his eyes and saw them clouded and confused. He shook his head, collecting himself. "Walk with me," he murmured, taking my arm. He was dreadfully skinny but still I felt his wiry strength. We began walking. "Don't talk; if I say something, just nod your head as if you agree completely," he whispered. He let go of my arms as we crossed a major street, almost bereft of traffic. "Stop walking like an American, like you own the world," he said softly. "You're a Romanian now. You own nothing. They own you."

It was true. In my excitement, I'd been striding along, swinging my free arm, my head held high. I switched back to a shuffle, looking down at the sidewalk. "That's better," he whispered. I took his arm back, feeling as if it were the most natural thing in the world. We walked for 20 minutes, in and out of side streets, faster than I was used to, not saying anything. Whenever my feet slipped on the icy surface, he steadied me, apparently unaware of the effect this was having. I had forgotten about the cold. He kept looking around, trying to check if we were being followed.

"Quiet now," he said as we reached the entrance to an apartment building several stories high. I had no idea where we were; this was not his home. He took off his gloves and rummaged for a key with frozen hands. "It's six stories up; the elevator doesn't work of course." He spoke musically with a kind of British accent tinged with what I now recognized as Romanian. We went in and started climbing. It was almost black inside the building; he kept a hold of my arm, hugging the wall with his body as we ascended. I was out of breath by the time we arrived, or perhaps I was just nervous, not knowing what I was going to say once we were alone. Again, he fiddled with the key.

Finally he got the door open and we went inside. He pulled off his cap and took off his satchel, tossing it on to a sofa; I removed the scarf and shook out my hair, trying to get my breath back. It was too cold even to think about taking off our coats. He turned a light switch and a feeble bulb came on, not much brighter than a candle. We looked at each other. He was older than in the picture I'd seen back in Eskew's office—tired, a little careworn. The first signs of gray were already creeping into his black hair, which looked as if he had recently cut it himself, hacked it away with a pair of blunt scissors. It made no difference. For some reason, I was drawn to this man like no-one I had ever met. It was scary, confusing and inexplicable—but also undeniably thrilling.

"Sorry about the cloak and dagger," he said, spreading empty hands in front of him in a gesture that may have been helplessness, or perhaps resignation. "Much of the time I am watched. I considered it necessary."

"I understand," I said, watching my breath dissolve in front of my face. "It was worth it to meet you face-to-face." It sounded banal but it was the best I could do. He grimaced awkwardly, a pained, apologetic expression, as if he had lost the ability to smile. My heart broke for him. Suddenly, without thinking, without considering or hesitating, as if another being had taken command of my body, I felt myself stepping forward, closing the gap between us.

Perhaps, I'd intended to deliver a morale-boosting hug, or a friendly peck on the cheek—but that's not what happened. Without being sure how, to my utter astonishment I found myself kissing him on the mouth—passionately. Instinctively, my left hand found its way to the back of his head and was stroking that spiky, uneven haircut, my middle finger poking its way through the hole in my glove to feel its texture.

I felt Petrescu stiffen, then relax into the embrace as his cold lips softened momentarily. A second later, his brain reasserted control; stepping back, he heaved me away like a sailor shoving off from shore, his body rigid with shock, not so much at my action, I think, as at his own response. We looked at each other like boxers breaking a clinch, both of us panting softly. I could hardly believe what I had just done. My pulse was racing but to my surprise, I felt unashamed. There had been a wonderful rightness about the kiss. I'd felt its power and I knew he had felt it too. How long had it lasted? Five seconds maybe, that was all. Yet it had changed everything. The air between us was charged, almost crackling with static. I was about to say something, what I didn't know, when he broke the silence, his voice hoarse and gruff.

"In God's name …" He sputtered for a moment, lost for words, then, "What are you doing? What was that about?"

"It was a kiss," I wanted to say. *"A perfect kiss."* But he was still talking.

"Who are you? Who sent you here? What do you want?"

I couldn't tell if he was really angry or just astounded. Now, suddenly, at exactly the wrong moment, my usual facility with words failed me. My mouth formed an apology but it wouldn't come out. The fact was, I wasn't sorry, not even a little. I could still taste him and I knew he tasted me. Still, I had to say something. By my actions, I had lost the right to remain silent.

Fumbling with the plastic bag, I extracted two cartons of Kents and offered them. "To help you through the winter," I said. As soon as the words were out, I understood from his expression it was exactly the wrong thing to say.

"Thank you. I do not smoke." It felt as if the temperature in the room had dropped a few more degrees if that were possible.

"But you can exchange them for food." Could anyone possibly have felt more foolish and exposed than I did at that moment?

"I do not eat much either," he said sardonically.

"Then give them to a friend." I knew I had hurt his pride, perhaps the only thing he had left. Every sentence I uttered was just making things worse. But the conversation kept sliding downhill, each word breaking the physical connection we had formed just a moment before.

"Which friend?"

"What about the woman in the church?"

"What about her?"

"She wasn't a friend?"

"Perhaps she was my sister, perhaps my lover."

"Was she your lover?"

Silence. Then, "This is scarcely the season for love."

"You have many admirers abroad, people who love your work. Ralph Eskew, editor of *The Brahmin*, for one. He worries about you. He was the one who asked me to bring you these." I put the cigarettes down on the kitchen table. If I could have snapped my fingers to make them disappear, I would have done so.

"So that's what this is, an offer of support? Tell me, is America sending beautiful female emissaries all over the Soviet bloc to cheer up poets and intellectuals with passionate embraces and Kent cigarettes? Is this a new kind of diplomatic initiative to stiffen spines and raise morale?"

I reddened. "It's not a diplomatic initiative." We looked at each other for a moment, realizing we had talked ourselves into a corner. Absurdly, tears were leaking from my eyes. I fumbled for a tissue and remembered I'd left them in my pocket book, now in possession of the woman I'd met in the church, his sister or his lover.

"Then what?" he demanded.

I tried to answer, stringing my disjointed thoughts together. "I work for *The Brahmin*; I'm writing an article about Romania. Ralph Eskew, my editor, published your poems. I read them; they moved me."

"And because of this, it was necessary to kiss me?"

I said nothing. And reading the silent plea in my eyes to give me a second chance, he must have realized he had a choice. He could continue making cutting remarks, or he could do what his instincts demanded and respond to me, this woman who had so unexpectedly entered his life. A second later, he was moving forward, placing his hands carefully around my shoulders, stroking my hair.

"It's OK, please stop crying, I'll take the cigarettes if it means so much to you." His voice was suddenly soft and gentle. I leaned against him, feeling his breath on my neck.

"Such beautiful, American hair," he whispered. "Such soft skin, such rosy lips." Our eyes met and then our lips. He tasted unexpectedly sweet. Breaking away, he licked a tear away as it tracked down my cheek and I laughed in sheer relief. Words just mixed things up. For the first time in our lives, we didn't need them.

Now began a third kiss, more demanding, more inquiring

than the second. His hands snaked inside my coat. I shrugged it off, trying to gain access to his body with my own hands. He seemed to be wearing at least four, maybe five layers of clothing. We fumbled like inexperienced teenagers, until at last, he broke away. "This is crazy. What are we doing? I don't even remember your full name."

"Elizabeth. My name is Elizabeth Graham."

"And you read my poems?"

"A couple of them. One about a horse …"

"Yes, of course. That poem."

"It was lovely, so sweet and haunting."

"I'm glad you liked it. I paid quite a toll for that little verse." The unwelcome thought made him take a step back.

"I know it got you into trouble. What exactly happened, if you don't mind talking about it?"

He shrugged. "They threw me around a bit, gave me black eyes, broke a rib or two, you know how it goes. Then I was locked up in my apartment for almost a year. I lost my job. I still can't publish anywhere." I understood from his look that his was the kind of face that could hold several layers of expression at once. Right now, there was defiance, but also below the surface the recollection of pain.

"How do you live?"

"I give lessons now and again to brave people who still wish to study great literature. People come; we discuss Shakespeare, Dante, Tolstoy, Eminescu. They bring a little food or money, whatever they can spare. I'm leading a seminar tonight on Shakespeare's sonnets. But that reminds me, it's past lunch time. You must be hungry. You Americans are used to eating, what four or five times a day?"

"I'm not hungry."

"Of course you are. And this is an essential part of your education. You want to write about us Romanians. You must eat like us; you must share our life, at least for a day. Now let's see what's in Simina's freezer?"

"Simina?"

"My sister. You met her in the church. This is her apartment.

It's not as carefully watched as mine, where all my comings and goings are of great interest to the powers that be." He opened the refrigerator, which was almost bare. "Ah, here we have chicken feet, a special delicacy. And what's this? Lard. Delicious. Have you ever eaten a chicken's foot fried in fat before?" I realized sarcasm was his method of survival, the way he asserted his independence.

"No."

"It is not the meatiest part of the bird; in fact it's almost entirely skin and thin, little bones that you must be careful not to swallow or they will stick in your throat. But it can be wonderfully tasty and nutritious when prepared correctly, as our great leader so often tells us." He rummaged in a cupboard and found a frying pan. "If only we had some bread, life would be perfect."

"But what about your sister? Won't she mind us eating her food?"

"Simina, at this very moment, should be ordering room service on your account at the Athénée Palace. After that, no doubt a bath with bubbles which is quite a luxury when you only have hot water in your home once a week. You know what they say about Romania—the only thing colder than the cold water is the hot water. So don't worry about Simina. She's enjoying ten Christmases and five birthdays all at once."

"Stefan, I don't want to eat your food," I said. But somewhere in the back of my mind, the journalist part of me was thinking I ought to try it. The chicken feet would provide color for my article.

"But Elisabeta, I insist," he said, using the Romanian version of my name.

"Maybe later."

"Then what do you want?"

I hesitated. "Just to spend some time together—talk, get to know you."

"What would you like to talk about?"

"I don't know—poetry, philosophy, freedom, your life—anything you like."

"Ah freedom, let's talk about that. Tell me, what is it like?"

"How do you mean?"

"To be able to go wherever you like, say whatever you think, think whatever you wish? These are things we Romanians can no longer do."

I looked into his piercing, bitter eyes. "Stefan, I don't believe there's anything I can teach you about freedom. We've just met but I think you understand more about freedom than anyone I've ever known. You may not be able to go wherever you like or say whatever you want, but nobody owns your mind or your soul. That's the definition of a free man."

He smiled, humoring me. "That's flattering, but how can you know this after such a brief acquaintance?"

Finding courage, I took his hand. "You'll call me crazy … but the first time I saw your photograph back in Mr. Eskew's office in Boston …" I stopped. What I had been about to say sounded silly even to me, like something from a cheap romance novel.

"Go on."

I steeled myself. "I can't explain it very well, not even to myself. I'm not a mystical person or a sentimentalist—but when I saw your photograph and read your poems, something happened. I think you touched my heart. Language can't quite describe it; it's beyond logic."

He made as if to reply but I gestured him to wait as my words gathered force.

"You spoke to me through your image. Isn't that crazy? Of course, I'm interested in your country and I want to write a good article and promote my career—but Stefan, if I'm honest with myself, you're the real reason I'm here. I saw your face and I wanted to talk to you, to know you, to …"

"To kiss me?"

"You're right to laugh. And yet … the first time we touched, when we met in the street, there was something … real … alive … a connection—and again, although infinitely stronger when we kissed. You felt it too, you can't deny it."

Silence. Then, "No, I don't deny it. There was something. Perhaps it was simply physical. After all, you are a beautiful woman, and I, despite everything they've done to me, am still a man."

"We both know it was something more. Stefan, I came thousands of miles and we only have a short time. I'd just like to know more about you, as much as I can. I need to know if this is real or whether it's just a fantasy."

I lifted my head to look at him. He gave that lopsided grin. "That's all?"

I shrugged. "For starters."

"Ah, another allusion to food."

"Sorry."

"And for the main course?"

"This is the main course."

"In that case there's only one thing to do," he said.

"What's that?"

"We must dance."

3 - Sinaia: October 2007

The 90-minute train ride north from Bucharest to Sinaia was a riot. Angela, Andrei, Cristina and half-a-dozen other friends had come to lend support to Mihai and to enjoy a beautiful autumn weekend in the mountains. Angela said Petra could stay with her parents who had a large house on a hillside overlooking the town. They piled into the train carriage, laughing and joking. Angela winked at Petra, then jumped on her boyfriend's lap and they started making out right there and then. When Mihai's cell phone suddenly went off, playing the theme of the *William Tell Overture*, everyone but the two lovebirds joined in, infecting the other passengers with their enthusiasm until the whole car was suddenly singing together. Mihai tried to take the call, clutching his instrument case between his knees, his garment bag over one arm, holding the phone right against one ear and sticking a finger in the other—but it was hopeless and he gave up the struggle.

Petra took a corner seat feeling a little excluded from the babble of words she was unable to understand. No sooner had everyone gotten settled in their seats when they started pulling out food for the 90-minute journey. Cristina grinned at her and tossed her an apple. Petra had always been awful at any sport involving a ball. To her relief, for once she managed to catch it. She ate while looking out the window as the train started moving. Within minutes, it had left behind the drab, crumbling Soviet-style housing blocks of outer Bucharest and was moving across a flat, green plain. She saw peasants driving horses and carts along dirt paths beside huge fields. Someone sat down next to her—without looking, she knew it was Mihai. He reached across and hung his garment bag up by a hook next to the window.

"Tuxedo," he muttered.

"Are you nervous?" she asked.

"About what? The concert?"

She nodded.

"Not really. I do these gigs to make a few euros but that's not what I really care about. Not that I don't love the music—I do, of course—but it's not what I see myself doing for the rest of my life, although my parents and my professors put pressure on me all the time to devote myself to the violin. Do you have tiny, little sparkles in your cheeks or is it just the way the light is catching you."

"It's just some powder Angela gave me to try. Do you like it?" she asked, pleased he'd noticed.

"Very alluring." She blushed and hurriedly got the conversation back on track.

"So Mihai, what will you do if you're not going to be a violinist?"

"I want to compose. Actually, I already compose but it would be nice to get something performed somewhere one day."

"Don't be so modest Mihai. I *googled* you. I know you won a big competition at the University of Indiana."

"You did?"

"Sure I did. I google almost everyone I meet. It's automatic. Don't you?"

"Not usually."

"So what kind of music do you write?" Petra asked.

"It's hard to explain, kind of a merging of avant garde and classical. I'm into something called 'sonification' right now. I'm trying to write a piece based on my impressions of New York City."

"Cool. What's it like?"

"Do you play sudoku puzzles?"

"Sometimes, if I'm bored and there's nothing else to do."

"Well this piece I'm working on is like the audio representation of the numbers in one of those puzzles. Each variable on the grid is reflected in the piece."

"This is electronic music?"

"Yeah, I compose on my computer. So how it works is, each number stands for a note. The way they're arranged in rows controls the resonance or sound quality; their place in the columns control the duration of each note and their position in the boxes the volume. Are you with me?"

"Not really. It doesn't sound like my kind of music."

"Keep an open mind, you don't know how you'll respond until you hear it. So here's where it gets interesting. I'm using an actual puzzle and I arranged the notes in the same order that I solved it. That creates a sonic connection between the notes, because each number provided the clue that led to the next. So it's not totally random."

"It sounds more like math than music."

"Well, music is math. In fact everything in the world can be reduced to math if you think about it that way. You should know this. I've seen you wearing a sweatshirt saying, *'Math Rocks the World'*."

"That was the old me."

"But you're correct in saying that music has to be more than just math. So what I've tried to do is turn the basic numerical theme I derived from the puzzle into a fugue, like in Bach. Actually, what emerges is quite haunting."

"What's it got to do with New York?"

"New York City is a grid like a sudoku puzzle. I'll play it for you when we get home. Actually, nobody but my composition professor has heard it yet so you would be the first."

"Not Angela or Cristina?" Petra asked, feeling absurdly pleased.

"They wouldn't get it."

While they'd been speaking, the scenery had changed. They were climbing through hills covered with trees ablaze with color—deep russets, different shades of yellows and oranges and the dark greens of the fir trees all forming a glorious tapestry.

"Wow," Petra gasped. "This is almost like fall at home." For a second, she spared a guilty thought for her mother who still thought she was in Providence, half a world away. Then she was back to the present, drinking in the scenery, thinking to herself with amazement that here she was, surrounded by new friends who accepted her, with a gorgeous guy sitting next to her pouring out his secrets, and that never, ever in her life had she felt so free, so ecstatic, so … happy!

"Maybe, I could stay here longer," she suddenly thought. "I don't have to rush home. I could enroll at the University of Bucharest, meet my father, learn Romanian—it shouldn't be difficult. Everyone keeps telling me, it's a Romance language." But then she thought she'd need money and her mother would have to agree, which seemed highly unlikely.

"Your father," Mihai said abruptly, bringing her back to reality. "We asked some questions. He's not married. He was for a few years but it ended."

"Children?"

"No children."

Petra felt a touch disappointed to let go of her fantasy of bonding with a long-lost half-brother or sister. But she was also relieved. One less complication.

"Did you get a reply to your email?" Mihai asked.

"Yeah, he messaged me yesterday. He said he remembered my mother and that I should call his assistant for an appointment or come to his class next week and he'd talk to me."

"So did you call?"

"Not yet. I guess I'll do it on Monday."

"And that was all? Nothing about your mother or their relationship?"

"That's all he said."

They arrived at the mountain resort of Sinaia to be met by a battered old Dacia at the station. An exuberant man with a spectacular mustache and a broad brimmed straw hat emerged from the vehicle and started toward her, arms outstretched.

"Welcome, welcome, welcome to Sinaia, Miss American girl," he bellowed. "I am Ion, father of Angela. You are welcome to my car, my home, my town, my country, our wonderful world." Before she could react, he had enveloped her in a mighty bear hug.

"Thank you," Petra mumbled, as her face was crushed against his tweed jacket. She emerged to see the others laughing at her.

"We should have warned you," Mihai said, as they squeezed into the back seat. "Angela's father is … what's the phrase in English? … Larger than life. Now you know where Angela gets it from."

"Is true, is true," he shouted from the front seat. "I am larger than life, but I make life larger than life." He turned on the cassette player and began singing along to Puccini's *'La Bohème.'* "You love opera?" he yelled, taking his eye off the road to look back at Petra.

"I guess."

"You guess? You guess? You cannot guess. No guess. Either you love or you hate. Me, I love. Puccini, Verdi, Rossini, Donizetti, Bellini. I love."

He abruptly pulled over next to another vehicle and started shouting at the driver. Both men got out of their cars; Petra thought for a moment that they were about to start a fight but instead they began slapping each other on the back. The second man opened his trunk and pulled out two cartons of Marlboro cigarettes which he tossed to Ion who stowed them in his own trunk.

"He owed me big favor," he explained to Petra and winked as they pulled away.

Driving way too fast, they hit a cobbled road with woods on either side and suddenly, through a clearing, Petra saw what looked like a Disney castle with white turrets, Tudor-style half timbers and neo-classical pillars painted with figures of knights in armor. It was an architectural mish-mash but somehow, here in these Transylvanian mountains, it worked.

"Peleş Palace," Ion shouted. "Builded by our first king, Carol, from Germany. Is *sehr schön,* very beautiful. Tomorrow, you will see inside."

They turned a corner and there was another, slightly smaller castle. "That one is called Pelişor—is queen's house because king's palace was too big for her," Ion explained. "Also *sehr, sehr schön*."

They screeched around another bend and Ion shoved the car into reverse; then started driving up a steep cobbled street backwards at 30 miles an hour. "Is here," he announced happily, as they lurched to a halt outside a house at what seemed like the highest point in Sinaia. The sun was just setting, casting a warm glow on the rocky mountain that towered over the town from the other side of the valley.

Inside, the three-story house was like a museum. Petra had never seen anything like it. Every inch of wall was covered with pictures, every inch of surface with collectibles of different kinds. One wall featured portraits of Lenin, Stalin and Ceauşescu and a glass display case of communist medals.

"I buy in flea market in Bucharest, very cheap," Ion declared when he saw Petra looking at them. "You think perhaps I red communist? Is not so. Once they own me, dirty bastards. Now I own them."

There was a large collection of knives and swords, another of oriental carved elephants gathering dust on a sideboard; yet another wall was covered with Japanese wood cuts.

"I see, I like, I buy," Ion chuckled. "Is good."

"Is dumb," Angela interjected, but her voice was affectionate.

"Is dumb, maybe, but good," Ion insisted, blowing a kiss at her.

Angela's mother entered the room and introduced herself as Clara. A small, self-possessed woman with close-cropped gray hair, she was as quiet and sedate as her husband was effervescent.

"My wife is German," Ion declared happily. "From very old family, very good. Doctors, professors, lawyers, all very clever." He pointed to some old photographs on the wall. "Here is my wife's grand-grandfather, Herr Doktor Heinrich Claussen. He builded this house 1885 and here is picture of him in this very house with family. This lady is grand-grandmother Magdalena, this one is her daughter, this one her son who was grand-grand uncle to my Clara."

Petra looked at the men in top hats and frock coats and the women in long dresses frozen in time.

"Awesome," she said, for want of something more intelligent.

"True, true, is very, very … how you say … *awesome*," Ion said, doing a pretty good imitation of a teenage American girl. "And now we drink. Clara, please to bring drinks for all young guests and for special American guest from United of States."

"I didn't know there were Germans in Romania," Petra observed.

"Yes, Saxons were here in Transylvania almost for 1,000 of years. Of course now, there are not so many. The pig Ceauşescu sold them to West Germany for deutsche marks to put in his personal pocket," Ion said.

Clara bustled in with glasses on a tray and some clear liquid which she announced was a homemade liqueur made from apples.

"Try, try," said Ion, pouring her a shot glass.

"I'm underage," Petra said, trying to wave it away.

"What is this?"

"I'm under 21. In the United States, that's the drinking age."

"You how old?"

"Um, 19," Petra said, aware of Mihai shooting her a quizzical glance. Now she was regretting having spoken.

"You 19, you old enough. Come, drink, drink to your health and this beautiful day in Sinaia." He started singing, *"May the Lord God Bless America, the wonderful United of States,"* to the tune of the *Marseillaise*, which should have been weird but sounded almost normal from his lips.

Seeing no escape, she lifted the glass to her lips and took a tiny sip. It tasted like medicine, only worse, and was followed by a searing, burning sensation in her throat and all the way down into her stomach. “Ugh,” she sputtered.

Ion burst out in a mighty guffaw. “Hey, little American lady. Is strong, no?”

Next morning, Petra toured the palaces with Angela. Mihai was rehearsing with his colleagues but he appeared after lunch, grabbed her hand and pulled her outside.

“Come on, we’re going to the hills,” he said.

They started walking, just the two of them, along a narrow road that climbed slowly out of town. After about a mile, Mihai veered off on a trail into the forest.

“Watch out for bears,” he said, as they climbed through a forest carpeted with fallen leaves.

“I hope you’re joking,” Petra said.

“Nope, there are lots of bears in these woods. You often see them at night. They come down to scavenge for food. Don’t look so scared. Just keep talking nice and loud and they’ll leave us alone.”

Sunlight slanted through gaps in the trees; Petra thought the air itself was golden. She was struggling a little to keep up, but pride prevented her from asking him to slow down.

After an hour, they reached a short stairway leading up to a viewing point. They were stuck out on a parapet overlooking the valley, the town spread out several hundred feet beneath them, with a tremendous view of wooded hills all around.

“This place is called *‘Franz Josef’s Rock’* after the Austrian emperor,” Mihai said. “For five bonus points, give me the years of his reign.”

“1841-1917,” Petra said.

“Seriously—you know that?”

“No. I was guessing. I know he died during World War I so the last date is probably in the ballpark,” Petra said.

“Wow! You’re amazing,” he said, only half sarcastically.

“Was he ever here, the emperor?”

“I have no idea. See over there, that’s the cable car to the top of the mountain. Soon, maybe in a month, the snow will come. Do you ski?"

"A little."

"In winter, perhaps I'll take you up there."

If I'm still around, Petra thought.

"Stand right there," he said, producing a small digital camera. "I want to remember you just like this." She smiled shyly as he snapped a couple, feeling pleased and self-conscious at the same time.

"Now I'll take one of you," Petra said. She looked at him through the tiny screen at the back of the camera, thinking how lovely he was with his cheeks flushed from the climb and his black hair flying in the breeze.

"Now both of us," he said, balancing the camera on a ledge and pressing the time release button. He rushed back to take his place by her side, putting his arm around her and pulling her close. A whoosh of electricity ran through her as the little flash lit up and the camera clicked. They looked at each other for a long minute. *This is where he kisses me*, she thought tremulously. Instead, after an awkward moment he released her and went to retrieve the camera.

"So Petra," he said, breaking the uncomfortable silence that followed. "Are you really 19?"

She hesitated.

"Come on, the truth."

"I'm 17," she told him reluctantly, resisting the temptation to add a year.

"Shit, you're still a child. You can't even vote yet, let alone drink. How did your mother allow you to come here all alone?"

"I will be an official adult soon. I have my driver's license," Petra protested, not meeting his eyes. She was almost ready to weep. If only she'd simply knocked back the foul liqueur the previous evening instead of getting legalistic about it!

"How soon? When will you turn 18?" he asked.

"Next April," she said, knowing that the moment had irrevocably passed and nothing was going to happen between them now. He turned to go.

"Let's get moving. I need to get ready for the concert."

Mihai seemed quite different in evening dress with his hair slicked back—somehow older and more serious. Nearly all men look good in a tux but Mihai looked great—suave, virile, confident, like a younger version of Sean Connery playing James Bond. His friends had all brought flowers to give him after the concert. Petra clutched a bunch of yellow and white chrysanthemums, only half-listening as the ensemble worked their way through an early Beethoven quartet. But after the interval, something changed. The quartet was playing a Schubert piece called '*Death and the Maiden.*' Petra didn't know much about chamber music but the tragic second movement drew her in. She'd never experienced a concert this way before. Her eyes stayed on Mihai, watching his every expression. It was as if she was inside his head, channeling the music the same way he did, feeling it at the moment of creation. A kind of rapture overtook her. Her scalp was tingling; she was on the verge of tears. And then she realized, *My God, I'm in love with him.*

4 – Bucharest: March 1989

Petrescu rummaged through a pile of records on the floor. "Simina doesn't have any real dance music but this ought to do."

"Stefan, I ought to warn you, I can't dance," I said nervously.

"Oh but you can." He rested his arms around my waist and I placed mine on his shoulders. The music began, a piano tune in three time. He started swaying ever so slightly with the music and I swayed along with him, a little to the left, a little to the right, shifting my weight from one foot to the other, feeling foolish like a girl at her first high school dance. He moved closer, his left hand exerting gentle pressure on the small of my back. I found my feet were moving and he was guiding me slowly around the cramped living room. Gradually, I lost my inhibitions.

"What is that music? It's haunting," I murmured.

"It's Chopin, the fourth ballade."

"It's so sad and lovely at the same time." The theme in a

minor key was based on five notes, rising and falling. I found myself humming them quietly, my mind silently inventing a five-syllable lyric to go with the melody. *"Could this truly be? Do you feel it too?"* I leaned into him, resting my head on his shoulder, closing my eyes, feeling the flow of the music and the gentle rocking of his body. His hands rose higher up my back; I nuzzled his neck, matching my breathing to his. It was as if we had entered a cocoon—a place we had created inside the music. Nothing I had ever experienced was half as sensual.

The piano grew more impassioned and agitated—but always that five-note motif returned. My mind sung, *"Is this real to you? As it is to me?"* Finally, the music erupted in a furious display of piano virtuosity and we could no longer keep up a rhythm. As we stopped moving, Petrescu placed his hands on my cheeks and kissed me once more.

Just as the piece ended with four tumultuous chords, the dim light in the apartment abruptly went out. I heard the record stop spinning and the background hum of the refrigerator fade away. We stood in total silence and perfect darkness. Reluctantly, our lips drew apart.

"Power cut," Petrescu said, stating the obvious. "Our wise leaders have decreed, enough dancing for now."

Now I felt the cold again. "Let's not stop," I said.

So we held each other a little more, humming the theme together almost soundlessly. Finally, he led me by the hand to a sofa.

"Come, sit down." By now, my eyes were adjusting to the darkness. He walked off into another room and returned carrying a blanket. "Here, this will keep us a bit warmer."

"I don't know how you stand this—the cold, the power outages, the chicken feet."

"We don't exactly stand it. We endure it because we have no choice. We sit in our apartments with our coats on from November to April. Why do you think people queue seven hours in the cold for tickets to see a Fellini movie or an opera? It's worth it just to remind yourself you are still human."

"Why don't people rise up?"

"Using what as weapons? Their bare hands? Against an army with tanks and submachine guns and artillery? Perhaps that day will come but for now, our beloved leader has this nation firmly under his thumb. So many Romanians have become corrupted and profit from the system. Sometimes I think we may have forgotten the meaning and value of freedom. But then I tell myself it's not true. We may be bowed but we are not yet completely broken. Somewhere, deep under the surface perhaps, we still long for freedom."

"Stefan, what makes you so different? You haven't forgotten."

He shrugged. "Perhaps it's because I live as much as possible in a different world, the world of literature, which is sometime more real to me than the so-called real world. And also, because I have faith in God. When I read the Bible, especially the Book of Psalms, the words strengthen and comfort me. But enough about me. What about you? So far, all I know is that your name is Elizabeth, you are a journalist and you dispense wonderful kisses to cold, lonely poets."

So I told him about my career and how I had married Tom hoping to have a family and why I had left him before coming to Romania.

"Is it really over?" Petrescu asked.

"Completely," I said, meeting his gaze, realizing that if it hadn't been before, it certainly was now. "Totally, utterly, absolutely."

He smiled wryly. "I too would like to have children some day. But who would take the responsibility of bringing new life into being in a place like this?" Stretching out on the narrow sofa, he pulled me toward him. "We only have a short time. Soon, you must leave. I have my seminar this evening and you should get back to the hotel. This has been a wonderful dream, but every dream must end." He stroked my face and I leaned forward to kiss him again, a gentle kiss full of regret. His breath became mine and then ours.

"You feel so different from a Romanian woman," he murmured. He himself was all bone and sinew; I could count his ribs through his clothes.

"How am I different?"

"Your body—it's lovely … womanly. And your face is so soft and smooth, it's almost unreal. We Romanians, men and women both, have become … coarsened and roughened, like sandpaper. When we couple, our bones grind together like old car parts."

I didn't want to think about him coupling. "Stefan, you shouldn't compare me to a Romanian woman. It's unfair. Of course my face is soft and smooth. I have all the advantages money can buy. You should see my bathroom back home. You wouldn't believe the number of skin products on my shelf and the amount of money I spend on them. Here, women have nothing. That doesn't make me unreal. Believe me, I am real and this thing that's happening to us is very, very real."

"Maybe to you. To me, it's like a dream."

"Please stop saying that. I don't want it to be a dream, at least not now while I'm living it. Later perhaps, but not now."

"Very well, we'll agree that it's real, even if my head is spinning and I feel drunk."

"Me too." We kissed again, little exploratory pecks on the lips.

"Can't I stay for your seminar?" I asked. "I'd love to see you teach. And I don't want to leave."

Abruptly, he released me. "Unfortunately you must leave. It's forbidden for Romanians to have contact with foreigners. I would be putting my students in danger if you stayed."

"But I thought they were your friends. Surely you can trust them. Who would know?"

Petrescu smiled grimly. "One of the apostles always plays the part of Judas."

"What do you mean?"

"Someone will be the informer. I just don't know who." Petrescu grasped my hand under the blanket and began stroking it gently. "Let me tell you a story, Elisabeta. If you wish, you can use it in your article as long as no names appear. Do you agree?"

"Of course."

"A colleague of mine, a fellow writer, told me this. He himself had a very close friend whom he had known since childhood. The two had no secrets, or so he thought. But he was wrong. One day, his friend came to him to make a confession. The friend said he had been forced by the government to become an informer; his one duty was to report on the doings of my colleague, the writer. Once a week, sometimes even more, the friend met his control officer in various apartments around Bucharest to deliver his reports. Eventually, he could stand the guilt no longer and so he confessed what he had been doing and asked my colleague for forgiveness."

"What did your colleague say?"

"At first, he was shocked, then disgusted and disappointed. But gradually he became used to the idea. He remained on good terms with his friend and neither of them ever mentioned it again. And yet, it was understood that the spying continued and that once a week the friend delivered his report to the *Securitate.* This situation went on for some time until one day the informer obtained permission to emigrate. Strangely, once he was gone, my colleague found that he missed him and not only as a friend. He knew that someone in his close circle, another trusted associate, must have taken his friend's place as spy and informer—but he did not know which one. Someone was writing reports on him, but who? It turned out that it was better to know than not to know. That is the situation I find myself in. I'm certain someone close to me is informing on me, but I do not know who. And the price my true friends could pay for unauthorized contact with you could be very high. That's why you cannot stay."

"And through all this craziness you continue to teach Shakespeare? Why?"

"Ah Elizabeth, such a question. I'm surprised at you. One never grows tired of Shakespeare. Anyone who believes in the power of words, in the power of literature, must read Shakespeare. He teaches us so much. He teaches us that everything, even this great evil we are living through, will pass. He teaches us …" He sat up, excited, pulling out a book from his satchel which had fallen under the sofa. "If only we had a light, I would show you. Where does Simina keep her candles for God's sake?"

He started rummaging around in kitchen drawers.

"Aha, here we are. Come here and read this."

I squinted over a book by the feeble candlelight and read.

Sonnet 29

When in disgrace with Fortune and men's eyes,
I all alone beweep my outcast state,
And trouble deaf Heaven with my bootless cries,
And look upon myself and curse my fate,
Wishing me to one more rich in hope,
Featured like him, like him with friends possessed,
Desiring this man's art, and that man's scope,
With what I most enjoy contented least;
Yet in these thoughts myself almost despising,,
Haply I think on thee, and then my state
Like to the Lark at break of day arising
From sullen earth sings hymns at Heaven's gate,
For thy sweet love rememb'red such wealth brings
That then I scorn to change my state with kings.

"Do you understand what he's saying and how perfect it fits for us today?" Petrescu asked, his thin face alight with enthusiasm in the dim light.

"It's a nice poem," I said skeptically.

"It's not nice. It's inspiring. No matter how miserable he is, no matter how isolated and unlucky and worthless he feels even to the point of self-disgust, the poet can always draw comfort simply by remembering the sweetness of love—and this thought transforms him utterly. What a powerful concept! One moment, he's complaining to heaven at his fate, the next he's singing hymns of praise at heaven's gate. Did you catch the way the words *'despising'* and *'arising'* give way to the word *'sing'* at the moment of transformation? The word *'brings'* in the next to last line actually sounds like a bell ringing. Try saying it, *'Brings, brings, brings...'*"

I tried. It did sound like a bell.

"And do you see how the imagery ascends from *'sullen earth'* upwards through the flight of the lark, finally arriving at heaven itself? And how heaven is deaf at the beginning of the poem but by the end is unable to resist the hymns sung at its gate?"

"You make it sound wonderful. I can see you truly are a passionate teacher. But Stefan, it's still just a poem. Unfortunately, it's not real life."

"I must ask you to let me decide for myself what is real and what is unreal. You tell me that you are real and these hours we have shared together are real—but soon you will be gone, back to your country, your magazine, your life. And I will still be here, staring at these four walls, isolated, unable to publish, doubting my own talent, cursing my fate. How will I do it? Do you have any suggestions?"

I had nothing to say. I felt an almost physical pain at his plight.

"I see you are silent," he said.

"I'm so sorry. I never thought about what might happen after we met. I couldn't see that far ahead. Perhaps, I shouldn't have come at all," I said.

He grabbed my hand and brought it to his lips. "No! Don't say that. This afternoon has been—wonderful, magical! I think for the last few years I have been sleepwalking through my life and now you have awoken me with your kisses."

"Perhaps that was a mistake," I said, fighting back tears.

"No! It's always better to be awake than asleep, even if it's more painful. Shakespeare gives me the answer; he tells me how to survive. He says that just the memory of love should turn my complaints into hymns of praise, which I can sing at the very gate of heaven."

"I think you put too much stock in memory. I'm a journalist, I know how unreliable memory can be. It changes depending on circumstances. I've seen it a million times. Two people live through the same event and when you interview them later, they remember entirely different things. People are always reconstructing their memories to fit the story they're trying to tell themselves and others."

"That won't happen to me. Elisabeta. I don't know how to explain these feelings I have experienced with you this afternoon. Perhaps it's a temporary madness. But I do know that for the first time in a long time, my spirit is light. And all because you saw my picture and read my poems and came halfway around the world to meet me. That's amazing. No matter what, I'll never forget it."

"And that's all we're left with?" I asked. "That's the end of our story?"

He didn't respond. More desperately, I said, "Can't we at least meet once again?"

He hesitated. "How long will you stay in Romania?"

"Maybe another two weeks."

"You know it's dangerous for me to meet with you."

"It's your decision. Whatever you decide, I'll understand."

For a long minute, I held my breath. Then he smiled. "What would I not risk for one more afternoon with you? Come to the same church next Thursday."

5 – Massachusetts: October 2007

To: Poneill@brown.edu

Fm: Lizgraham@tmail.com

Petra, I don't suppose you realize how sad I was to receive your message saying you may not come home for Thanksgiving. I think you should reconsider. *I've delayed replying to you until now so as not to be over-emotional. (Liz backed up and deleted this.)* It's important. Even though Tom is dead, we are still a family. Thanksgiving is the one time we all come together. It's especially important this year. Even if you're angry, I'm asking you to come home for the sake of your brothers who want to see you and their kids who love their "Auntie Petra."

On another note, I'm interested in your new Shakespeare course. Stefan Petrescu once explained one of the sonnets to me. I think it was number 29. If you read it, you'll see that it's all about how the memory of love endures. We ended up disagreeing on whether memory has the power to banish sorrow. He thought it could; I disagreed. *I wish I could ask him now if he still thinks the same way, after everything that has happened. It would comfort me to know that he does. (And again, Liz hit the delete button to make those last two sentences disappear)*

Love,

Mom

6 - Bucharest: October 2007

Petra and Angela slipped quietly into the classroom and took seats at the back. Twenty minutes before the lecture was to begin, already the room was filling up, mostly with young women. Soon, there would be standing room only.

Petra looked around at the grubby, peeling walls, the creaky old wooden desks covered with the scribbles and carvings of generations of students and the exposed hot water pipes running along the sides of the room. One window was broken and boarded up with a piece of cardboard. She had persuaded Angela to accompany her; she felt too nervous to face Petrescu alone. Mihai had refused to come; he thought she should have responded to Petrescu's email invitation and made an appointment to see him one-on-one. He couldn't understand her hesitation.

"Petrescu clearly wants to meet you. He says he remembers your mother." But Petra wanted to attend the class anonymously, observe from afar, and then decide how to approach him. She'd also started worrying about what would happen after they met. What if they just had a polite conversation and promised vaguely to keep in touch? Then, she'd have no further excuse to stay in Bucharest and would have to go home—which meant leaving Mihai behind, an unbearable thought.

A distance had opened between them in the past week. Mihai seemed to be avoiding her. Petra felt confused and hurt. *I was a lot happier before*, she thought. *Now I can't sleep, I feel like I'm on the verge of tears all the time and I'm behaving like a total moron. Is this what love's like? If so, it sucks.*

She wrenched herself back to the present. "Who's that?" she asked, pointing to a poster tacked to the wall showing a handsome man with thick, sensual lips, swept-back hair and a haughty expression.

"Mihai Eminescu, our national poet. He was a big romantic. He loved this woman but she was married so he could never be with her. Just like your mother," Angela said.

"You don't know that," Petra replied. By now, students were crowding into spaces between the desks, leaning against walls and sitting cross-legged on the floor. It couldn't have been more different from Brown, where every student always had a comfortable chair, clean desk and Internet connection wherever they were on campus. But there was an air of excitement that Petra had never felt in any of her classes back home. "Is it always this crowded?"

"Petrescu draws lots of people, even though he insists in giving the class in English. He's almost like a pop star. He limits the number of students taking the class for credit but the lectures are open to everyone," Angela said.

"Why don't they give him a bigger room?"

Angela shrugged. Just then, there was a rustle of anticipation. Students turned off cell phones and removed earphones. The door opened and Petrescu strode in, took off his leather jacket, threw it over the front desk and faced the class.

"Shakespeare, sonnet number 15," he announced and started handing out copies.

Petra gasped. "Why didn't you tell me?" she hissed at Angela.

"Shush," Angela whispered back.

Petrescu wasn't very tall but he was a solid, beefy fellow who looked as if he had put in long hours at the gym. His black turtleneck could hardly contain his stocky upper body and muscular neck. He wore his gray hair shorter than was fashionable and a bristly gray mustache. Then there was the large, black patch over his left eye.

The handout reached them and they each took a copy. Petra

read the poem half-heartedly, unable to concentrate. She kept peeking glances at Petrescu, drawn as if by magnetism to the eye-patch which seemed both theatrical and unsettling. This man was her father? He was speaking about the structure of the sonnet and how the rhyming scheme worked. *What had happened to his eye? Did it have anything to do with 1989, with her mother?* He was handsome all right, even in middle age. The patch only added to his mystique, lending him an edgy, piratical allure. Half the girls in the class seemed to be in his thrall, staring at him with adoring eyes. Petrescu himself appeared indifferent, or maybe he was just used to it. He started reading the poem aloud, his voice husky and melodious with just the faintest accent:

When I consider every thing that grows
Holds in perfection but a little moment,
That this huge stage presenteth nought but shows
Whereon the stars in secret influence comment;
When I perceive that men as plants increase,
Cheered and checked even by the selfsame sky,
Vaunt in their youthful sap, at height decrease,
And wear their brave state out of memory;
Then the conceit of this inconstant stay
Sets you most rich in youth before my sight,
Where wasteful Time debateth with Decay
To change your day of youth to sullied night,
And all in war with Time for love of you,
As he takes from you, I ingraft you new.

"Comments," he said when he had finished. His good eye scanned the class. "Come on ladies and gentlemen. What's this poem about? Who can tell me?"

"It's about a debate that's going on between Time and Decay," said one youth sitting in the front row, one of the few males in the class.

"Very good," Petrescu said. "And what do we learn about this debate, or war as the poet also calls it? Is anyone else involved? Who are the human characters?"

"There's the poet and the poet's lover," said another student standing against a wall. "The lover is beautiful only for a moment, but eventually he will die. Meanwhile the poet tries to keep his beauty alive by capturing it in a sonnet."

"Excellent. Notice how the poet's viewpoint encompasses the entire world, or more accurately the entire universe including even the stars. He compares it to a stage, which is a common Shakespearian metaphor, which we also see where?"

"*As You Like It*," Petra blurted out, her years of general knowledge competitions asserting themselves. "'*All the world's a stage/And all the men and women merely players.*' It's the '*Seven Ages of Man*' speech."

"Very good," Petrescu said, his eye alighting on her at the back of the room. He stared at her for a long minute, taking in her newly-tinted dark-bronze hair, eye makeup and the black velvet choker around her neck, all Angela's of course. Her mother would hardly have recognized her. Petra met his gaze. He cleared his throat and asked, "Your name, please?"

"Um, um Angela. Angela Radu," Petra mumbled, ignoring the sharp kick in the calf administered by the real Angela. Petrescu hesitated, apparently about to say something, but thought better of it and turned his attention back to the class.

"What's with you?" Angela hissed. "Why are you behaving like such a jerk?"

"I didn't want him to know. Not like this, in front of everybody. It's too impersonal," Petra whispered back.

Petrescu was explaining how the author's perspective changes during the course of the poem.

"One of the central themes of all the sonnets is the search for immortality and the transitory nature of life. All great writers ask the same 'big question,' namely, '*What is the ultimate purpose of life, since we all must die?*' Of course, this is a great theme in religion as well. I refer you to Psalm 103. He extracted a small, leather bound Bible from his breast pocket, obviously well-handled, opened it at a previously-marked page and read:

'As for man, his days are like grass. As a flower of the field, so he flourishes.
For the wind passes over it, and it is gone.
Its place remembers it no more.
But God's loving kindness is from everlasting to everlasting
With those who fear him.'

"The Psalmist uses similar imagery to Shakespeare's but offers a very different answer to the question of how we should face mortality. He says we must have faith in God. That doesn't work for Shakespeare, who had little regard for religion. His approach is not to accept death but somehow to outwit it. In sonnet 29, for example, he points to memory as a defense against the ravages of time. In sonnet 12, which we studied last semester, he urges his beloved to progenerate children, as if by passing on his seed he could in some sense continue to live after his death."

At this, Petrescu's good eye wandered inexorably back to Petra.

A student in the middle of the room raised his hand. "What does he mean by *'ingraft'* in the last line?" he asked.

Petrescu nodded. "Good question. There's some discussion about the exact meaning. Some think he's urging the beloved to marry—to join, or graft himself to another in order to procreate. But the majority believes what Shakespeare means is to immortalize, in the sense that it is, he, the poet who gives his beloved a form of eternal life through his writing. A similar theme, of course, is expressed in the most famous sonnet of all, beginning, *'Shall I compare thee to a summer's day'."*

"But how does this poem immortalize the beloved?" a girl sitting near Petra asked. "We don't even know the beloved's name. We only know that he's beautiful in an abstract way. What kind of immortality is that?"

"Another excellent point," said Petrescu.

Petra's hand flew up in the air. From her first day in kindergarten, her hand had always been shooting up with answers and opinions and she was powerless to stop it. Petrescu spotted her immediately, almost as though he'd been waiting.

"Yes, Ms. ... Ms ...um ... Radu, you have something to add?"

"I don't think that Shakespeare himself believes in what he's saying," she said, starting nervously but gaining confidence as she spoke. For her at this moment, Petrescu had become another in a long line of teachers and professors with whom to cross intellectual swords.

Petra continued, "If you read the *'Seven Ages'* speech in *'As You Like It,'* you see he regards aging and death as inevitable and there's nothing anyone can do about it. The lover grows up and becomes a soldier, who in turn becomes a judge, who becomes an old man, who finally sinks into his second childhood. I don't believe this sonnet has much to do with the beloved. It's all about Shakespeare himself bragging about what a great poet he is. Writers always care more about themselves and their work than other people. This poem doesn't offer a real solution to what you called *'the big question.'* It's just Shakespeare on an ego trip, showing how great he is with words At the end of the day it's just a poem, it's not real life."

"It's just a poem, it's not real life," Petrescu repeated, as if in a trance. He sat down heavily on the desk, swinging one leg below him, apparently lost in space. The class waited patiently, pencils poised for the next nugget of wisdom. Then, he collected himself, glanced at his watch and said, "Well, Ms. ... Ms. Angela Radu has had the final word. Same time next week please."

"Quick, let's get out of here," Petra said, grabbing Angela's arm.

"Aren't you going to meet him?"

"Not today. I can't. I'm not ready," Petra said. Suddenly, she was crying. She looked toward Petrescu, but he was surrounded by students clamoring for his attention and she could no longer see him.

"But you impressed him. Everybody could see that."

"I can't meet him. Not here, not now. It's too much. This is all wrong. Don't you see?" Petra said, trying to control the onrush of emotions she was experiencing.

"OK, we'll go," Angela said. They slipped out of the door.

7 - Bucharest: March 1989

The day after my encounter with Petrescu, I interviewed Marius Gavril, chief spokesman of the Romanian Foreign Ministry. We met in the coffee shop of the Athénée Palace. I ordered hot tea. Gavril, by far the plumpest, best fed Romanian I'd encountered, was drinking Pepsi which the waitress poured carefully from a china tea pot as if it were Early Grey.

"If you don't mind me asking, why are you drinking soda from a porcelain teacup?" I asked after the woman had withdrawn.

"This is the real thing, just like you would drink in Manhattan or London," said the diplomat, who had shown up wearing an elegant charcoal gray suit obviously acquired in the West. "However, I feel no need to flaunt it or make other people feel bad. Unfortunately, in our current situation, not everyone can enjoy such a luxury. Better to let them think I'm drinking tea."

"Actually, Coke is the real thing," I said. But the allusion was lost on Gavril.

"No madam, I assure you, *this* is the real thing," he insisted, picking up a napkin and gently dabbing his thick, fleshy lips. "Why don't you have some? Then you will see." He was a large, moon-faced man who clearly took pride in his appearance from his carefully blow-dried hair to the yellow silk handkerchief sticking out of his breast pocket.

"No thank you. I'll stick to tea," I said, dropping a lump of sugar into it. "So tell me, Mr. Gavril, how would you assess your country's position in the world right now?"

"Romania plays a unique role, poised between East and West and between Europe and the Middle East," he said as if reciting a prepared text. "You are no doubt aware, for example, of President Ceauşescu's special role as an interlocutor between Israel and the Arab world. While enjoying diplomatic relations with the Israelis, he also maintains a long-standing friendship with Chairman Arafat of the PLO. Our President would like to see an Israeli-Palestinian dialogue begin and offers his services as an intermediary. This is just one example of Romania's special mission in the world."

"But isn't Romania itself rather isolated right now?"

"Not at all. What gave you that idea?"

"You no longer have *'most favored nation'* status with the United States."

"We hope that is temporary. It is true that we have been the unfortunate victim of a sordid and unjustified smear campaign in your country. That's one reason we welcome journalists like yourself to come here and see the truth."

"And your ties with the Soviets under Gorbachev?" I asked. "One reads about strains in that relationship as well."

"Let me explain something, Madam Graham. For most of our history, we Romanians have been squeezed between powerful empires—the Ottomans to our east, the Austrians and Hungarians to our west and the Russian bear on our doorstep in the north. Each of them have at times gobbled up pieces of our historic homeland. Of course, the Ottoman and Austro-Hungarian empires are no more and these days the Russian bear is mostly content to stay in the forest where he belongs. But occasionally, the bear tries to come into the kitchen to warm himself by our fire. That's when problems arise."

The idea of anyone trying to warm themselves by a Romanian fire seemed far-fetched. But Gavril was still in full flow.

"It is not easy living alongside such a powerful neighbor," he intoned. "It took an act of extraordinary courage by President Nicolae Ceauşescu in 1968 to condemn the Soviet invasion of Czechoslovakia—just one example of his inspired leadership. Remember, we are an island of Latin culture in a sea of Slavs. And yet, the friendship between the Romanian and Soviet peoples ultimately remains unbreakable because both are committed to the path of socialism and justice. So we shall walk on together, on the same unstoppable path, despite occasional temporary strains."

I shook my head, trying to make sense of this torrent of contradictory words. "Isn't Romania actually becoming a pariah nation right now, isolated from both the East and the West?"

Gavril dabbed his forehead with his handkerchief and shifted uncomfortably in his chair. No doubt, he knew about the hidden microphones placed all over the hotel. He stiffened his back and began to speak, slowly and clearly, so there should be no misunderstandings.

"Those are very strong words, Madam Graham, not at all the language one would expect from a guest we have welcomed into our midst. Have we not shown you true hospitality? Have we not opened the doors of our ministries to you? Indeed, tomorrow are you not traveling to visit one of our factories, in accordance with your own request? But let me answer your impertinent question anyway."

He took a deep breath. "Romania is a proud, independent country that answers to no-one. Under President Ceauşescu's strong leadership, we have rid ourselves of the burden of foreign debt. Who else in the entire world can say that? Can the United States say so? I think not. Your country cannot boast the economic independence achieved by little Romania, achieved I might add, without so-called *'most favored nation'* status."

He poured out the rest of the Pepsi from the teapot and drained it in a single swig. "That's the real thing," he said proudly, and stood up to leave.

Back in my room, I decided to call Eskew. He'd phoned the previous day when I was out, leaving a message to get back to him urgently. I knew what he wanted. The old buzzard was running out of patience; he was getting anxious for me to write my story and get it into the magazine.

I knew my time here was limited. But I was determined not to leave before meeting Petrescu at least once more. The truth was, I'd been thinking of little else since we parted. At night, I tossed feverishly in bed, thinking of him alone in his freezing apartment. Every time I ate, I thought of his skeletal body.

I ordered the call to Eskew from my friend, the hotel switchboard lady, to whom I'd been giving regular, small payoffs. Five minutes later, I was put through.

"Ah Elizabeth, I was hoping to speak to you today at long last," he wheezed. "I've been trying to reach you but you were never in your room."

"I've been so busy."

"Excellent," he brayed. "I'm anxious to see your story. They're working on the cover art as we speak—which brings me to the nub of the matter. When do you expect to start writing?"

"Mr. Eskew, I'm not quite ready to leave here yet. There's more to do. For example, I finally got permission to visit a tractor factory."

"Could be interesting. I recall once publishing a fascinating article about how tractors were a major symbol in official Soviet art in the 1920s and 1930s representing modernity and the end of the old order. Later, tractor production lines were transformed into tank factories and became a symbol of Soviet resistance to Hitler."

No matter how obscure the subject, Eskew had always published a "fascinating" article about it some time or another over the past 35 years.

"This particular visit may be revealing," I said, taking advantage of his interest. "They're taking me to a factory near the city of Braşov in Transylvania where there was some serious labor unrest a couple of years ago. I hope to try to gauge the mood."

"How will you do that? I assume you'll be kept on a tight leash," Eskew observed.

"Yes, I'm sure everyone I speak to will have been carefully chosen in advance and told exactly what to say. And of course, I'll have a Ministry of Information minder with me. Still, they can't stop you seeing things and you can often read between the lines of what people tell you."

"And after that, what are your plans?"

"The other thing I'm working on has to do with the horse and the apple," I said, hoping the allusion to Petrescu would be too obscure for any government eavesdropper to catch. "I'll need a couple more weeks here to complete my research into that angle."

"Too long. I have you penciled in for the cover story of the April 10 edition, which means I need to receive your copy for editing April 7 at the very latest. Of course I understand one can never do too much research. There's always another interview to conduct, another place to visit, another angle to investigate. But there comes a time when you have to say 'enough.' By all means, visit your factory and give my regards to the horse man if you see him. But after that you must leave, lock yourself in a quiet room somewhere and start writing."

My heart sank but I knew there was no appeal. "OK, I'll come home at the end of next week."

"Actually I had another idea. If you were willing to stay in Europe a little longer, I would definitely have more stories for you to cover—unless you absolutely insist on returning. I assume from the increasingly frantic calls my secretary intercepts from your husband every day, that the two of you are not reconciled."

I wasn't getting into that. "What kind of stories?"

"As we discussed before you left, interesting things are happening within the Soviet Union and Eastern Europe. Now that you've experienced Romania, I could use your expertise elsewhere. Did you know for instance that the Soviet Republic of Lithuania recently adopted its own flag? I'd like you to go to the Baltic Republics and report on their growing independence movements. Poland may soon have a truly free election, the first under communism anywhere. I'll need someone to cover that as well. We are living in a momentous time. I tell you, the evil empire is creaking. The signs are clear."

"Not here."

"So that's your story—Romania remains apart. I'll give you another week, Eliza, but then it's time to leave."

"Where should I go if you don't want me to come home?"

"The magazine owns a small apartment in London which you could use as a base for the next few weeks and as a quiet retreat in which to write your articles. Nobody is occupying it right now."

"OK. I'll fly to London."

The road north from Bucharest to Braşov next day was icy and treacherous and the mid-sized Dacia supplied by the Romanian government offered a ride that was far from luxurious. The suspension felt like it was made of wrought iron. We frequently found ourselves stuck for long stretches behind farmers driving horses and carts or trucks wheezing along at 25 mph, belching great clouds of noxious fumes behind them. Even when the road was clear, the driver had to be careful of potholes.

I was sharing the back seat with a British correspondent from the Reuters news agency, a small, pointy-faced man who introduced himself as Peter Pringle.

"Hope you don't mind me coming along on your trip," he said in a plummy British accent. "I'd been asking to see one of their factories for some time but they always turned me down until now."

"Glad of the company," I replied politely.

Inside the vehicle, it was as cold as the grave. Either the car heater did not work or for patriotic reasons the driver refused to switch it on. "God, how I hate this fucking country," Pringle mumbled under his breath at one point, as the car skidded from one side of the narrow highway to the other, narrowly missing a cart piled high with firewood.

"What brings you here?" I asked.

"It's part of the territory I cover for my sins." He extracted a red and white woolen cap emblazoned with the legend *"Arsenal FC"* from his pocket and pulled it down over his ears as far as it would go. I tried not to laugh, but he did look like one of Santa's elves who had taken a disastrous wrong turn somewhere on the way from the North Pole.

"Where are you based?" I asked.

"Vienna. I'm in charge of covering Czechoslovakia, Hungary, Bulgaria, Albania and Romania. I have to come here every once in a while, even though it's usually a waste of time."

"How so?"

"I'll tell you later. They're listening to every syllable," he mouthed. "Probably have the car bugged as well."

Our Romanian minder, a grumpy, middle-aged lady who had

introduced herself as Madam Cobalcescu, sat up front next to the driver, both of them smoking furiously. I could see her face in the rear-view mirror, lips perpetually pursed as if she were sucking on a particularly sour, green apple. No-one spoke as the car started climbing into the mountains, occasionally passing through small, bedraggled-looking towns, avoiding the chickens and turkeys that wandered freely down the middle of the road. It took half an hour to crawl through the ski resort of Sinaia and the air in the car grew ever thicker, fouler and more oppressive.

After an hour, Pringle started coughing ostentatiously and patted Cobalcescu on the shoulder to attract her attention.

"Pardon me, Madam, can you not smoke any more?" he asked. "It gives me asthma."

"What?" She turned reluctantly, favoring him with a bad-tempered grimace, exposing a set of teeth as yellow as old parchment.

"Asthma." He demonstrated by wheezing—a nasty, high-pitched, gurgling outtake of phlegmy breath that made him sound as if he needed instant hospitalization.

"This is not caused by our smoke," said Cobalcescu, profoundly unimpressed. "I suggest you see a doctor to verify the true cause."

"Excuse me?" Pringle said. "What did you say?"

Cobalcescu didn't answer. As far as she was concerned, the conversation was over. Pringle sat back seething. "You see what I mean?" he told me. His face was as red as his hat; he seemed on the verge of exploding. "The nerve of it, the fucking nerve," he muttered, coughing ostentatiously to signal his extreme displeasure.

"Madam Cobalcescu, could you perhaps explain to us what we are about to see today?" I asked hastily, hoping to avert a confrontation.

Without looking back, she answered frostily, "When you see it, you will have seen it. It will speak for itself." After that, there was no further conversation until the car pulled up in a vast, deserted parking lot outside a rusty gate. The factory, if such it was, did not appear to be functioning. There was no rattle of machinery, no funnels belching smoke, no engine sounds—nothing. It appeared to be abandoned. Cobalcescu got out of the car and walked into a small building by a chain-link fence. While we were waiting, Pringle and I decided to stretch our legs, breathing the cold air, which came as a relief from the poisonous buildup inside the vehicle. Eventually, the minder returned.

"An unfortunate mix-up," she said, not sounding in the slightest bit apologetic. "We are not expected today. The papers did not arrive from Bucharest."

"You mean we came for nothing?" Pringle asked.

"You will receive a briefing but you will not enter the facility itself."

"We can't go in?"

"Perhaps next time."

I was afraid Pringle was on the verge of an aneurysm, he was so furious. I patted his hand. "Let's see what comes out of the briefing," I said. "We can always complain afterwards."

He calmed down a little and we trooped into the building to be greeted by a skinny individual wearing an ill-fitting, toxic green polyester suit. The briefing was not illuminating. We were shown slides of the various tractors produced by the plant and given a handout in Romanian containing columns of figures signifying production, sales and exports. All the trends were up.

"Why is it so quiet here?" I asked. "It's not Sunday. Where are all the workers?"

"You prefer it to be noisy?" the briefer asked.

"One expects some noise in a factory," Pringle said. "It's a good indication that there's work going on."

"Today is a holiday."

"Which holiday?" Pringle persisted.

"An important anniversary," the official said. "More, I cannot say."

That completed the briefing and further questions were not invited. Instead, we were ushered back into the car.

"Could we take a look at the city center?" I asked. "I hear Braşov has a lovely medieval square."

Cobalcescu shook her head. "Nothing was said about that. It

was not in the plan approved by the ministry." So we returned to Bucharest.

That evening, I had dinner with Pringle in a small restaurant that was patronized almost exclusively by foreigners paying dollars. He started in on a bottle of wine, which he quickly polished off without much help from me.

"Tell me why you hate it here so much," I said.

"You need to ask? It's so depressing, so utterly miserable," he said, slurring his words only slightly. "Almost anywhere else in Eastern Europe nowadays, you find signs of change, a sense of hope. In Poland, they're negotiating to allow free elections."

"My editor wants to me to cover them."

"You should. It's going to be a great story, an important one too. I've been covering Eastern Europe for 20 years and nothing remotely like it has ever happened. Of course, nobody knows what will follow if the opposition wins. That's what makes it so fascinating."

"You think the communists will lose?"

"If people are really allowed to vote freely, the communists will lose in a landslide. The opposition has internal divisions but everyone hates the government and the Soviets and everything to do with them."

"So what would happen if the opposition won?"

"It would be a moment of truth for Gorby. Remember, it was only eight years ago the Polish commies with Soviet support crushed the opposition, threw all their leaders in prison and slapped the country under military law. I was there. But it's not only Poland that's changing. In Czechoslovakia, thousands of intellectuals have signed statements against the regime. A few years ago, they would never have dared. In Hungary last year, the parliament passed a law to create free trade unions and even freedom of the press. Can you imagine? Press freedom under communism?"

"Hard to believe."

"And then you come to this shithole and what do you find?" He waved to the waiter for a second bottle of wine.

"What?"

“A ruthless, puffed up dictator and a beaten-down population starving and freezing half to death. Look into their eyes and you see a people utterly broken. All the times I’ve come here, I’ve never once met a single Romanian with any spark of life. And it’s just going to get worse. The economy is collapsing—you saw that factory today.”

He was becoming louder with every gulp of wine but I wanted to keep him talking. The man evidently knew his stuff.

“Why do you think they wouldn’t let us in?”

“Wasn’t it obvious? Either they’ve run out of parts or they have no fuel to run the assembly lines. I tell you, there’s no hope for Romania as long as the crazy Ceauşescus rule the roost. I hate to say it but the place is totally fucked.”

Later, back at the hotel, he tried to make a pass at me, pawing ineffectually at my breasts with an unsteady hand. I briskly swatted him away like a troublesome fly.

“No hard feelings, eh Lizzie? Chap had to give it a shot,” he burbled.

“Go to bed Peter. Sleep it off.”

8 - Providence: October 2007

Dear Ms. Graham,

I am writing to ascertain the academic status of your daughter, Petra O’Neill.

I regret to inform you that Ms. O’Neill is currently in danger of failing all of her courses. She has failed to attend any of her classes since the beginning of the month and has not produced homework assignments or taken part in class quizzes. Her roommate, who reported her absence, has not seen her for several weeks and has not heard from her apart from one brief email in which she said she was taking care of a ‘family situation.’ Our inquiries as to her whereabouts have not been productive. We have reason to believe Ms. O’Neill is presently not at the university.

If Ms. O’Neill is suffering from illness or mental distress, she should inform the university as soon as possible. We try to be understanding when such circumstances occur and we would be prepared to consider allowing Ms. O'Neill to resume her studies, either next semester or at the start of the 2007/8 academic year.

Please feel free to call to discuss this and any related matters at your convenience. I must stress that unexplained and unexcused absences are not condoned and that if Ms. O'Neill wishes to remain a student in good standing, she must come forth with an explanation as soon as possible. Naturally, academic and residential fees already paid for the current semester cannot be reimbursed.

Sincerely,
Dr. J. R. Lovett,
Dean of the College of Arts and Sciences

9 - Bucharest: October 2007

In the past week, Petra had signed up for Romanian classes and now she was driving her flat-mates crazy, forcing them to engage in simple dialogues with her over and over.

"What is your name?"

"My name is Petra."

"Do you speak Romanian?"

"I speak a little Romanian?"

"Do you understand Romanian?"

" I understand a little Romanian."

"Do you speak English?"

"I speak English"

"What is your name?"

"My name is ...."

Finally, Angela rebelled. "Enough with the stupid Romanian. I have to get out of this apartment. Let's go dancing."

So here they were, walking down Strada Lipscani, a pedestrianized, cobbled street in what was left of the historic old city center, headed for her favorite night club for an evening of heavy metal, grunge and punk rock.

"Are you going to Professor Petrescu's class again tomorrow?" Angela asked as they walked.

"Planning to. Will you come too?"

"Nah. You can sit there making brainy remarks on your own. You don't need me for that. Did you email him for a personal appointment yet?"

"I tried. I just haven't been able to make myself do it."

"Why not? Isn't that why you came here?"

"It was, but after I saw him last week, everything kind of changed in my mind and I got confused and now I can't decide what to do. Maybe after I see him tomorrow …"

"I don't get you, Petra. Everything is such a big drama. You're the same way with Mihai. You really like him but you won't tell him. What's the problem?"

"Mihai thinks I'm jail bait."

"Jail bait?"

"Too young. He thinks that because I can't vote, that makes me a little girl. He's avoiding me. He wouldn't even come out with us tonight. He won't stay alone in the same room with me anymore, let alone kiss me."

"He would if you grabbed his hand and put it where it wants to go."

Petra stopped walking. "Angela! Where do you get such gross stuff?"

"OK, so maybe that wouldn't be the best approach with Mihai," Angel said, entirely unrepentant. "But I still think you should introduce yourself to your father."

"Don't call him that. That's one of the problems. When I saw him, I suddenly remembered that I already had a father. His name was Tom O'Neill and the day he died last summer was the worst of my life. If I suddenly got another one out of the blue, it would be like Tom wasn't really my Dad. Yeah, he lied to me but I still love him and he loved me. For 17 years, I called him 'Daddy.' I carry his name, O'Neill. But I also carry this other guy's name—Petra. So who am I? And then, I also keep thinking, what if Petrescu isn't interested in knowing me at all? What if we just have a polite conversation, he asks me how my mother's doing, I say she's fine, and then we say goodbye and that's that? Then I'll have lost everything."

"How interesting being you," Angela said, leading them into a doorway. "OK, this is the place. I hope it's not too loud and uncultured for you." She paid the entrance fee and they went downstairs into a cellar where they were immediately assaulted by a wall of sound blasting from massive speakers at the far end of the room. It was so crowded they could hardly move. The place smelled of stale beer, cigarettes and sweaty, unwashed bodies.

"I'll get us a drink," Angela shouted.

"What?"

"Drink," she mouthed, tipping her hand toward her mouth. She began shouldering her way through the mob and was lost to sight, somewhere in the impenetrable cloud of cigarette smoke. Petra felt someone tap her and turned around to be faced with a guy probably in his mid-twenties wearing a red muscle shirt, dancing in time to the music. He put his hands on her shoulders and before she knew it Petra was dancing too, or at least moving in time to the heavy base, which rumbled through the floorboards, making her entire body reverberate.

The guy slid his arms down to her waist and she started gyrating her rear end the way she'd seen people do it on MTV. He pulled her toward him. His arms were wet with sweat and his hair hung over his face in greasy strands. But he was well built and had a nice smile and he was looking at her as if he never suspected she'd been the nerdiest girl in the class since kindergarten.

Angela shoved her way back through the smog, two drinks in hand.

"Try this," she yelled, offering Petra a large plastic glass containing clear, sparkling liquid with a slice of lemon floating on top.

"What is it?" Petra shouted, still moving in time to the beat.

"Just try it."

Petra took a sip and made a face. "Nasty." It burned all the way down her throat as she swallowed. But she drank it down anyway in two long gulps and turned back to her dance partner, putting her arms around his neck, and just like that, they were moving, body to body once again. Angela gave her a broad grin and disappeared.

A strobe light came on, making it seem like everyone was moving in slow motion. Petra kept dancing. At some point, she lost the guy in the red shirt but before she had time to miss him, his place was taken by a bearded dude wearing black. Her head was spinning from the drink and the constant flashing lights and there was a roaring in her ears. The guy kept shaking his extensive mop of hair in Petra's direction and trying to paw her breasts, so she shook loose from him, shimmying her way between swaying, bouncing bodies, looking for Angela. All the time, the music kept up a relentless, pounding beat. Petra felt disoriented, as if she had left her regular self somewhere far behind. She felt a hand tap her on the shoulder and turning around, there was the guy in the red again.

"You American?" he shouted in English. She nodded, still keeping time with the music. "Where from?" It was too loud for conversation so she just smiled and kept moving. He grabbed her and before she knew what was happening, he was kissing her, trying to shove his tongue down her throat. She thought of resisting but it was unexpectedly thrilling. A small part of her thought this was not how she would have wanted her first kiss to be, in a smoky nightclub with some skanky guy in a red shirt whose name she didn't even know tasting of beer and cigarettes. She'd wanted it to be Mihai, at the Franz Josef Rock, overlooking glorious scenery. But he'd had his chance and he blew it. His loss was this dude's gain. She draped her arms around his neck and kissed him back, exploring his mouth with her tongue. One of his hands cupped her ass and she wriggled pleasurably, all the while still kissing Mr. Red Shirt. The hand on her ass started trying to sneak down inside her jeans, while its partner looked for an entry point into her blouse.

The feel of his intruding fingers brought Petra back to her senses. What the hell was she doing? She wrenched herself out of his grasp and wriggled away through the crowd. Finally, she spotted Angela. Petra grabbed her arm.

"Got to get some air," she sputtered and headed for the exit.

Climbing the stairs, she emerged into the street, breathing great gulps of Bucharest pollution. Her shirt and underwear were soaked with sweat. She felt grimy, tipsy, a little ashamed, a little frustrated and totally exhilarated. She'd really done it, she'd kissed a guy and as far as she could tell, she wasn't terrible at it. *Watch out Mihai, like it or not, you're next,* she thought.

"Had enough?" Angela asked, coming through the exit.

"What was that drink you gave me?"

"Vodka and fizzy water. Did you like it?"

"Disgusting. But it loosened me up, I guess."

"I'd say. I saw you kissing that guy in red like you've been doing it all your life. What were you trying to do, stroke his tonsils with your tongue? Who would have thought our little virgin would be such a natural?"

Petra felt herself blush. "He was nice. Until he started pawing my body. Then I thought enough was enough."

"Well, I guess it's time to head home. Petra has a big day tomorrow. She's finally going to meet her new daddy," Angela said, grabbing her hand. They started walking arm in arm as young Romanian women often did, taking care not to slip on the cobbles. Suddenly, Petra felt a sharp pain in her left leg. She turned in time to see a large, shaggy dog disappearing into a dilapidated building.

Looking down, she saw her pants ripped to shreds and blood dripping down her leg.

"Oh my God, I've been bitten, that dog bit me," she screamed. It had happened so fast, she'd never even seen the animal approach. But there was no doubt; blood was oozing out of two puncture wounds and she could see the bite marks. And then it was all too much—the drink, the kisses, the smoke, the noise and now this. Petra found herself sitting on the sidewalk, sobbing, "It bit me, it bit me. Now what do I do?"

"Let me see," Angela said, peering over, her voice worried. "OK, we've got to get you home and clean you up and get you disinfected. And then probably a doctor." She whipped out a cell phone. "Hey, Mihai, this is Angela. Listen to me. You've got to come. Petra's been bitten by a dog. Call a taxi and meet me at the corner of Lipscani and Victoriei. Fast. I'll never be able to find a cab off the street around here at this hour."

Bending down again to Petra, she asked, "Can you walk to the main road? It's just a short distance. Mihai will be there with a taxi in 10 minutes or less."

The pain was not terrible—just a dull, throbbing ache— and the blood flow was little more than a trickle. It was more the shock. Where had the dog come from? How could she not have seen it? Petra stood up and took an uncertain step, her shredded pants trailing behind her on the pavement. Angela grabbed the material and ripped it clear.

"OK, let's go. Lean on me."

Petra found she could walk. She didn't want to look at her leg again. They made it to the end of the street. Five minutes later, a taxi pulled up and a worried-looking Mihai jumped out.

"Are you OK?"

"This is so your fault," Petra yelled at him, surprising even herself.

"What?"

"If you'd have just kissed me that day none of this would have happened. I wouldn't have come here and danced with some sweaty, skanky guy, and kissed him and the dog wouldn't have bitten me."

"You kissed some skanky guy? Who?"

"One kiss in my whole, entire life, and now I'm going to die a horrible death from rabies," Petra shouted, and burst into tears again.

"It's all right, it's all right," Mihai said, helping her into the taxi. "You're not going to die of rabies. We're going to take good care of you. We've all been bitten at one time or another." He got into the back seat beside her while Angela sat upfront next to the driver.

"Mihai," Petra said, the alcohol making her brave.

"Yes."

"Why didn't you kiss me at the rock?"

He looked away. "Do we have to talk about it now?"

Angela turned to them from the front seat. "Don't talk about it at all. Just do it. Stop being such a wimp! Kiss her and get it over with. You know you both want to."

Mihai looked at Petra, she at him. Then, bending forward, carefully avoiding contact with her injured leg, he gently kissed her.

When they arrived back at the apartment, Mihai and Angela washed the wound and dabbed alcohol on it, making Petra howl. It wasn't all that deep but they could clearly see where the animal's upper and lower incisors had penetrated the flesh, leaving two half-oval shaped wounds.

"She has to see a doctor," Angela said. "She needs to start rabies injections as soon as possible."

"Mihai, kiss me again," Petra mumbled. "You're a good kisser, you taste much nicer than the guy at the club." His lips had sent her entire body into overdrive, driving away the pain of the bite.

"Yes, but where?" asked Mihai, ignoring her. "It's almost midnight. I don't want to go to the emergency room in the middle of the night. The hospital is horrible and she could wait there for hours. We need a private doctor—but I don't have the money."

"Wait, I have an idea." Angela scrabbled in her pocket for a piece of paper and dialed a number on her cell. A short conversation in Romanian ensued. Then she made a second call. Petra couldn't understand what was going on. Her head started spinning again. She felt vaguely nauseous. She lay down on the sofa and closed her eyes as the Romanian talk continued. She caught the word "professor" a couple of times but otherwise it might as well have been Swahili.

An arm shook her awake and she struggled to open her eyes. "Sorry," she mumbled. "Must have dozed off. How long have I been asleep?'

"Only about an hour," said Mihai. "And there's someone here to see you. He's going to take care of you and get you to a doctor first thing tomorrow morning."

"Who?" Petra asked, still confused.

“Me,” said a deep voice. She turned to see Professor Stefan Petrescu looking down at her.

10 - Massachusetts: November 2007

To: Poneill@brown.edu

Fm: Lizgraham@tmail.com

Petra, have you taken leave of your senses? How long did you plan to keep your trip a secret from me? Can you imagine how I felt receiving a letter from the dean of your college telling me that you’ve disappeared and were about to flunk out. I was in a total panic. I thought you must have been kidnapped or worse. I didn’t know who to call first—the police, the FBI, the Missing Persons Bureau? Then I had an idea and decided to contact your bank. I knew you had to be getting money from somewhere. Luckily you’re still a minor and after a bit of persuasion, they gave me access to your account. So now I know from your ATM cash withdrawals where you are. *Are you totally crazy? What on earth do you think you’re playing at in Bucharest of all places? (Liz backed up and deleted this. She wanted Petra to know how angry and worried she was but there was no need to completely alienate her. The main thing was to get her safely home as soon as possible.)*

Petra, I want you to call me as soon as you get this and tell me you’re OK. I need to hear your voice. I have to know where you’re staying and how you’re managing. I want to know, above all, that you’re safe and well. I’ll be waiting by the phone. If I don’t hear from you, I’m coming over there to bring you home myself.

Why did you keep this a secret from me? There was me sending you brownies and all the time you were in Romania. Why all the lies, the deceptive emails? I suppose you went to find your father. Did you see him? What’s he like? Does he still remember me? (Liz hit the delete button and removed the final paragraph).

Love,

Mom

11 - Bucharest: March 1989

Petrescu closed the apartment door and turned to look at me. I returned his gaze for a second, then I was in his arms.

"My God, how I waited for this. I've thought of nothing else for a week," he gasped, pulling away for air.

"Me neither," I said, drawing him back in.

This time, despite the risk of being spotted, he'd brought me to his own apartment. It was no warmer than his sister's, despite the fact that outside the temperature had risen a few degrees. In the past couple of days, the sun had come out and thc mountains of ice lining the streets had begun to thaw, forming dirty puddles of slush. Suddenly, spring was in the air. Inside, it was still darkest winter.

He shucked off his coat and started unbuttoning mine, pulling me toward his tiny bedroom.

"Yes, yes," I panted as it dropped away from my shoulders.

We fell on the bed in a tangle of limbs. "Come quickly, get under the covers," he said. "It's too cold otherwise."

As much as I had fantasized about leaping into bed with Petrescu, I hadn't dared hope it might actually happen. The truth was, I hadn't known what to expect from this encounter. Maybe we'd have another discussion about poetry. Perhaps we'd eat chicken feet. Whatever he wanted, I'd decided to go along with it. But it was clear Petrescu was not thinking of poetry or chicken feet.

"Wait, wait." I bent to unzip my boots. "OK, now." I slid under the covers, still dressed. We lay, pressed against each other, feeding off each other's warmth. He started wriggling out of his pants. I pulled my own down, kicking them to the bottom of the bed. We stopped to kiss again, our legs entwined. He sat up and pulled off his sweater and shirt. I hastened to follow. It was so cold I had to resist the urge to curl up in a ball. The sheets felt rough and coarse against my flesh. Of course, nobody in Romania had laundry driers, I thought, my journalistic mind still working. I'd seen how people hung their clothes on washing lines inside their balconies, where they froze solid in the cold, and wondered how they ever got dry. It didn't matter; the roughness of the sheets made what was happening all the more real. And Petrescu himself felt wonderful, his skin smooth and silky except for his strong, tapering fingers which were rough and calloused from repeated washing in icy water, I supposed. I felt myself beginning to melt. Now we were both naked.

"Your feet are cold," he panted. "Give them to me, I'll warm them."

"Are you sure? They're like blocks of ice." But he had already taken them between his own. Our pace slowed as we adjusted to each other. I began running my finger tips up and down his body, learning its contours, drawing moans of pleasure from him. Then Petrescu took the initiative, sliding me on my back, lifting himself on top. God, he was skinny—all hard bones and knobs and sharp angles like a Cubist portrait come to life, pressing down into me. He began exploring slowly with hands and tongue. I lay back, eyes closed. I felt as if I were a violin and he was playing me, now with soft caresses, now with powerful bow strokes until I was vibrating all over, every nerve end tingling, my entire body taut and tense.

"God, Stefan, what are you doing to me? Stop playing me. I need … I need …"

He gasped, "Birth control?"

"Yes, do you have something?"

He reached across her to a bedside table and pulled out a package of condoms. "German, black market," he said, rolling one on. He positioned himself and slid inside.

Neither of us lasted much longer after that.

We lay back in silence for a long while. Perhaps we dozed. Then, I became aware of his hands again, searching, probing, stroking, strumming, coaxing me awake. I shivered as my body began to respond. "Stefan," I gasped.

"Don't talk. No words, now."

We made love again, slower this time, bringing each other to the edge, then drawing back, making it last until it became unbearable.

"I have to get up," I groaned, after I'd regained control of my senses.

"You have to go already?"

"Just to the bathroom."

"Over there. But I warn you, you won't find any hot water." It was frigid outside the bed, a bone-numbing cold that raised goose bumps on my arms and legs. I searched for my discarded coat, threw it on, and rushed into the tiny bathroom. Two minutes later, I was back in his arms, pushing against him to get warm again.

"You're like a plucked chicken," he observed, rubbing my legs.

"Now I'm like a real Romanian woman."

"Hardly," he said, stroking me. "Try six months on our diet. Then we'll see."

"In America, women pay thousands of dollars to lose weight. Here, your government provides the service for free."

"Very funny." He dived down under the covers and began to attack me with little nips until I cried out for mercy. Then we just lay there, not talking, hands lazily caressing each other.

"Stefan," I said at last, unwilling to break the spell but knowing I had to.

"Yes."

"I have something to tell you, something painful. I'm leaving Romania in four days. My work here is done. I have no choice. I have to go."

He said nothing for a while. Then, "I knew this would be, of course. But still ..."

"I know. It hurts so much. But what can I do? My editor told me to leave. He wants to see my article. And when it appears, your government isn't going to like it. It won't paint a pretty picture."

"So this afternoon—this is the entirety of our story?"

"Couldn't we meet again before I leave?"

He hesitated, his face a picture of misery. "I think it would be unbearable, knowing it was the last time. Perhaps it would be better just to cherish this moment as long as it lasts and then say farewell."

I felt tears gathering but willed myself not to cry. Later, there would be time enough for that.

"Stefan, isn't there some way for you to get out of this country? So many Romanian intellectuals have left. Couldn't that happen to you too?"

He was silent for a long minute. "I always swore I would never leave or allow the government to get rid of me. No matter how bad it gets here, I told myself, someone has to stay to bear witness. If all the poets and the writers and the philosophers leave, who will be left to tell the truth?"

"Isn't that a terrible burden to carry? You have a right to live your life too."

"Don't think I haven't thought of leaving. But then I ask myself, what makes me so special? Even if I leave, there are 22 million others who must stay. Anyway, nobody ever offered me the chance. Until last week, that is."

"Last week? What are you saying?"

"Just after our first meeting, I was paid a visit by an officer from one of the organs of state security, I'm not even sure which one."

"Because we met? We were so careful."

"No, I think it was just coincidence. I'm fairly sure the authorities know nothing about our meetings or they would have acted by now."

"What did the officer say? Did he threaten you?"

"Not exactly. He said that if I applied for an exit visa, perhaps to attend an international conference, the government would look favorably on such an application."

I raised myself on one elbow, scarcely believing it. "But Stefan, that's wonderful."

"Naturally, there was a condition to their offer."

"Yes?"

"If I leave, I can never come back. They would not physically bar me but the officer made it clear that the consequences of returning would be extremely unpleasant. In other words, they've had enough of me and they want me gone."

"But Stefan, why is that so terrible? To me it sounds like the most wonderful thing. It means there's hope for us. You could get out of here and we could be together." I threw my arms around him, aware of a great flush of happiness spreading through me. A moment later, I sensed he was not returning my embrace with equal enthusiasm.

"What's the matter?"

"It's not as easy as that," he said. "I keep telling myself I should just take their offer. I could teach at an American university, live a normal life and yes, you and I could spend time together and get to know one another. All this is most tempting. But then I think that I owe it to myself and to my fellow citizens to remain. I'm afraid that if I leave, my conscience will never rest easy."

"What about us? We could be together. What we've experienced isn't something that happens every day. The way we fit together, the way our bodies join and our minds and our very souls—how can you dismiss that?"

"I don't. But it's based on two meetings, a few short hours under unusual conditions to say the least. What do you really know about me, or I about you?"

"You know we share a powerful physical attraction."

"How do we know it wouldn't wear off after a few weeks or months? I may be impossible to live with. You don't know anything about my moods, my ups and downs, my annoying little habits."

"What do any two people anywhere who have just met know about each other? You learn as you go along. I never felt the way I feel now with anyone else. I think back to when I met Tom. I'd convinced myself I was in love with him—talked myself into believing it. It's not that way now. All I want is to be with you, talk to you, hold you, make love to you. Don't you feel the same?"

"You know I do. In normal circumstances, I'd do anything to spend more time with you, to get to know everything about you. But leaving the country is a big step when there's no way back. I can't so easily throw away my entire identity, my whole life however miserable. You must understand, I'm not just a poet.

I'm a Romanian poet. That's how I define myself; it's the identity that gives my life meaning. And if I take their offer, I will become a poet in exile, without a voice, without a language, without readers, without a role in the life of my country. What would I write about, cut off from my country and my people?"

"You could build a new life, a new career."

"Anyway, I don't have the exit visa yet. What they offer with one hand, they can just as easily take away with the other."

"Will you apply at least?"

"I want to think about it some more, think also about what has happened between us. Perhaps everything will become clearer in my mind after you have left."

We lapsed into silence, neither of us knowing what to say next. Finally, Petrescu stirred himself.

"One thing: you must not write about me in your article. You mustn't quote me or give any hint you've spoken to me," he said, looking at me with those intense, blue eyes. "That would be extremely dangerous. It could ruin everything."

"Don't worry," I said quickly. "You know, it's funny. Ralph Eskew, told me to visit you, see how you're doing and offer you some money or cigarettes. But I think what he really wanted was to see if I could persuade you to publish some more poems in his magazine. I guess that wouldn't be such a great idea right now."

"So jumping into bed wasn't part of the plan?"

"No. Ethically, I've violated one of the Ten Commandments of journalism—*thou shalt not sleep with thy source.* That's right up there with plagiarism and fabricating stories."

"Am I a source?"

"A source of joy and infinite pleasure."

I kissed him long and deep. He sighed and murmured, "In that case, maybe I should accept a few more packs of cigarettes."

"Stefan, can I ask you, are you still writing?"

"Of course. I have to."

"That's what Eskew said. A true poet always writes because he has no choice. But what do you do with your poems if you can't publish them?"

"I write them in tiny, almost microscopic handwriting and

pass them to various contacts who copy them and pass them on to others. I know I'm widely read, which is why the regime still fears me."

"Would you like me to smuggle your work out of the country? We wouldn't publish any until you gave your permission."

"Not really. I write in Romanian for Romanians. I don't really see why anyone else would care."

We lay back in silence again, still idly stroking one another. Finally, Petrescu rose.

"Well, it's getting late. You must be hungry. Unfortunately, I don't have much to offer. I tried to do some shopping yesterday but I didn't come up with much, just a couple of apples and some bread. If you decide you need to return to your hotel to eat, I would understand."

"Don't be silly," I said. "I'll have whatever you're having. If apples are good enough for Bogdan the horse, they're certainly good enough for me."

"Good, so it's apples and bread. How long can you stay? Don't you have other appointments?"

"Nothing. I'd like to stay in bed with you for the next four days until I need to leave for the airport … but I know that's not practical."

"Unfortunately."

"Could I at least stay the night? I'd like to wake up next to you in the morning so that the first thing I see is your face."

He didn't have to answer.

12 – Massachusetts/Bucharest: November 2007

"Hey Mom, it's Petra."

"Petra, thank God. You got my email? How are you? Where have you been staying?"

"I'm fine Mom. I mean, I got bitten by a dog and all, but it's fine now."

"You got bitten? Oh my God, did you go to a doctor? Where did you get bitten? Did you have stitches? Is your tetanus up to date?"

"Slow down, Mom. It was just a little bite on the leg. It hardly broke the skin so I didn't need stitches. I went to the doctor. I've already had two rabies shots and I have three more to go. I had a tetanus shot before I went to college, remember?"

"Rabies? They have rabies? I have to get you out of there immediately. What were you thinking, rushing off to Romania?"

"Mom, chill out. The doctor said there haven't been any rabies cases in Bucharest for years. It's just a precaution. The shots don't hurt that much."

"And there's no infection around the wound? Oh my God, I just thought of something else. Did he use a clean needle, this doctor? In my day, they'd re-use the needles over and over again. That's how they spread AIDS through the entire country."

"I think things have changed since then."

"Petra, this is serious. You may feel fine now but sometimes these infections develop weeks or months later. It would be much safer if you came home immediately. I'll have my travel agent buy you a ticket. Then maybe, we can sort out your status at Brown and…"

"Mom, I'm not coming home now. The needles were clean. I saw the doctor take them out of the package. Stefan said he's one of the best doctors around."

"Stefan?"

"Stefan's the one who found the doctor. I think he had to pay him a bribe to see me so quickly and we had to buy the shots from a pharmacy but that's the way they do things around here."

"Stefan Petrescu?"

"Of course Stefan Petrescu. Who did you think?"

"You met him?"

"Duh! That's why I came here. He's been great; he's so cool, so fascinating. He has such amazing stories."

"I'm … I'm speechless. I don't know what to say. Isn't he married?"

"Divorced. He's right here with me now. Do you want to talk to him?"

"Stefan is with you right now? Oh my God. And he's

divorced?"

"He sends his love and says hello."

"He says hello?"

"Mom, could you please stop repeating everything I say."

"OK, OK, let me get this straight. You got bitten and Stefan Petrescu, whom you had somehow met, brought you to the doctor."

"That's right, his own personal doctor, the one who treated him after he was wounded."

"OK, so what else should I know?"

"I dunno. What do you want to know?"

"Well, for starters, where have you been living? What have you been doing apart from getting bitten by wild dogs?"

"OK, I was staying with these three students, really great people, one of them I met on the plane over here. His name is Mihai and he's really nice. I guess you could call him my boyfriend, kinda."

"Boyfriend? You have a boyfriend?"

"Kinda boyfriend. I mean we really like each other and he kissed me one time … but it's not like we're officially dating or anything."

"He kissed you? I can't believe I'm hearing this. And you were living with him?"

"Not in the same room or anything. Don't worry Mom, he's been the perfect gentleman. He's totally cool, you'd really like him."

"How old is this boyfriend?"

"I guess maybe 22 or 23. He's a musician. Last week he took me to the opera and guess what? I didn't even hate it that much, at least until I fell asleep in the second half because it was four hours long. He plays the violin and he wants to be a composer. He's super-talented …"

"He's 22 or 23? Does he know how old you are? What kind of a man messes around with a young girl like that? What the hell is going on here Petra?"

"Mom, I knew you'd be like this. That's why I didn't call before. I knew before we were speaking for three minutes you'd start treating me like a little child."

"OK, OK, let's both of us take a deep breath. I certainly don't think you're a little child and I didn't call to fight with you. You were the one who upped and disappeared without saying a word to anyone. You were the one sending misleading emails, not exactly the behavior of a mature person."

"Yeah, I'm sorry about that."

"Just tell me you're taking precautions and you remembered all those talks we had about HIV and sexually transmitted diseases."

"Jesus Mom!"

"Well are you?"

"That's just so typical. I said I'd kissed a boy and you immediately assume that, not only am I sleeping with him and not only am I not taking precautions but he's also infected with HIV and gonorrhea and probably lice and crabs as well. And by the way, which precautions did you take before I was born? Whatever they were, they didn't work because, hello, here I am. So don't go preaching to me. I just kissed him for Chrissakes. Actually, he wouldn't even touch me because he thought I was too young. But he changed his mind after the dog bite."

"He did, did he?"

"Mom, he's wonderful, handsome, smart, talented, sexy. I love him."

"Nonsense, you're too young."

"I'm not. I've grown up a lot in the past month."

"So it would appear."

"And Stefan is wonderful too. He invited me to move in with him, so now I'm here in his apartment, which should make you happy."

"What would really make me happy would be for you to come home. I'll make the arrangements tomorrow and email you."

"You should see this place. He has all this artwork on the walls by modern Romanian artists, and some of them are his friends. And he has great furniture—hand-made by craftsmen—and all kinds of other interesting stuff."

"So you're living with Stefan now?"

"He said we needed time to get to know one another. Mom, it was the weirdest thing. I went to his class on Shakespeare's sonnets …"

"He still teaches Shakespeare's sonnets?"

"Yeah, it's like a legendary class. It was packed with students. Anyway, I raised my hand and made a comment, and he said he knew right away I was your daughter the moment I opened my mouth. Something about the way I spoke or the way I looked. He just knew."

"Really?"

"Mom, are you crying? There's no need to cry, you should be happy."

"Excuse me, just give me a moment."

"Do you want to speak to him?"

"Speak to Stefan? Maybe a little later; not just yet. It's too sudden, too much. I can't … I can't!"

"I totally understand why you fell for him. He's still dreamily attractive, especially with that romantic patch he wears over his eye. He must have been really sexy when he was young."

"He wears an eye patch?"

"To cover up his wound."

"When I knew him, he didn't need an eye patch. In fact, his eyes were the most attractive part of him. Poor Stefan. I had no idea. I knew he was wounded of course. I mean, I was there of course …"

"You were? You never told me."

"I have been telling you. I've been writing an account of everything that happened between Stefan and me. I sent you several letters—but of course you never received them. They were all sitting in your mail box at Brown, along with the moldy brownies I baked for you."

"Yeah, sorry about the brownies. But Mom, I'd really like to see those letters."

"They'll be here for you as soon as you get home"

"Mom, how have you been doing? I never even asked."

"I'm fine. I find your behavior very hurtful but I suppose I'll get over it. I guess that's what mothers are for."

"I'm sorry. I needed to come here and I knew if I asked, you'd say no."

"Maybe I wouldn't have."

"We both know that isn't true. Tell me honestly, if I'd asked for your permission to come here alone, would you have said yes?"

"If you had asked if you could just leave college in the middle of your first semester to waltz off to Romania, after I paid $28,000 for your tuition and housing, which by the way is not refundable, then of course I would have said no. But we could have taken a vacation together in Romania if you were so insistent. All you had to do was make a reasonable request in a reasonable way."

"I'm sorry about the money. I needed to come here alone."

"Well you did it. And now I want you home."

"Mom, that's not going to happen. I signed up for Romanian classes. I'm already picking it up fast because it's a Romance language, like Spanish."

"What about your family? What about Thanksgiving?"

"Hey, that's a great idea, I'll make a Thanksgiving dinner here. I can invite my friends Angela and Mihai and Stefan of course, and I'll cook a turkey and stuffing and pumpkin pie—the works."

"Right. You, who hardly ever set foot in a kitchen your whole life."

"I bet Angela will help. Anyway what does it matter to you how it comes out? You won't be here to criticize. The point is, Mom, I'm going to stay here for a while. I'll take a year off from Brown, like a gap year. I'm a year younger than everyone else at college. Why shouldn't I?"

"And what are you going to live on for this year?"

"I forgot to tell you, I got a job. I'm a waitress in a place called Café Vienna. I started last week."

"How can you get a job? You don't have a work permit. The whole thing is ridiculous. Don't they have laws there?"

"They said it didn't matter, they'll pay me under the table in cash. They prefer it that way. Everything here is in cash; they don't trust credit cards. Anyway, they gave me an outfit to wear, a white puffy blouse and skirt. It has a green and brown striped bodice on top and a green and brown apron on the bottom. And the other girls who work there are really nice. They're all students, like me."

"So this is a sleazy bar where the waitresses dress up as Little Bo Peep? Petra, tell me I'm imagining all this. Tell me this is just a bad dream and I'm going to wake up and get my little girl back."

"I'm not your little girl any more Mom, how many times must I say it? And there's nothing sleazy about the Café Vienna. It's not a bar, it's a café. They play waltzes and polkas on the soundtrack all the time and serve cappuccinos and lattes with lots of whipped cream and different kinds of hot chocolate and all kinds of desserts. It'll help my Romanian to work there and when I get home I'll be able to get a job at Starbucks as a barista."

"Petra, this is too much for me. OK, you wanted to meet Stefan. I guess I can understand that. But why would you want to spend a whole year in a nasty place like Bucharest?"

"Bucharest isn't nasty, it's quite beautiful. There are so many neat, old mansions with lovely scrollwork and carvings and great wrought iron balconies and they're renovating all the time."

"Doesn't sound much like the Bucharest I remember."

"Of course, there's too much trash lying around and the sidewalks are all broken up and the traffic is horrible. But it's getting better. Places change as well as people."

"How else have you changed? What else should I know about?"

"Well I do look a bit different, not so dorky. My friend Angela took me shopping for new clothes. Plus I got my hair colored a bit."

"Oh heavens. Are you possessed? Tell me it's not purple or blue."

"No, it's just bronze, kind of dark red. Angela says it makes me look hot. And I wear my lenses every day now, even though the solution is really expensive here. Mom, Stefan really wants to talk to you. He's making signals to me. Maybe he can make you understand. Will you speak to him?"

"Petra, you didn't get anything pierced did you? You know you can get Hepatitis C from some of these hole-in-the-wall tattoo places."

"No Mom, no piercings."

"Thank God for that."

"Mom, please talk to him … Just a few words. He really wants to. He says he can explain some things that will put your mind at rest. Just listen; you don't have to say anything ... Mom, are you still there? Where did you go?"

"I'm here."

"So you'll talk to him?"

"All right, very well, put him on if you must."

…

"Hello."

"Hello Stefan."

"How are you Elisabeta?"

"Oh God, nobody's called me by that name since … since then."

"It has been a long time. It's good to hear your voice."

"Yes."

"A long, long time."

"Yes."

"And I hear from Petra that you're well."

"I'm quite well."

"And just as beautiful as ever."

"Ha! You wouldn't recognize me if you saw me now."

"I'm sure I would. Neither one of us is as young as we were. But you, I'm sure, are still lovely. And now you have sent me your daughter, who is just as beautiful as you."

"I did no such thing. She sent herself. It was an irresponsible, immature thing to do and I want her to come home immediately."

"Why so anxious? She's quite safe here with me; you know I won't let her come to any harm. She's spending her time constructively studying our language, working in the coffee shop.

Why shouldn't she stay a little? Don't I deserve the chance to get to know my own daughter?"

"She's not your daughter. I mean, biologically she is of course, I don't deny it, but her real father was Tom O'Neill and we should all remember that before we get carried away. Sure, she thinks she's living in a romance novel; she finds her long-lost father and he turns out to be a glamorous Romanian poet. But it's not a novel; it's real life. She's an American girl and her place is here. She's still a minor and I'm still her parent, her only legal parent, so I get to decide."

"She may not be my daughter, other than biologically as you put it, but, that was your decision, not mine. Thank God, she found her own way to me. I could have been a father to her—but I was not consulted. Now, suddenly I have that chance and it's the greatest gift anyone has given me for many, many years since … since then. And Elisabeta, she's wonderful—brave and kind—so bright and delightful to be with. She reminds me of you—her wit, her independence, the way her mind works. I really must congratulate you for raising such a daughter—and Tom of course, may he rest in peace."

"Well thank you for saying so."

"And also, she may be a minor for now, but she won't be much longer. Soon, you'll lose whatever legal power you have over her and she will decide her own future. So even if you drag her from me today, surely she will be back next year or the year after. You can't keep us apart now that we've met. And you know, she really is an adult already in all but name. She's perfectly capable of making up her own mind. Wouldn't it be better to let her stay for a while? You owe it to me. Even more you owe it to Petra."

"But I worry about her in that strange city."

"The city is not so strange and you wouldn't be apart for such a long time. You and I both know how fast time can pass. How long is it since I've seen you? Seventeen years. And yet, now that I'm talking to you, it seems that all that time was like nothing."

"Stop trying to change the subject. This conversation is about Petra, not us."

"You should know that Petra keeps asking me about us. She wants to know what exactly happened between us."

"What have you told her?"

"Nothing specific. I wanted her to speak first with you. But she deserves an answer. She needs to know the truth."

"I'd started writing an account of what happened. I guess I could mail it to you in Romania if she's going to stay a while."

"Perhaps with your permission, I will read it too. I'll be interested to see what you remember and how you remember it. I recall we once had a conversation about the unreliability of memory. It was that first time we met, at my sister's apartment. Do you remember the music we danced to?"

"Chopin's fourth ballade. I can't listen to it without wanting to cry."

"I can't either."

"Once I was at a recital at Carnegie Hall, and the pianist played it. I had to leave the auditorium. Tom couldn't understand what was wrong with me and there was no way I could explain it to him."

"Elisabeta, are you crying now?"

"Maybe … a bit. I can't help it. I don't even know what I'm crying about. Excuse me, don't go away; just give me a second."

"And I thought you'd forgotten everything."

"No."

"It's interesting, you once told me that two people would always remember the same event differently. I wonder if that's the case with us."

"Probably. Excuse me, I feel so foolish. Stefan, your voice, it's the same, the same as then."

"And yet, according to you, as I recall, you insisted that memory is subjective and unreliable."

"Not in this. I remember everything."

"Yes. I also."

"And now life has come full circle and you have my daughter. Perhaps it's poetic justice after I took her away from you."

"Oh don't be so silly. Why make such a drama out of it? Petra isn't some possession to be passed from hand to hand. She's her own person and she loves you very much. She also loved her father, Tom. And perhaps, one day, there will be a small place in her heart for me, also."

"I'm sure there will be. I'm sure there is already."

"So you'll allow her to stay."

"Perhaps for a little but a year is too long. I'm alone now. What will Christmas be for me this year, without either Tom or Petra?"

"Why not come here? We could all three of us spend Christmas in Romania. After that, she could decide whether she'd like to stay the rest of the school year here with me or go home. Although I should warn you, with that boy on the scene, my guess is she's not going to want to leave so quickly."

"That's another thing. This boyfriend; I don't like the sound of him. He's much too old for her."

"I've met him and I can assure you he's an excellent fellow, very polite, well-spoken, good family, well educated. But of course, if you don't believe me, why not come at Christmas? You could meet him and decide for yourself."

"I don't know."

"Why not?"

"Stefan, you know why not."

"Actually I don't."

"Because of what happened between us, the way I abandoned you. You're too polite to bring it up directly, but it's always going to be hanging there between us. Why aren't you bitter about it? You certainly deserve to be."

"For many years I was bitter. But I don't feel that way any longer. You did what you had to do for the sake of your daughter, I understand that now. You wanted her to have the best life she could have. And now, she's come here to me and through her, I'm talking once again to you. Isn't that a miracle? So why shouldn't you come? It's not about us anymore, it's about her, our daughter."

"Well perhaps. I need to think about it."

"Promise me you will."

"OK, I promise you that much."

"And we'll talk again soon?"

"I suppose we'll have to. You have my daughter in your keeping."

"I promise I'll take good care of her, like she was my own child."

Part III: Remind my heart

And if the clouds their tresses part
And does the moon outblaze,
It is but to remind my heart
I long for you always.
- Mihai Eminescu

1 – Massachusetts: November 2007

Dear Petra,

I hope by now you've received all my earlier letters. I mailed them to you care of Stefan's office at the university.

Since we spoke last week, I've been trying to continue with my writing. I have to say that talking to Stefan on the phone has made it much harder than before. The truth is, I'd long ago stopped thinking of him as a real person leading an independent existence. In my mind, he was still frozen in 1989 like a character in a movie or a novel. I never allowed myself to think about what kind of life he might have led since then or might be leading today. But he's not frozen any longer. Like one of those prehistoric creatures in a science fiction movie, he's thawed out and come back to life and now he's prowling around in my brain.

I still haven't decided whether I'm coming at Christmas. Of course, I'd love to see you, but I'd also have to face him. Perhaps it's better to leave our story, with its pain and heartbreak and betrayal, in the past. Clearly it has no future.

Today I ordered my Thanksgiving turkey from the supermarket. There will be 11 of us—your brothers and their families and me and of course Ralph Eskew. Maybe we'll call you that day so everyone can say hello. I know your little nephews and nieces will miss you.

I was thinking about your idea of cooking a Thanksgiving dinner for your friends. You should definitely do it. It would be a nice way to repay them for their help and hospitality. Let me know if you need any recipes. I'm assuming you can get proper food in Romania these days, although the only turkeys I ever saw there were wandering down the middle of the streets of the villages I drove through.

Petra, it's going to start getting cold there soon and I'm assuming you didn't take any winter clothes. Bucharest in winter is no joke; the year I was there was brutal. I still remember the icy cold of Stefan's apartment. You'll need a decent coat, boots and lots of long underwear. I can send you some if you like, or wire you money so you can buy whatever you need. Let me know which you prefer. And now, I'm going to get back to my writing,

Love,

Mom

2 – Bucharest: November 2007

Petra met Angela to go shopping for the grand Thanksgiving dinner in the Amzei open-air market just off Calea Victoriei, the fanciest shopping street in Bucharest. Angela had promised to help with the cooking. They kissed on both cheeks.

"So how's it going back there with the professor?" Angela wanted to know. She was wearing black leather pants and a tight black velvet waistcoat that left a couple of inches of bare midriff and she had a little chain with a silver heart pierced by an arrow dangling from her navel. For mid-November, the weather was still mild.

"Is this your dominatrix look?" Petra asked.

Angela gave a little pirouette and curtseyed. "You like?"

"What does Andrei think?"

"Andrei's history."

"Oops, sorry."

"Don't be. He was starting to get too serious. What is it with men nowadays? Can't they just enjoy honest, healthy sex without wanting to get all mushy and sentimental? I don't understand it. You put out but they always want more."

"What did he want?"

"Commitment." She spoke the word as if uttering a deadly curse. "I told him we could keep on hanging out and having fun but there's no way I'm getting into a serious relationship."

"Why not?" Petra asked.

"Are you crazy? This time next year, I'll have my degree and it will be 'goodbye Romania.' There's a big world out there and I want to be part of it. Anyway, no problema; plenty of fish in the sea. I see you're back to your old dorky look." Petra was wearing her *Quizmaster Classic 2005* sweatshirt.

"Yeah, I decided it was part of my identity. Maybe I can help invent a new trend—intellectual but sexy at the same time."

"Ha!" Angela snorted contemptuously. "I let you move out and look what happens. God, I miss you, even your retarded Romanian dialogues. Mihai is being a real drag. I wish you'd come back."

"I miss you guys too. I even miss the smell of Mihai's dirty socks. Stefan smokes a pipe. He walks around with his own personal cloud of pollution hanging over his head."

"Gross!"

"He thinks he has to be my dad, but he doesn't know how to do it. It's like he's trying to pick it up on the fly. It's sweet in a way but it can also be incredibly annoying. Every time I step outside, he's like, 'When will you be home Petra?' and 'Take the cell phone and call me when you get there Petra' and, 'Don't forget to let me know where you are, Petra.' I can't stand it when my mom does that, and it's no better from him."

"My parents are the same way. It's like a parental disease."

"Plus he has this weird religious streak. I didn't notice at first but he always wears this gold cross around his neck under his shirt. Last Sunday, he tried to get me to go to church with him. He said it would be interesting for me hearing the choir and the service. I didn't know what to say. In the end, I told him I've been brought up as a total atheist and I wouldn't feel comfortable."

Angela squeezed her arm. "That's one problem we don't have in my family. We're strictly twice a year Christians —Christmas and Easter."

"We weren't even that. My dad—my real one, I mean—couldn't abide religion. You know, I never appreciated what a great dad he was until now. I really miss him. These two weeks with Stefan have made me realize nobody can ever take his place."

As they walked, they were approached by a man holding out boxes of L'Oreal mascara. Angela engaged in a rapid-fire conversation with him; Petra caught a word here and there but that was all.

"What was that about?" she asked, as they moved on.

"Oh just another peddler. God knows what they put in those boxes. You'd have to be crazy to buy one, although this guy assured me his stuff was genuine. He said he stole it himself only yesterday."

Petra laughed. Angela said, "Seriously, if the professor is being a drag, maybe you should move back with us."

"I could never do that to Stefan," Petra replied. "I probably exaggerated a bit. He means well and I do like him a lot. He's really smart and interesting and he has so many great stories. I don't want to move out; I just need a little break, maybe another weekend in the country with no so-called adults around. Could you arrange something?"

"Sure, we could go to Sibiu—that's pretty."

"Sibiu?"

"It's a medieval city in Transylvania. I'll get Mihai to come as well and fix it so you two end up in the same room. He really misses you. I can tell by the grotesque sounds he's cooking up there in his room on his computer, some new composition. It sounds like a cat dying a painful death in slow motion. I mean, get a life! You guys badly need to sleep together and get it over with."

Petra reddened.

"Well what?" Angela asked. "Don't look so shocked. It's what adults do; they have sex."

"Maybe I'm not an adult after all. I only just had my first kiss," Petra said.

"Come on Petra, what are you waiting for? Mihai is absolutely the right guy for you. He's had some experience so he knows what to do and I'm sure he'd be gentle. He should definitely be the one."

"I don't know," Petra said, uncomfortable with the conversation.

"If you didn't want to go all the way the first night, you could try just sleeping with him, no sex. That can be nice too. But Petra, you just have to take the plunge sooner or later. It's not such a big deal. You can't stay a virgin for ever."

"I'm only 17," Petra protested.

"Exactly my point."

"What if he doesn't want to?"

"Don't worry. We'll go shopping. Once he sees you in the lacy camisole we're going to buy, he'll want to all right."

Petra gulped. "So when can we go for this weekend?" she asked bravely.

"Maybe over Christmas vacation?"

"No. Can't do it then. My mom's coming. She finally decided."

"Maybe your mom and the professor will hook up again. Hey, maybe you could write a screenplay based on their lives and sell it to Hollywood for a million dollars."

"Hah! I don't even know the full story yet. I started reading the letters my Mom sent me about how they met in 1989."

"What are they like?"

"If you ignore all the times where she writes that I'm too young and immature to understand or appreciate the glory and splendor of their love, it's really interesting. But I wish she wouldn't keep telling me what a huge sacrifice she made for my sake by going back to Tom O'Neill in America instead of staying with Stefan. I knew my parents were never lovey-dovey—but I didn't realize what their relationship was really like. It makes me feel weird reading it. I am looking forward to the bit when she describes the revolution but she hasn't sent me that yet."

"You know my parents were in the revolution too. I asked them about it once. They said they left me with my grandma to go out and demonstrate against the government and they wound up down in the metro checking people for weapons. There were rumors that terrorists were running wild in the city. People were shooting each other without even knowing which side they were on."

"How old were you?"

"Four. I don't remember anything about it. The other thing they described was that everyone was singing this really sappy song, *'And I fell in love with you.'* Then they got misty-eyed and started humming the tune and I had to leave the room before they started smooching. There's nothing nastier than old people in their fifties not acting their age."

"That's all they told you?"

"You have to understand, people here don't speak much about the revolution or life under the communists. It's like a taboo subject, a closed book. They don't like to remember. I think too many people have skeletons in the closet. So many were working for the regime in one way or another. OK here's the market. Now what do we need for this big feast of yours?"

3 – London: August 1989

When I left Bucharest shortly after my night with Petrescu, I wasn't sure I'd ever see or hear from him again. I thought of him constantly, recalling our brief time together, the words we'd spoken and those left unsaid. As the weeks went by, I had no way of knowing whether he'd decided to apply for an exit visa as we'd discussed or when it might be granted. There was no way to communicate with him—letters and phone calls were certain to be intercepted and would only cause him trouble.

Every so often, I called Clint Aldrich at the U.S. embassy to see what was happening in Romania. I'd asked him to keep an ear out for any news about Stefan but there was nothing, either good or bad.

The only thing I could do was to drown myself in work. It helped that Eskew kept me busy with one amazing assignment after another. I was in Brussels for the 50th anniversary of NATO. In early June, I flew to Poland for what turned out to be the first free election anywhere in the Soviet bloc. It was won decisively by Solidarity, the anti-communist, independent trade union party. I remembered how Peter Pringle had told me this would be a moment of truth for the Kremlin. Since meeting him, I'd been reading his dispatches on the Reuters wire and had learned to respect his judgment.

Throughout that summer, everybody was wondering, what would Gorbachev do; when and how would he act? Ralph Eskew was sure he'd do nothing.

"Hasn't got the stomach for bloodshed," he told me in one of our regular phone calls. "He's too anxious to be liked around the world. Stalin must be rolling in his grave. Gorby enjoys cavorting in Western capitals with his fancy wife, and he has this naïve idea of wanting to be a personality rather than a dictator. He's not going to unleash the dogs of war."

"Isn't that a good thing?" I asked.

"It's a great thing for the United States and the West. We're only too happy to be dealing with a weakened Soviet Union under an indecisive leader. It's also wonderful for the people of Eastern Europe, who have the chance to grab more freedom than they've had for 50 years—if they have the courage to take it. But Gorbachev won't last long, you mark my words Eliza. The Russians don't respect weakness. They're only truly comfortable when some tyrant is oppressing and abusing them. Ivan the Terrible, Peter the Great, Lenin, Stalin—these are the leaders the Russian people admire."

By coincidence, I ran into Pringle a couple of weeks later in the lobby of a Budapest hotel. We were both on our way to Heroes Square, where hundreds of thousands of Hungarians were gathering for a ceremony to rebury leaders of the 1956 uprising who'd been executed by the communists and dumped in unmarked graves. We decided to walk together. Pringle seemed half-drunk with excitement, although he'd probably also gotten started early on the beer.

"I've been waiting for this half my life," he yelled as we weaved our way through a massive crowd, streaming slowly and quietly down Andrassy Boulevard, the wide avenue leading to the square.

"Twenty years of covering the Soviet bloc; 20 years of reporting the lies of apparachiks and their fake economic statistics and their orchestrated party conferences—and now the whole system is falling apart before our eyes. I never thought I'd live to see it. It's amazing."

I didn't much like Pringle. He was a crude, stuck-up, opinionated Brit who drank too much. But I had to admit, he knew what he was talking about when it came to Eastern Europe.

"So what's next?" I asked.

"Fucked if I know Lizzie. If the commies allow an event like this to take place without doing anything, I can only conclude that they've lost the will to resist. The big question is, what's going to happen when the freedom bug spreads, because it will. It's not stopping here. This is just the beginning. You watch, 1989 will go down in history."

The atmosphere in the square was solemn, the tension palpable. Many of the Hungarians I spoke to seemed in shock that the ceremony was actually happening without Russian tanks rolling in to stop it. Hour after hour, people filed past, sinking to their knees to lay wreaths, or sometimes a single carnation, beneath the caskets of the dead leaders. The organizers had left one coffin empty to symbolize the countless unnamed victims of communist oppression. Deeply moved, I saw people on crutches limp by to pay their respects; others rolled by in wheelchairs. A grim silence hung over the scene. The massive Corinthian pillars were bedecked in black crepe; Hungarian flags with the Red Star symbolically burned out of the center flew all around. There was a sense of an entire people reclaiming their past and taking possession of their future. Along city streets, black flags fluttered from every villa and apartment block.

Pringle was almost overcome. "What a day," he kept saying. "What an incredible, fucking day."

At one point, I asked him if he'd heard anything interesting from Romania.

"Not a dicky bird. I don't know why you even bother asking. You've been there; you know what it's like. Nothing's going to happen in Romania. It's the one exception to this drive for freedom, the one hopeless case. Look at the people here today, look into their eyes. These are people who aren't afraid any more. Did you ever once see anyone in Romania with eyes like that?"

Actually yes, I wanted to tell him. *I did see one man with eyes like that.*

"Forget about Romania, Liz," he was saying. "Keep your eyes on Hungary and Poland. That's where it's at. And Germany, that's the lynchpin of the whole rotten system. If the East Germans start getting restless, watch out and hold your hat."

A couple of days after the reburial ceremony, I called Clint in Bucharest.

"Where are you?" he asked.

"Hungary."

"Hot damn, I wish I was there."

"What's going on where you are?"

"Same old, same old. Even more surrealistic than usual. Every night on state TV lately, instead of regular programs they've been scrolling long lists down the screen of production figures from the collective farms, each one showing record harvests. Real entertaining. It makes the usual images of the Ceauşescus visiting factories seem almost interesting. I don't know who they think they're fooling because the people are still almost starving, even though it's summer and food should be plentiful. You know what the top news is here?"

"No."

"Soccer."

"What?"

"You know, the game where Europeans kick a stupid ball around, instead of throwing it like real men. Well, one of the local teams, Steaua Bucharest, is pretty good and they were having a hell of a season. They reached the final of the European Championship, which is a really big deal for a tin pot country like Romania. The whole place was going crazy, like it was the greatest thing that ever happened. Only, when they played the big game a couple of weeks ago, the Romanians got whopped by an Italian team, four zip. I tell you, I really enjoyed watching those Romanians having the shit kicked out of them. Now the whole country is back to its regular depression."

"How are the authorities reacting to what's going on here? Are they taking it calmly?"

"Are you kidding me? The government here is paranoid about Hungary at the best of times—there are a couple of million ethnic Hungarians living in the country—but now they're totally freaked. The Foreign Ministry condemned the reburial ceremony as fascist, anti-socialist and anti-Romanian—and those were some of the milder terms they used."

"Nice."

"The Hungarians and the Romanians have hated each other for ever but it was kept dormant while they were both under the Kremlin's heel. Now, with the Hungarians heading for freedom, Uncle Nick can't be sleeping too well at night."

"But there are still no signs of actual dissent?"

"Nothing that I've seen or heard about. So when are you coming back?"

"I applied for another visa just in case something happens there. I was surprised they granted it after what I wrote about them. Still, it seems pointless coming back if nothing's really cooking and there are so many dynamite stories everywhere else. My editor would never buy it."

"Not even to see me?"

"Ah, now you're talking."

"I ask you Liz, what could I possibly have done to deserve getting posted to this backwater? All over Europe, history is unfolding and I'm stuck here."

During that period, I also spoke to Tom a couple of times to tell him I wasn't going back to him and we should start thinking about a divorce. He swore he was a new man, he'd seen the light and if it was kids I wanted, no problem, we could have half a dozen. I didn't want to listen to him—my head was too full of Stefan—but I didn't do anything about the divorce either. I was just so busy and figured there'd be time later. I only hoped it would be an amicable parting.

It must have been about six weeks after the Hungary trip that the phone rang in my London apartment early one morning. It was August and I was packing my suitcase for yet another trip.

"Yes, who is it?"

"Elisabeta."

I'd have known it anywhere, that gravelly voice calling me by a name that only he ever used.

"Stefan," I breathed. "Where are you? How are you?"

"I'm in Rome. They let me out. I'm free."

4 – Italy: August 1989

I flew straight to Rome where Petrescu had been invited to address a writers' conference. We met in his hotel room. Seconds later, we were in each other's arms.

"I never felt sheets so soft," he murmured as we lay together in bed afterwards. "You have no idea how I've dreamt of something like this. We should stay here forever."

"We'll need to leave the room at some point to eat."

"Why? They have this amazing thing here called room service. You call on the phone and 20 minutes later they bring you whatever you want, day or night, in very large portions. It's amazing. Whatever you want! I see heaps of leftovers lying on trays in the corridor every morning. Such waste! A Romanian family could live for three days just on what they leave over. And they just throw it in the garbage. It's unbelievable."

"How can you afford all these meals? Room service is expensive."

"They never ask for money. You just sign something and they go away."

I wasn't sure whether to laugh or cry. "But Stefan, you know it's all going on your account for when you check out, don't you?"

"I'm not a complete idiot. The conference organizers will pay as long as I'm here."

"How long will that be?"

"Until tomorrow. Checkout from paradise is at 11 o'clock sharp."

"What will you do next?" I asked, unsure where things stood between us.

"I haven't decided. I've only been here a few days and everything is so overwhelming; this chaotic city, the traffic, the stores, the strange money, the plastic cards everyone has in their wallets to pay for things—all the choices people have. I feel like I landed in another planet."

I sat up and gently stroked his spiky hair. "You just need time to adjust. I can help you find your way around, help stiffen your resolve, so to speak." I took his hand, pressing it over my breast.

He looked at me with those dazzling eyes. "My resolve is already stiffened whenever I see you. But to be serious, if I want to stay in the West, I'll need money. I have only a little that they gave me for speaking at the conference and it won't last long. The prices here are unbelievable."

"You could come to London and stay with me while you get settled. No strings attached—you'd be free to leave at any time," I said carefully. Suddenly, everything that had seemed simple in

Bucharest had become delicate and sensitive.

He smiled. "That's generous. But I would need to find a job. I can't live off you."

"Of course," I said, deeply aware of the danger of offending his pride. "It would just be for a while. I'm sure a university in England or America would snap you up."

"You think so?"

"Absolutely. And Ralph Eskew will print some of your poems—he pays very well—and he'll also introduce you to other editors. We'll need to get them translated into English as soon as possible. I'm sure a publisher would be interested in bringing out a book of your work."

"So you think we should go to London together while I try to sort out some of these things?"

I had an idea. "Why don't we get away somewhere first for a few days, just the two of us? We need some time to get to know each other properly. Then you can decide if you want to chance it with me in London."

"But the cost…"

"Don't worry about that. I'm being very well paid for my work. You can pay me back later when you have a job. I know just the place. Do you agree?"

He looked doubtful for a few seconds, then smiled and nodded.

I stood up to go to the bathroom.

"Stay like that, just for a second," he said, as I returned. "I've never seen all of you before properly. It was too cold and dark in Bucharest." I twirled around, enjoying the look of lust on his face.

"So beautiful," he breathed. "You know, you're so unbelievably gorgeous."

"Not really, but it's nice to hear you say so."

Next day, I rented a car and we drove south, past Naples, down the Amalfi coast, weaving around hair-pin bends on the narrow road, avoiding buses driving at breakneck speed in the other direction, admiring the spectacular mountain vistas. We ended up in a *pension* overlooking the Mediterranean in the hillside village of Positano.

The next few days passed in a blur of lovemaking, sun, food and wine. After blanching at the price, Stefan bought himself a pair of running shoes, and soon he was trotting up and down the steep stairways that connected the winding streets of the village and doing push-ups and sit-ups on the patio. He'd seen the bodies of the Italian men on the beach, bronzed from the sun and gleaming from hours in the gym, so different from his own undernourished frame. Already, after a few days of local cooking, he was beginning to put some meat on those bones and his skin had lost its pallor.

"Skinny poets are all very well in Romania but not here," he said. "I don't want you to abandon me for a young gigolo."

"I like you fine the way you are," I assured him.

"Soon there'll be more of me to like," he promised.

While still in Rome, Stefan had discovered cable TV. He was particularly fascinated by the all-news channels.

"In Romania, we hunch over our radios hoping to pick up Radio Free Europe or the BBC without interference for just a snippet of real information from the outside world," he said. "Here, you have news all the time day and night and nobody pays attention."

"That's not true. I'd have no job if it were," I told him. "Maybe here in Positano, where everybody's on vacation, people aren't paying much attention, but this isn't the real world. You'll see, in London life will be more normal."

Stefan couldn't get enough of the beautiful Italian churches. Whenever we entered one, I would consult the guidebook to check whether there were any famous works of art we should see, but Petrescu seemed relatively uninterested in the frescoes and sculptures. Instead, he would light a candle and stand before the altar, praying silently. I was surprised. I'd never really known anyone truly religious before.

"What are you praying for?" I asked him once.

"For my country, my people, my sister Simina, all those I love back home. I don't ever want to forget that while I'm here with you in heaven, they're still suffering in hell."

I remember thinking religion might become an issue between us if we stayed together long-term but it didn't seem relevant at that moment.

Over the next few days, we fell into a rhythm. Mornings, we'd wake up, make love, shower, drink a cappuccino on the veranda overlooking the sea, then wander down to the beach for a swim and lunch in a local *trattoria.* Already, after a few days, Stefan was able to converse fluently with the local waiters.

"Romanian is almost like Italian; they're both Romance Languages," he explained.

In the hot afternoons, we'd sleep for a couple of hours or read. After that, we'd explore some of the neighboring villages and finish the day with another huge meal before returning to bed for more love-making. In between times, we talked and talked—about our childhoods, past relationships, politics, religion, movies, books, music. It turned out we shared a love of the Beatles and Jane Austen and both of us named *Casablanca* as our all-time favorite movie. Stefan had seen it almost a dozen times and knew whole chunks of dialogue by heart. "It's one of the few things they didn't censor because the government approved of the anti-fascist message," he explained.

One thing we didn't discuss was the future. It was too soon for Petrescu to make plans, I told myself. Everything was too new and strange; he needed more time to acclimate to freedom.

I knew our idyll couldn't last, but it ended more suddenly than expected. Two days before we were due to leave, we wandered down to the village for a coffee and croissant and I bought the *International Herald Tribune*. The lead story was about how two million people from the Baltic Republics of Latvia, Lithuania and Estonia had joined hands, forming a human chain hundreds of miles long, to demand their freedom and independence from the Soviet Union. Stefan read the article carefully, his coffee sitting forgotten on the table. Afterwards, his mood darkened perceptibly.

That night, his love-making seemed particularly urgent and desperate, almost frenzied. When it was over and he had extracted one last climax from my exhausted body, I saw he was crying.

"What is it?" I asked. "What's the matter?" But he would not say.

In truth, I knew him well enough by then that I didn't need to ask.

"You've decided to go back there, haven't you?" I said, choking back sobs.

He sat up in a tangle of sweaty sheets. "How did you know?"

"I saw the way you reacted to that article. How could one newspaper story do that? It's unthinkable. Please, Stefan, please don't do this. I can't bear the thought of you going back there. I'm so scared for you," and I broke down completely, pushing him away as he tried to comfort me.

He drew back. "I have to," he said flatly, holding out his hands in supplication.

"But I love you. Can't you see how much I love you? I'd do anything for you. I thought you felt the same way about me."

"I do Elisabeta. I love you more than I can say. But love is not everything; it cannot be everything."

"What else is there?"

"There's the future of a people, my people who are suffering and deserve the chance to be free. I saw in that article how the people in those little Baltic nations are rising up for their freedom. They had it much worse even than us all these years. They were occupied by the Soviet Union. We never were. For 50 years, they lived as slaves to the Russians—but now they are rising up. If they can do it, with the help of God, why not us? Why not?"

I collected myself. If he wanted a debate, a debate he would have. Perhaps, he needed to be talked around; perhaps he was troubled by a guilty conscience that just needed soothing.

"You know why not, Stefan. Those Baltic people have lost their fear. They don't believe Gorbachev will send in tanks and guns to crush them. That's not the case in Romania. If there were ever an uprising in Bucharest, we both know that Ceauşescu wouldn't hesitate for five seconds. It would be a bloodbath. My heart breaks for the Romanian people but nothing's going to change any time soon. All the experts tell me so."

"Which experts?"

"The U.S. embassy in Bucharest for one. And colleagues who have been covering Eastern Europe for years."

"Bah, foreigners. They know nothing about my country, my people. I saw what you wrote about us in your magazine article. You think we Romanians are crushed. I say we are just biding our time, awaiting the right moment. Elisabeta, we are a proud nation, descended from the legionnaires of the Roman Empire. We have always fought for our freedom, our independence. We are also a devout Christian nation and we have not abandoned our faith. All over Europe, people are rising up. You'll see, eventually the tide of revolution will reach us too. We will not remain the last European nation still living under tyranny. It is inconceivable."

"Stefan, I can understand why you feel that way. It's brave and splendid and inspiring and idealistic… but it's a fantasy. You'd just be making yourself a martyr, like those saints you pray to all the time."

"It's not a fantasy and I have no desire to become a martyr," Stefan said, his expression suddenly cold and determined.

"No? I remember you yourself telling me back in Bucharest how you couldn't imagine the Romanian people rising up any time soon."

"That was before all this happened in Eastern Europe. Everything is changing; things that used to be impossible are becoming possible every day."

We left it at that with nothing resolved, but I could see that in his mind he was already back in Bucharest. Eventually, we slipped into a restless, unsatisfying sleep.

The next day was our last in Positano. As if by mutual consent, neither of us mentioned the matter in the morning. After a silent breakfast, Stefan went off for his usual run up and down the stairways of the village, while I spent the morning mustering my mental resources. After lunch, when we returned to the room, I launched a final effort to change his mind.

"Even if you're right and the Romanian people rise up, why do you have to be there?" I took both his hands in mine. "Why do you have to give up this?"

"When the hour strikes, my country will need voices, leaders, people with credibility, with integrity. Exiles and émigrés do not have that credibility because they fled to a better, more comfortable life leaving the rest behind. The people will not believe them, will not listen to them. But I do have the ear of the people. I have earned their trust."

"But what if you're wrong? What if that time never comes? You would have thrown away everything—your freedom, our love, our future together, your physical safety, perhaps even your life—and for what?" I asked, my voice rising almost hysterically. Already I could see it was useless; his mind was made up.

"Nothing in this world is certain," he replied calmly. "So yes, I may be wrong. I may look back on this moment years from now and curse myself as the greatest fool the world has ever seen. But I do feel in my heart and in my bones that a big change is sweeping Europe and Romania must be part of it, and will be part of it. If that is so, I must be in Romania."

I recalled Ralph Eskew talking about this in his office in Cambridge six months before. Then, it had been a purely theoretical discussion with nothing at stake. Now, everything lay in the balance. I had never loved Petrescu more or admired him more but I was convinced he was making a huge mistake.

"I'm just so scared," I said. "The authorities warned you never to go back. You'd be putting yourself in such danger."

"I don't think they will do so much. Perhaps they will place me under house arrest for a few months or send me to jail. I can survive that. I'm not afraid of them and I don't want you to be either."

He reached out and began to stroke my arm. I felt the tears come again—I tried to blink them away but could not—and realized I was defeated. There was nothing more to say.

"Ah, my poor Elisabeta, our troubles are not so great," he murmured. "With God's help, it will turn out all right." He kissed me. I returned his kiss, sucking the air from his mouth. His hand ripped open my blouse. I moaned, tearing his shirt from him, biting hard on his neck. We fell back on the bed, discarding our remaining clothing, clawing at each other.

"Wait," he gasped. "The birth control; we used the last one." He pulled away.

"No Stefan," I commanded, refusing to let him go. "Don't leave me. Not now. Make love to me like you know it's the last time." *Because it is*, I added to myself silently.

After it was over, I must have fallen asleep. I awoke several hours later, alone in the bed. For a moment, I thought he'd already gone. Then I saw him hunched over the desk, scribbling furiously on a piece of hotel notepaper.

"What are you doing?" I asked, blinking encrusted tears out of my eyes. I felt as if I'd run a marathon, stiff and spent.

"I'm writing a poem for you, a sonnet."

"In Romanian?"

"In English, my first poem in English."

"Can I see?"

"It's not finished. I'll give it to you tomorrow."

The evening passed quietly. I had never known such despair but I was determined not to cry any more until after he had left. Now the decision was taken, I owed it to him not to make things harder than they already were. We ate moderately, speaking little. Stefan kept taking my hand, stroking my fingers, caressing my wrist. We returned to the room, I to shower, he to continue work on his poem. Eventually, we climbed into bed but did not make love again.

Next morning, I awoke to find him writing once more. The rising sun slanting into the window cast a strange radiance over his head like the halos surrounding the Byzantine saints that adorned the churches he loved so much.

I lay watching him, trying not to cry, still unable to believe he would soon be gone. He sensed I was awake and turned to gaze at me wordlessly. I got dressed and silently packed my bag, noting that his was already packed. An hour later, we drove to the railway station in Naples and I stood beside him as he bought a ticket to Rome. He'd fly from there back to Bucharest while I took the direct connection from Naples to London.

Petrescu turned to me. "Remember what Rick tells Ilsa near

the end of *Casablanca*?"

"What?"

He put on his best imitation of Bogart, but it still came out sounding odd.

"I'm no good at being noble, but it doesn't take much to see that the problems of little people like us don't amount to a hill of beans in this crazy world. Someday you'll understand that."

I smiled through my tears. "Here's looking at you kid," I said. "May God protect you. I'm not a religious person but I'll pray for you every day."

He took both my hands and raised them to his lips.

"Farewell Elisabeta. Never doubt that I love you. I know we'll meet again and sooner than you think. This is not goodbye. This is only *au revoir* or as we say in my language, *la revedere*."

Back in the car, I finally allowed myself to break down. Great racking sobs tore through me. I wanted to rip out my hair by the roots, shred my garments in ritual mourning. I pounded the steering wheel with my fists. Eventually, the tempest subsided and I collected myself, glancing in the rear-view mirror at the wreckage of my face. That's when I saw the envelope lying on the back seat. Reaching back, I picked it up and ripped it open.

"Dear Elisabeta,
We cannot know what tomorrow will bring.
But please, please believe...
Never stop believing...
All my love,
Your Stefan."

And below, his sonnet:

For Elisabeta

The sun upon your golden hair, your skin, your breasts,
is glowing.
Don't fear, my love, I know I'll see such loveliness again.
Raw winter winds may come—I hear them, howling
shrieking, blowing.

If I could but command the sun, like Joshua—Remain!
And plead with God to stop time's arrow,
halt planetary motion,
And order Eden's skulking snake, be silent, crawl away,
Enough! Such foolishness defies both logic and emotion
And soon you will be waking, stirring, rising to the day.
Perhaps, like Shakespeare, I could make this moment
seem eternal
With rhyming quatrains, words that flow,
perfection on a page,
But still the clock would march along, would do its
work infernal,
And into that good night we'd go, it matters not we rage.
The sun upon your golden skin, your breasts,
your hair, the glowing.
We live between the blessing and the curse—
the never knowing.

5 – Bucharest: November 2007

In the end, Petra had to settle for two chickens for her grand Thanksgiving feast because turkey was impossible to find. They were five around the table at Angela and Mihai's apartment: herself, Petrescu, Mihai, Angela and her new boyfriend, a scruffy individual called Constantin who sported blond hair down to his shoulders, sideburns and a goatee that was little more than a tuft of hair glued to his chin. He barely spoke English so Petra had no idea what he was like.

Angela and Petra had done the cooking together and they brought the food proudly to the table: sweet potatoes glazed with raspberry preserves, stuffing, green beans cooked with onion and garlic, a home-made relish made from little orange berries they found at the market, and of course the two roasted chickens. Waiting in the kitchen for dessert was real pumpkin pie.

"So Petra, what do you do at Thanksgiving in America?" Stefan asked.

"In our house, my dad and my brothers would always park themselves in front of the TV and watch the football—you know, our football, not yours. Then, if it wasn't raining, they'd go out in the yard and throw a ball around while my mom and I prepared the meal."

"How quaint. And then what?" Angela asked.

"And then we'd eat," Petra replied. "We'd eat and eat and eat and keep on eating until we couldn't force another bite into our bodies."

"Sounds pretty boring," Angela said. "Didn't you guys do like we always see Americans doing in movies about Thanksgiving—you know, joining hands, bowing your heads and telling God all the things you had to be thankful for?"

"I already told you my dad wasn't keen on religion."

"I too have seen this in the cinema and I think it's a very beautiful thing," Stefan said. "We should certainly do this here today; perhaps we can create a new tradition."

"Okay," Petra said slowly, reluctant to contradict him. "If you say so. Who wants to go first?"

"I'll begin since it was my idea and I have so much to be thankful for," Stefan said. He closed his good eye, bowed his head and took Petra's hand. She in turn grabbed hold of Mihai and the chain continued until the circle was complete.

"Thank you, dear Father in heaven, first of all, for this wonderful meal cooked by these very special young ladies. And thank you for the freedom to enjoy good food, tasty and plentiful, which we did not always know in our country. And thank you for friendship and good fellowship around this table. And most of all, Lord, thank you for sending me this lovely young woman, my darling Petra. Amen."

There was an awkward hush around the table as the rest of them waited for someone else to speak. Finally, Mihai broke the silence.

"I'd also like to give thanks for the great food, which I hope to eat before it gets cold, and for good friends."

Again silence. Petra knew she should step into the vacuum but she didn't want to. It seemed phony and saccharine. She was the only American, for heaven's sake, the only one who had ever experienced a proper Thanksgiving. This was her celebration and she felt slightly miffed at the way Stefan had taken over.

Finally, Angela raised her head, opened her eyes and cleared her throat, winking at Petra.

"I'd like to thank the heavenly father for Constantin and his huge you-know-what and for the three orgasms he gave me last night. Thank you baby." She blew him a kiss across the table. Constantin grinned back uncomprehendingly. There was an uncomfortable silence and then Petra burst out in hysterical laughter. She was laughing so hard tears ran down her face. She tried to take a sip of water but had to put the glass down before she spilled it. Then she tried stuffing a napkin in her mouth but that didn't work either. After a second Mihai joined in; even Petrescu, who had looked grim, permitted himself a tiny smile.

Later, on the walk back to his apartment, Petra asked Stefan why he still refused to answer her questions about the revolution.

He said, "I know your mother is writing her own account. I think you should read what she says first. I don't want there to be two dueling versions, so you can go rushing back and forth between us trying to figure out the real truth, if such a thing exists."

"But your perspective has to be different."

"When she's finished telling her story, perhaps I will add my own viewpoint. We'll see. I know this is of great interest to you, but I learned to stop dwelling on the past a long time ago. It is not productive. Now I prefer always to look forward."

It was a damp, chilly evening and the streets were almost deserted. Feeling bold after a glass and a half of wine, Petra grabbed his gloved hand. "But there are still so many things about you I want to know that have nothing to do with the past."

"Very well, ask me something. Let's say, three questions. But there are ground rules: Whatever you ask should be only about the present, or possibly the future, not the past. And for every question you ask, I get to ask you one as well."

"That's only fair I guess. OK, first question, do you still write poetry?"

He laughed. "You don't mess around. Well, I said I'd answer, so I will. The truth, dear Petra, is that I haven't written poetry for some years. It seems my inspiration melted away with the Ceauşescu regime." He sounded sad. "You know, I was seriously wounded in the revolution; it's when I lost my eye. For quite a long time, I was in the hospital. I contracted an infection while I was lying there and almost died. It took me many, many months to regain my strength. Then, when I finally felt well enough, I began the task of tracking down all the poems I had written over the previous 10 or 15 years, which were scattered in the homes of friends and acquaintances all over the country. There were over 200; some I had almost forgotten writing. They had to be edited and prepared for publication. That took quite a while. After they appeared, I was invited to read and lecture in many places here at home and also around Europe. After years of working in secret, I suddenly became a minor celebrity. And then one day I realized I had no more poetry left inside me. It was as if God gave me a poetic voice for one reason alone and that was to speak out against the evil that was here. When that went away, so did my gift. I see you tricked me into speaking about the past after all."

They passed the Mihai Eminescu bookstore and stopped to look at the window display.

"You know, before the revolution, virtually the only books they sold here were either written by the dictator Ceauşescu or in praise of Ceauşescu," he said. "I often used to pass this shop and look in the window and all I saw were the faces of Nicolae and Elena, our twin rulers, mocking me, mocking the very idea of literature. Now look, the Ceauşescus are nowhere to be seen and instead, there are several books by me." He pointed at a small poster showing his face and a pile of volumes underneath.

"But you said you don't write anymore."

"Is that another question?"

"It's just a follow up. It doesn't count."

"OK, I'll allow it. To answer, in the last 10 or 15 years I have of course written and published several books of literary criticism and essays as well as many editorials, political commentaries and lectures. Just not poetry. For a while, I tried to write about nature and sunsets and mountains but what I was producing was banal and unworthy so I left it behind. Okay Petra, enough about me. My first question to you: do you write poetry like so many of the young people I see in my classes?"

"That's easy. The answer is no."

"Never?"

"I guess I did at school a couple of times but it wasn't any good. Don't look so disappointed, I have other talents. Next question to you: why do you wear an eye patch instead of a glass eye?"

"You are very direct. Do I have to be honest?"

"Totally."

"Well, they put the patch on after they operated and told me I needed to wait a while before the false eye could be fitted. In the meantime, I became accustomed to looking at myself that way. The patch reflected, in some way, how I felt—incomplete and damaged. It reminded me of what I had lost. So I left it. And to be frank, it helped a lot with my public profile and book sales. Instead of one poet among many, I became the poet with the eye patch."

By now, they had passed the University Square and crossed through the underground passageway, emerging on Regina Elisabeta Boulevard.

"OK, Petra, my second question to you," Stefan said. "What do you see yourself doing when you complete your studies?"

"Oh, that's hard. I like politics and history but I also love language and literature. I'd like to do some good in the world. Maybe I'll go to law school. I'm hoping it will become clearer as I get older. Remember, I only just started college."

"Whatever you do, I'm sure you will succeed brilliantly." He squeezed her hand.

Petra said, "Damn, we're almost home. OK, here's my third." She took a deep breath and decided to go for the jugular. "Question number three: are you still in love with my mom?"

There was a long silence as they turned the corner and reached the apartment building. Petra tried to see Stefan's expression, but he turned his good eye away from her. They stopped at the entrance, still arm-in-arm. She waited for what he would say, although she knew that through his silence he had already unwittingly given his answer.

He cleared his throat. "Petra," he began huskily. He coughed, then began again. "Petra, since today is Thanksgiving, I feel we should adopt American rules of procedure. Therefore, as they say in your country, I'm going to take the fifth."

6 – Massachusetts/ Bucharest: December 2007

To: Spetrescu@ubuc.ro

Fm: : Lizgraham@tmail.com

Thank you for your kind *and totally crazy and inappropriate (deleted)* invitation to stay in your apartment during my visit to Bucharest but I think I will respectfully decline. I believe it would be better *for all concerned, but especially me, (deleted)* to find a hotel. Perhaps you can suggest something modestly-priced but comfortable, well located in the city center. I would have liked to stay at the Athénée Palace for old times' sake but at $350 a night, it's beyond my means. Putting me in a hotel will give us both the space we need during this *emotional (deleted)* period and allow me to have some quality time with my daughter.

Thank you also for your regular reports on her progress which are welcome since I rarely hear from Petra herself. I guess she's busy with her life, which is all to the good. I'm glad to hear her Romanian is progressing so well. Please tell her I have arranged everything with Brown University. She'll return in September and she may even be able to get credit for the Romanian she is taking now.

Stefan, I want to ask you to support me in insisting that she come home to the United States to resume her studies, no matter how attached she becomes to Romania, to her friends and to you. She can maintain those relationships through visits but she must complete her education here at home.

I've been doing some reading ahead of my trip and I must say I've become curious to see how Bucharest has changed.

Actually, I don't care how much Bucharest has changed; I've been thinking of little else but you. I'm as nervous as a young virgin on the eve of her first date. How utterly ridiculous at my age! (deleted)

Thanks for your offer to meet me at the airport but there's really no need. I'll take a taxi. *The last thing I want is for you to see me emerge looking like a wrinkled old hag after a 16-hour airplane ride. I can't help my age of course but with the magic of modern cosmetics, perhaps I can repair some of the worst devastation before I meet you.(deleted)* I fear this visit is not going to be easy. I only hope I can maintain control of my emotions. I have so many memories, both good and unspeakably painful.

My best regards,
Elizabeth

To: Lizgraham@tmail.com
Fm: Spetrescu@ubuc.ro

I found a nice little hotel in the center for you, Hotel Opera. The rates are reasonable and it's only a 10-minute walk to my apartment. I booked a room with twin beds so that Petra can stay with you while you're there if she wishes. I promise to be an unobtrusive host and will leave you as much time alone with your daughter as you need. *It's crazy but all I want to do is see you. I haven't slept for a week. You keep warning me of how you've aged. I don't care, I just want to see you again. (deleted)*

The city is especially pretty now with the Christmas lights. It's been a mild winter—the temperature rarely dips below freezing point even at night, so different from the winter when we met. But bring a good thick coat just in case. *Do you remember the feel of my body that first time we went to bed as we hugged each other so tight to get warm? (deleted)*

Regards,
Stefan

To: Lizgraham@tmail.com

Fm: Poneill@brown.edu

mom—i've been going through all the latest stuff you sent me about how you met stefan. wow! *hot stuff, it even kind of turned me on a bit. (deleted)* i stayed up most of last night reading, then today i went and found that church where you switched coats with stefan's sister. by the way, i asked what happened to her and guess what, she teaches math at a college in tennessee of all places. i stood in that church trying to imagine the scene the way you described it, but i totally couldn't. there was a service going with a male choir singing all the responses. it was almost like a concert. whatever you do, please don't tell stefan i went to a church, it will only encourage him. i just wish you wouldn't keep writing how you gave up the love of your life for me, so i could grow up privileged in the united states. How's that supposed to make me feel? it's too much to put on my shoulders. stefan told me you decided to stay in a hotel, probably a good idea , *i wouldn't have wanted to listen to you two old lovebirds getting it on in the next room, yuck, how gross is that? (deleted)* it will give you the space you need to be totally comfortable. i'm going away next weekend with some friends to a town in transylvania, should be nice. maybe we can talk on the phone next week, looking forward to seeing you, love ya, petra

7 – Massachusetts: December 2007

Petra,

I've set myself the task of finishing this account before coming to Romania. I'm sure you'll have questions and I'll try to answer them as best I can when we're together. I guess we'll also walk around the city and I'll show you some of the places I reported from during the revolution as I remember them.

When I left off in my last letter, I'd reached the point when Stefan decided to return to Bucharest. Naturally, I was devastated. I told myself we'd only been together for an absurdly short time—really only a few days—and I should forget him and move on. But I couldn't.

There was, of course, no way to communicate with him. The only thing I could do was call Clint at the U.S. embassy and ask him to try to find out what had happened to Stefan on his return. I was afraid the authorities had thrown him into jail, or even worse. Clint reported back a few days later that according to his sources Stefan was back in his apartment in Bucharest but under house arrest. That came as an immense relief. Now I knew where he was; I could even picture him in his tiny kitchen, trying to scrape together something to eat.

Well, life went on despite my broken heart. Events in the Communist bloc were moving very fast. In September, the Hungarian government opened its borders to refugees from East Germany. That turned out to be a momentous decision. Thousands of people immediately poured through the open frontier heading straight for the West. Communist East Germany plunged into crisis. By early October, I was in Leipzig where huge crowds were on the streets, chanting "We are the people," and demanding freedom. The demonstrations continued night after night, widening to other cities, growing larger and larger with each day that passed. You could feel the foundations of the communist regime shudder.

I remembered how Peter Pringle had told me back in the summer that if unrest ever spread to East Germany, the endgame was approaching. Now, it was happening. The communists had no idea what to do. It was too late to send in the tanks; there were literally millions of people on the streets. In desperation, they fired their veteran leader Erich Honecker, who had been in charge since they built the Berlin Wall in 1961. But the crowds refused to disperse; the cries for freedom just got louder.

By this time, something else was happening. At the end of September, I missed my period. At first, I didn't give it a second thought. I thought maybe it was because of all the travel I'd been doing and the stress I'd been under. It wasn't the first time I'd been a week or two late. Then, I started feeling queasy, especially in the mornings. As you know, I love to start my day with a cup or two or strong coffee and I need regular refills every couple of hours. Suddenly, coffee revolted me. The only thing I wanted to drink was ginger ale. I thought it would go away but it just got worse. Soon, food seemed nauseating and the smell of cooking became unbearable. That made life difficult because the revolution was accompanied in the best German tradition by a strong flavor of beer and sausages.

One night, when I was out covering a protest, I had to duck into a side street to throw up. I'm sure anyone who saw me must have thought I was a terrible drunk, but I wasn't the only one. Half the protesters were drunk on alcohol and the other half on freedom.

Petra, it took me forever to put two and two together. I was convinced that I'd picked up a stomach bug that wouldn't let go. Here I was covering the biggest story the world had seen in 40 years and I could hardly drag myself out of bed. Finally, I could take it no longer and returned to West Berlin to see a doctor. That's when I found out I wasn't sick at all.

The news that I was pregnant came as a thunderbolt from the blue. At first, I couldn't figure out how it had happened. Stefan and I had always been careful ... except that one time on the last day we'd spent together when he'd run out of condoms. The doctor saw my face and asked me ever so politely if I needed information about 'safe and healthy options for termination.' Confused and shocked as I was, I didn't think twice. I told him no.

Initially, I think I was more stunned and disorientated than anything else. The timing was terribly inconvenient and I was still feeling wretched. I'd wanted a child, yes, but I'd never considered bringing one into the world without a father. However, over the next couple of weeks, I started getting used to the idea. I told no-one. It was my joyful, wondrous secret. I started having little, silent conversations with you, Petra, inside my head. For some reason, I knew you'd be a girl. Strangely, the knowledge that I was pregnant gave me new strength. I stopped feeling sorry for myself and started looking to the future.

The doctor figured I was around eight or nine weeks along. He advised me to take it easy for a month since morning sickness usually wears off by the 12th or 13th week. Naturally, I didn't take his advice. I wasn't about to sit on my butt while communism was falling apart a few miles away. I went back to East Berlin and forced myself to get out on the streets and do my job. That's where I was on the marvelous, incredible, transcendent day of November 9, 1989, and Petra, you were right there with me, inside me.

How can I describe that day? Nobody who lived through it will ever forget it. It began innocuously enough when a member of the East German leadership announced in a TV interview that citizens of his country would finally be able to travel abroad. When a reporter asked when this would begin, the man hesitated for a few seconds and then said, "Immediately." Whether this was planned or he just blurted it out, we may never know. Another reporter asked whether that meant people would be able to use the crossing points in the Berlin Wall to leave the country. The official said, yes they would.

Within minutes, crowds gathered all along the Wall and forced the gates open. And just like that, the Iron Curtain was breached. A huge celebration erupted in both sides of Berlin, the biggest party ever. I remember going to the Brandenburg Gate where the Wall was lower and wider than elsewhere. On the East German side, a thin line of troops still remained in place, nervously holding their Kalashnikovs, not knowing what to do, utterly bewildered by the amazing sight of hundreds of young people in front of them, standing on top of the Berlin Wall.

On the Western side, people were singing and dancing, waving flags, flying kites and taking pictures. Many strangers kissed and hugged me that day, when it seemed, for the first and only time in my life, that all men and women really were brothers and sisters. And I will never forget the predominant sound of that day: the pick, pick, pick of hundreds of hammers and chisels hacking at the Wall, taking it down chip by chip. After a couple of hours, cranes arrived and lifted away entire slabs and people poured through the gaps in their thousands.

At some point, I think it was late afternoon, I ran into Peter Pringle, an East German policeman's cap on his head, swigging champagne straight from a bottle.

"Hey Lizzie, what do you think of this?" he shouted, slurring his words.

"Amazing. And Peter, you saw it coming."

He grinned and took another slurp. "Damn right I did. So Lizzie, how about coming back to the hotel with me?"

"Oh Peter, you never give up do you? Don't you have something better to do, like filing a story to your agency?"

"I've filed thousands of words already. Now I'm celebrating. I thought maybe if the Berlin Wall came down, that Lizzie Graham's knickers might follow."

I laughed. "Communism may be crumbling, but Lizzie Graham is standing firm."

Much later, from my hotel room, with fireworks lighting up the night sky and the party still raging outside, I called Eskew in Cambridge. He's one of the toughest old buzzards I ever knew but I swear on that day he was crying tears of joy.

"I cannot believe what I'm seeing, I just can't believe it. I only wish I were there with you."

I was almost in tears myself. "Thank you Ralph, from rescuing me and sending me on this adventure," I gushed. "Thank you for allowing me to witness this amazing sight."

"Just keep sending colorful stories," he said. "Make us feel what it's like to be there. Everyone in America—that is, everyone who matters—has been reading you religiously."

After the Wall was breached, the rest of the dominos tumbled quickly. In Bulgaria, the communists gave up power without a struggle, just quit and left the stage. In Poland and Hungary, they had already surrendered. Next, strikes and demonstrations broke out in Czechoslovakia, marking the beginning of what became known as the *'Velvet Revolution.'* Events followed the East German pattern; first the communists tried replacing their old leaders; then they offered to negotiate with the opposition but in the end they had no choice but to give way and quietly disappear. By the end of the year, apart from tiny Albania only one last outpost of tyranny remained in Europe—Ceauşescu's Romania.

I returned to London and began packing my things. I'd promised Eskew I'd stay in Europe until the end of the year but after that I needed to return home for personal reasons. I had no idea where I would live or exactly what I would do but at least by early December the nausea had subsided and I was feeling more like myself again, able to look ahead and face the new challenge that awaited me. My waist was thickening and I had to let my clothes out a couple of buttons but nobody could yet tell I was pregnant just by looking at me.

Then one morning—I think it must have been around December 17 or 18—I received a telephone call. It was Clint calling from Bucharest, sounding more excited than I'd ever heard him.

"Liz, I think you'd better head back this way."

"What's happening?"

"Trouble has broken out in Timişoara. It seems quite serious."

"What kind of trouble?"

"It started with the authorities trying to arrest a dissident pastor, Lazlo Tokes. But it's gone beyond that now. There are crowds on the streets yelling *'Down with Ceauşescu'* and *'Down with tyranny.'* They've been setting vehicles on fire and smashing store windows."

"In Timişoara?" I said, remembering the gray, faceless city where I had spent my first weeks in Romania. "Hard to believe."

"I can hardly believe it myself. This could get nasty very fast. There's no way Ceauşescu's going to give up meekly. This is not going to be another *'Velvet Revolution.'* If the unrest spreads across the country, there could be huge massacres."

"So you think I should head for Timişoara?"

"I'd come straight to Bucharest. If there's going to be a confrontation, it will be decided here in the capital, not in the provinces. Either the authorities will snuff this thing out within a day or two, or it will gain strength, in which case the big action is going to be right here. If you go to Timişoara, you might get stuck there and miss the real story. Who knows how long the trains and planes will keep running if there really is a revolution?"

"But they're still running for now?"

"At the moment, everything here in Bucharest seems normal. On the surface nothing has changed. People are going about their business as usual. But I have to say Liz, there's a weird kind of electricity in the air—almost like the way it feels before a big thunder storm, almost too still, too quiet. Everybody knows about the uprising; they all listen to Radio Free Europe and the BBC. I think something is going to happen here very soon. I can't say when exactly, but the pressure's building. Do you have a visa?"

"I applied earlier in the summer just in case."

"Then get your ass over here. The government may seal the borders at any minute. I gotta run. Call me when you arrive."

"Thanks for tipping me off. I owe you big time."

My first thought was of seeing Stefan again and telling him my news—our news—and my heart beat faster. I was immediately on the phone to my travel agent. It was impossible to get a flight to Bucharest that day so I ended up flying to Sofia, the Bulgarian capital. By the time I arrived and checked into a hotel, Radio Free Europe was reporting from Timişoara that the Romanian army had opened fire on unarmed demonstrators in front of the cathedral, killing or wounding hundreds.

I called Clint and after an hour of trying managed to get through.

"Where are you?" he asked.

"Bulgaria. I couldn't find a flight to Bucharest but I've got a ticket on the night train. I should arrive early tomorrow morning. What's the latest? What I'm hearing on the radio sounds horrific. Is it true hundreds of people have been killed?"

"Nobody knows for sure. It could even be thousands. We hear the *Securitate* has been removing piles of bodies from the morgue to hide the true death toll, which is just fueling the rumor mill."

I was amazed the fighting was still going on considering that it was unarmed civilians against the army's tanks and guns. Clint couldn't even say for sure who actually controlled Timişoara and there were reports of trouble spreading to neighboring towns and villages.

"And get this, Ceauşescu has chosen this moment to fly to

Iran for a three-day visit," Clint said.

"That would suggest he's pretty confident the army will put down the uprising quickly," I said.

"Either that or he's become totally detached from reality."

"What about Bucharest? Have you seen any protests there?"

"No, it's still quiet here. But I think it's only a matter of time."

I called Eskew, who sounded grim. "Whatever you do, be careful. I don't want you wandering into the middle of gun battles. I should never forgive myself if something happened to you."

I told him not to worry. "I'm more concerned I'll wind up in the wrong place. The world's press is converging on Timişoara like a herd of stampeding elephants because that's where the action is. Meanwhile, I'm headed for Bucharest where right now nothing is happening."

Eskew said, "I'm sure your instinct is correct. Revolutions are always decided at the seat of power. If the regime is going to be challenged, the capital is the place to be."

"It's still hard for me to imagine it happening, not when Ceauşescu can mobilize such overwhelming force—the army, the police, Interior Ministry troops, the *Securitate*. The regime has already shown it's more than willing to spill blood."

"If he retains the loyalty of all those organizations, obviously Ceauşescu will win. What you want to watch for is whether some of the armed forces start changing sides. At that point, it's a real revolution, not just an uprising."

"That might mean civil war," I said.

"Indeed."

I didn't sleep a wink the entire train ride to Bucharest. I kept thinking about Stefan. Was he still shut in his apartment? Would I be able to see him? I wanted to hold him and kiss him and tell him how right he'd been about the courage of the Romanian people and also that we were going to have a child together. Then I started worrying the regime would turn against known dissidents and neutralize them before they could add their voices to the protests. I had awful visions of what they might do to him.

The train was full of Romanians heading home, talking quietly to one another. I kept hearing the word *"Timişoara"* but when I asked what they were hearing, they clammed up. I'd been nervous the Romanians would close the frontier but we crossed the Danube and breezed through the border checkpoints with less trouble than usual.

Next morning, December 19, 1989, I found myself back in Bucharest, checking into the Athénée Palace Hotel.

8 – Sibiu, Romania: December 2007

Mihai was not pleased when he discovered only four of them were going on the weekend trip to Sibiu—himself, Angela, Constantin and Petra. Angela had originally told him their flat mate, Cristina, would also be coming. Mihai gestured to Angela as she shoved their bags into the trunk of her car.

"We need to talk."

"What?" They moved away from Petra, who stood there feeling like an idiot as they began arguing in Romanian.

"You set me up. You said there'd be five of us. Now, I discover it's just us two cozy couples," Mihai shouted.

"Don't be such an old woman!" Angela snapped back, pushing him in the chest. "Do you expect me to provide a chaperone every time you're out in public?"

"I know what you're planning and it's not going to work. What are you trying to do—turn Petra into a clone of yourself?"

"Don't be ridiculous."

"Is it? Look at her wearing your clothes, your makeup, your jewelry. Soon she'll be fucking every second man that comes around, like you," Mihai said.

"Actually, the only one she wants to fuck is you, in case you didn't get it. Why don't you just get it over with? You know you want to."

"Because, unlike you, I don't let sex rule my life. And Petra is a sweet, innocent, young girl who knows nothing about sex. I'm not going to be the one to corrupt her."

"Suddenly you're Mr. Morality? I don't remember you being

so fussy before. Anyway, you've no need to worry. All four of us will be sharing the same room, so nothing's going to happen."

After that, everyone was in a sour mood during the four-hour car ride. Constantin showed up in bad need of a shampoo. He wore the same jeans and denim jacket he'd worn every time Petra had seen him. He was a man of few words at the best of times and all of them were in Romanian. The times he did open his mouth, Angela rudely cut him off. Eventually he pulled a pair of earphones out of his bag and retreated into his own universe.

Angela cursed loudly each time they got stuck behind a horse and cart on the twisting mountain road, leaning into the horn to make the startled animals get out the way. Peasants shook their fists at her as they sped by. Apparently, honking at horses was a major breach of Romanian road etiquette.

In the back seat, Mihai was either asleep or pretending to be. Petra tried nudging him awake but he refused to respond. Eventually, she fell back on figuring out what percentage of the horses they passed were white. She was out of math practice and it took an annoyingly long time to divide 13 by 37 and multiply by 100. Her mind kept getting distracted by what might happen that night.

Petra had been fantasizing about this weekend with a mixture of excitement and dread for the past two weeks, thinking about how it would be to finally get Mihai alone in a room for a night. Would she have the guts to undress in front of him, to stand in front of him, naked flesh to naked flesh, to feel him become erect? At that point, her imagination always went blank. She couldn't visualize herself actually engaging in sexual intercourse. At Angela's urging, she had bravely gone into a pharmacy back in Bucharest and equipped herself with a packet of condoms. The choice was bewildering. What was the difference between lubricated and unlubricated, supersensitive and super-thin, ribbed and unribbed?

Sibiu turned out to be a lovely town with medieval fortifications and a large Gothic cathedral whose spire, intricately patterned with black and white tiles, dominated the city. Nearby, narrow cobbled streets converged on two picturesque, adjoining squares that reminded Petra of Italy. Many of the houses were painted pink, rose or yellow; others had curious little windows set in their ancient tiled roofs like slanted eyes. Constantin walked with them for a few minutes and then announced he wasn't interested in historic buildings and stalked off, muttering that he'd join them later at the hotel, maybe.

"Where's he going?" Petra asked Angela.

"Probably to score some dope to make his brain even smaller than it already is. He's got druggy contacts all over Romania. I've had about enough. I swear, if it wasn't for this trip, I'd have finished with him already. The man's a Neanderthal. You can't have a conversation with him, he just grunts."

"Yeah, we noticed," Petra said.

"I thought all you cared about was his sexual prowess?" asked Mihai, who seemed to have recovered his good humor. He could never be mad at Angela for long.

"Sex isn't absolutely everything, you know," Angela said. "Occasionally, I do like to talk, either before or after."

They climbed the winding staircase of the ancient tower overlooking the main square and were rewarded with a brilliant view of snow-capped mountains to the south. Then they retreated to a bar which boasted a menu with 23 different types of hot chocolate imported from Italy.

"This is the life," said Mihai as he sipped a concoction so thick and rich it barely oozed out of the cup. But his good mood vanished when they checked into the hotel and discovered there was no room big enough for four and they would have to keep the two doubles Angela had booked.

"Do you think I'm some kind of moron?" he snapped at her.

"No sweetheart, why would I think that?"

"Was this just your idea or did the two of you cook this up between you?" he asked, giving Petra a dark look. She blushed a deep red. This wasn't turning out the way she'd planned at all.

"Sorree," Angela said, not sounding very sorry at all. "They told me there was a room big enough for all of us. I must have misunderstood."

"So you sleep with Petra and I'll bunk with Constantin," Mihai said.

"No way. I'm with Constantin. We're not giving up our fun just because you've turned into such a pussy. It could be my last chance; we're not going to last much longer."

Constantin eventually returned to the hotel and the four of them went out for dinner in a pizzeria on the central square. It was a muted meal. Angela tried her best to carry the conversation single-handedly, getting little help from the other three. Petra was too nervous to say much, but did put away two and a half glasses of Romanian pinot noir, earning more disapproving glances from Mihai. After dessert, Angela said she'd heard of a decent jazz club in the old town but Mihai begged off, saying he was too tired and would head back to the hotel.

"I'm tired too, I'll come back with you," Petra said, feeling a little woozy. The wine, as intended, had given her a modicum of courage.

Mihai shot her another look but said nothing and they left together.

"It's lovely here, so much history. I'm glad I came," Petra said, trying to break the ice that had built up between them.

Mihai started walking faster, forcing Petra to break into a trot to keep up. Back in the room, he went into the bathroom without a word, slamming the door behind him.

Petra sat on the bed. The room seemed to be revolving slowly. What was she supposed to do now? Should she change into her camisole and wait for him in bed? Maybe she should skip the camisole and just get naked. But then, why go to the trouble of buying the camisole in the first place? What would Angela do? While she was thinking about it, Mihai emerged, wearing shorts and a T-shirt and climbed under the covers.

"Goodnight, see you in the morning," he said curtly and snapped off the light. It dawned on Petra that she wouldn't be losing her virginity that night.

Suddenly, she felt horribly embarrassed. So much for the lacy nightwear which he would never see, and the condoms he would never use! How had she gotten herself in this situation?

"Stop crying, Petra," he said after a while.

"I can't," she snuffled.

He switched the light back on and sat up in bed, looking devastatingly attractive with his dark, curly hair, all damp and gleaming from the shower. That only made things worse.

"Don't look," she wailed. "I feel bad enough without you staring at me like I'm a total loser."

"I don't think you're a loser. Why don't you blow your nose and wipe your eyes?"

"Don't treat me like a little girl," she shouted, shoving aside the box of tissues he offered.

"I'm not."

"So why are you ignoring me? I know I'm not sexy like your other girlfriends but I thought you still liked me." She changed her mind, grabbed a tissue and loudly blew her nose.

"Of course I like you. You're very cute."

"Cute? A teddy bear is cute. I wanted to be sexy. I brought a camisole, peach colored, especially for tonight."

He looked at her, red-eyed, red-nosed with tears still trickling down her cheeks, and smiled. "I'm sure it's adorable."

"Adorable isn't sexy. I knew it. Just say it Mihai; you're not attracted to me."

He hesitated, knowing that the truth would put him on thin ice. "That's not exactly true," he said slowly. "I am attracted to you. That's what makes this hard. I do think you're sexy, even without the peach-colored camisole."

She brightened. "I can put it on real quick if you like."

"That's OK. Not tonight."

"Why not? I know you got turned on when you kissed me after that dog bit me. I felt you responding. But since then, you've been ignoring me again."

"Well, I'm not going to make love to you, no matter how turned on I was, and no matter what devious juvenile scheme you cooked up with Angela to get us into this room together."

"Why not?" she asked sadly, although part of her was also relieved. "Angela said everything would be OK once we were alone together. She said men always want sex when they get the chance."

"That shows how much Angela knows about men. Not

much!" It was a valiant lie.

"But you just told me you found me attractive. Why shouldn't we sleep together? I have to lose my virginity sooner or later."

"What's the rush? You're still young. Maybe they should pass a sex law like they pass drinking laws in your country. Maybe you shouldn't be allowed to have sex until you've voted in a presidential election. Sex is a lot more serious than voting."

"So that's the reason? You think I'm too young?"

"That and the fact that I promised your father I'd look after you."

"My father? My father's dead."

"I mean Stefan Petrescu."

"Screw him! He has no right. He's not my father, despite what he thinks." She started sobbing gently again, speaking through her tears. "And who gave the two of you permission to start deciding things for me behind my back? It's my life. Who elected you my guardian?"

"Nobody. I just care about you—more than you know. And I don't understand why you're in such a hurry to jump into bed with the first guy that comes along, even if it happens to be me."

"But you're not a virgin. You've slept with women. Why is it OK for you and not for me? Lots of girls my age and much younger are having sex. It's not a big deal. In my high school, the other girls were always talking about what they did with their boyfriends. It was like they were all members of a club I could never join. I was probably the only virgin in the class by the time I graduated."

"So you want to be like all the other girls?"

"Yes, I just want to be normal. If you're worried about getting me pregnant, you don't have to. I bought condoms. I have them in my bag, a dozen of them."

Mihai was speechless, not knowing whether to laugh or cry.

"Stop looking at me like that," Petra said. "They're ultra-thin and supersensitive for maximum male pleasure. It says so on the box."

"That was thoughtful."

"I asked Angela which type to get."

He stopped smiling. “I wish you wouldn’t copy Angela all the time. Why can’t you just be yourself? Do you really want to be like her, picking up sleazy types she find in clubs and bars and taking them straight to bed? Do you think it makes her happy? Whatever she says, I think it makes her feel like crap. Angela’s almost like a sister to me; I’ve known her forever. But I hate what she’s becoming. I know you think she’s super cool but she’s not. She’s actually quite pathetic. And for heaven’s sake, stop pacing around. You’re making me dizzy.”

Petra sat back down on the bed and thought about his words. Mihai waited. Finally she said, “But I don’t want a sleazy type I picked up in a club or bar. I only want you, nobody else.” She closed her eyes, swallowed hard and took the plunge, her voice quivering. “I love you. Don’t you see that?”

Mihai was taken aback at her courage. To his surprise, a lump was forming in his throat. He found he couldn’t look her in the eye. “Petra, I’m honored,” he said, trying to eliminate the tremble in his voice. “But how do you know it’s not just a teenage crush?”

His words were like a slap in the face. “I can see what you’re trying to do,” she said bitterly. “If you keep telling yourself this is just a teenage crush, you don’t have to take me seriously. But it’s not. This is the real thing.”

“How do you know? You talk a good game, Petra, but you have zero experience.”

“I know what I’m feeling right now. I know that I think about you all day and dream about you every night. I know how I felt when you kissed me. I’ve been honest with you. Why won’t you do the same with me? You’re supposed to be the grown-up here. What are you afraid of?”

“I’m not afraid.”

“Then tell me the truth. You owe me that. Tell me you don’t have feelings for me and I’ll leave you alone, no matter how much it hurts. I’ll go home to America. I’ve done what I came here to do; I’ve met Stefan. I don’t need to be chasing after someone who doesn’t want me.”

He hesitated, feeling like a fraud about to be exposed. “It’s not that I don't have feelings …"

"Then what?"

He paused for what seemed like a long time. "I think maybe I do."

"Maybe? You're not sure?"

"OK, OK, Petra, please wipe your eyes. Look, it's true; I do have feelings for you. You're not the only one who's been miserable these last few weeks. I think about you too. I want to take you in my arms and kiss you too."

"So why don't you?"

"Can't you see I'm wrong for you? I'm 23, you're 17. That's a pretty huge difference at your age, more than a third of your entire life. You're barely out of high school. I've got my masters degree. In terms of life experience, I'm like 100 years ahead of you. Plus I live here in Romania while you'll soon be going back to America. What's the point of starting a big romance? We'd only end up hurting each other. I'm just trying to protect you—and myself too."

"Are you saying what I think you're saying? Really?" she asked, her eyes suddenly shining through her tears.

A long silence but Mihai realized he'd been checkmated. "I didn't want to tell you," he said gloomily, not meeting her gaze. "What's the point? It won't do either one of us any good."

Petra grinned, her tears suddenly forgotten. "Then you love me too?"

"Unfortunately."

"Then say it!"

"OK, I love you too. Are you happy now?"

"Yess!" She pumped the air, like a tennis player who just made a spectacular winning shot. But there was no time to celebrate—not while she had him on the defensive. "So why are you so scared? Are you afraid what my so-called father, the hero of the revolution, would say if he saw us together, or what other people will think?"

Suddenly, without him knowing exactly how it had happened, the advantage in the conversation had completely switched.

"That's not it at all," Mihai protested weakly. "If I felt it was right, I wouldn't care what anyone else thought. But it's just wrong. You've never done this before; you don't know how much love can hurt. You have no idea what you'd be getting yourself into. How could you? You're so young."

She hurled a pillow at him but it fell wide. "Just stop it. OK, I'm only a teenager, I admit it. But I act a lot older. People my own age bore me. I'm emotionally very mature for my age."

"Really? This whole adventure, running away from home, coming to Romania—how mature was that? It worked out OK, but it was totally crazy. It could have gone horribly wrong. And you've changed so much since you've been here. You look different, you act different—it's obvious you don't have a clue yet who you really are."

"You sound like my mom. All I've done is color my hair and paint my fingernails. I haven't changed anything fundamental like my opinions or my religion. I'm still the same inside. And even if I've grown up a bit, what's wrong with that? People do change throughout their lives. They learn, they grow, they develop. It would be weird if they didn't."

Mihai had no answer. It was obvious she was slaughtering him in this discussion.

"It's not like I'm asking to marry you," Petra continued. "All I wanted was to go to bed together. And actually, that isn't even the main thing. Really, all I wanted was to be together."

Mihai sighed. What did he have to say to get through to her? Gently, he took her chin and looked directly into her eyes. "Listen Petra, I know whatever I say, you'll always have a dozen answers for me. If this were a high school debate, you'd win, no question. That still doesn't make you right. This isn't about words; it's about how we act, what we do—what we're going to be toward each other."

"So what are we doing to be?" she asked in a small voice.

"I guess I thought we could just be really good friends."

"Liar! That's not what you want, not really. You just admitted you loved me. Lovers are more than just friends. What do you really want?"

He winced. "What I want is really not the point. I may desire all kinds of things but I've learned to accept reality. And the reality is, you'll be leaving Bucharest soon. Once you get home, you'll forget me. There'll be no shortage of smart, attractive guys lining up for the chance to be with you. You can decide who to go to bed with. And I'll be back here in Romania."

He swallowed hard, not wanting to imagine it.

"I'm not going anywhere for another six months at least," Petra shot back. "And I already told you, I'm not interested in other guys. I can't imagine being with anyone except you."

"That's what you say now," he said morosely.

"Why isn't that good enough for you? I know, don't tell me —it's because I'm too young. It always comes back to that—too young for sex, too young for love, too young for commitment, too young for everything. You really think I just got out of kindergarten don't you?"

"I only meant you should be free to live your life."

"But this is my life, dummy! I didn't wake up one morning and decide it would be cool to fall in love with you. It just happened. Who cares what might or might not happen six months from now or a year from now? Maybe you're *not* destined to be the love of my life—but you are my love of right now. You have to be honest to yourself."

"That's a nice slogan."

"It's not just a slogan. Don't you believe in the power of love?"

"You've been reading too many romance novels."

"It's not just romance novels. It's life. Lovers overcome huge odds all the time. During the war, people waited for each other for years on end. Stefan has been in love with my mom for 18 years—he as good as told me. How realistic is that? If you love someone, you can't just avoid it or deny it, the way you've been avoiding me. That's living a lie."

Mihai sighed. She really was amazing. He'd never met anyone quite like her. He'd be crazy to let her go. And in truth, she sometimes was incredibly insightful for her age. That crazy mixture of youth and maturity was part of what had entranced him. Plus she was forcing him to be honest like no-one had ever done before.

"OK, I admit it. Trying to stay out of your way was dumb. I don't want to do that any more. I just didn't know how to act around you. I still don't."

"Why not just be together? You don't want to have sex with me right now? OK. I'll wait. I'll be old enough to vote in April, if that's so important to you. We can still go on dates, hang out together, go clubbing, see movies, take hikes, go skiing—whatever! You could play me your music, take me to concerts, help with my Romanian. Maybe once in a while, you'll even kiss me and put your arms around me and we'll feel close to each other."

Mihai smiled. She was relentless; it was impossible to resist her, and he had to admit he no longer wanted to. "OK, I suppose we can go out on some dates."

"And all the other stuff as well?"

"Some of it."

Petra smiled. "I think I'll keep those condoms around. Just in case."

9 – Bucharest: December 1989

"Welcome back to Bucharest, Miss Graham. How long will you be staying with us this time?" asked the desk clerk at the Athénée Palace.

I thought, *Depends on if there's going to be a revolution*. But I could hardly tell him that. "Three weeks perhaps." That ought to give the masses enough time to rise up.

The first thing I did on reaching my room was phone Clint at the embassy. I needed reliable information. It was already Wednesday; stories for *The Brahmin* had to be filed by Friday afternoon so that they could be edited in time for the magazine to hit the newsstands Monday morning. I was in an embarrassing situation. I'd made it to Bucharest but I had no idea what was happening elsewhere in Romania and few ways of finding out. I hadn't brought along my short-wave radio, fearing the Romanian border police would confiscate it. Ralph Eskew certainly knew more than I did, sitting in his office reading *The New York Times* and watching CNN.

I was put on hold for five minutes and then informed that Clint would be in meetings for much of the day but would try to get back later.

What I really, desperately wanted was to talk to Stefan. I longed to hear his voice and know that he was well. But I dared not take the risk. Assuming he was still under house arrest, one call from a foreign journalist might be enough to persuade the authorities to remove him from the city.

I began leafing through my organizer, searching for the numbers of the Romanian officials I'd met on my previous visit, not that I expected them to provide accurate information. Still, I was curious to hear the official Communist Party line and it might be possible to learn something indirectly from their tone of voice or by reading between the lines of what they said. But Marius Gavril, the man from the Foreign Ministry with a taste for Pepsi, was unavailable and no-one even answered the phone at the Trade Ministry. However a secretary picked up at the Government Press Office and put me through to the chief spokesman, Mr. Bărbulescu. He was the runty little man I'd interviewed sitting under a vast portrait of Ceauşescu, who had shown an unexpected human side by complaining about having cold wet feet the entire winter.

"Ah yes, Elizabeth Graham, I remember you of course," Bărbulescu said without enthusiasm after I introduced myself. "I have to say we were quite disappointed when we read your article, especially after all the efforts we made to open our doors to you."

"I did very much appreciate your assistance. Perhaps you can help me again," I said, ignoring the jibe. I was certainly not about to apologize for what I had written.

"I doubt it," Bărbulescu said sourly. "Not after the last time."

"What can you tell me about the situation in Timişoara?"

Except for his wheezy breathing, there was silence on the line.

"Mr. Bărbulescu?"

"Why don't you go there and see for yourself, Madam Graham? The trains from Bucharest are running normally. I believe there are several departures each day."

"But I'm not there, Mr. Bărbulescu. I'm here. That's why I'm asking you."

He paused again and she heard him rustling through some papers. "There isn't very much to tell, Madam Graham. As you know, there have been some incidents of disorder and lawlessness, blown completely out of proportion in foreign news reports, but now the situation is returning to normal," he said in a monotone. I assumed he was reading from a prepared statement.

"So the reports of thousands of casualties..."

"Ridiculous lies manufactured by anti-socialist, anti-Romanian, revisionist forces outside the country and cynically and irresponsibly spread by your colleagues in the Western news media."

"Are you saying nothing is happening in Timişoara?"

He cleared his throat. "No. I believe I just told you there were some incidents of disorder and lawlessness, instigated by fascists beyond our borders. The authorities are acting to restore order. And the rest of the country, including the capital, is quiet as you can see for yourself." His voice took on a shrill, self-righteous tone. "I invite you to take a walk on our streets, Madam Graham. People are going about their business. Nobody will molest you, nobody will mug you or rape you or shoot at you or attempt to sell you illegal drugs. Such is not the case in your own capital of Washington D.C. I'm afraid you have wasted your time coming here again, Madam Graham, you and all the other foreign correspondents descending on our country like a flock of vultures. You are all wasting your time. The story you are all hoping to write is not going to happen."

Stymied, I decided to go down to the lobby to see if there was anyone to talk to. The usually-bustling lobby was virtually deserted; so was the coffee shop. There were far fewer hotel staff around than before and those on duty seemed subdued and preoccupied. At the English bar, I saw one solitary figure wearing a tattered tweed jacket with patched elbows slumped in front of an empty beer tankard.

"Hello Pringle," I said. "Haven't seen you since Berlin."

"Lizzie," he said, turning his pointy little face to me without surprise. "Come for some jolly seasonal cheer in Romania, have you? You're looking in the pink, I must say. Have you put on some weight? It suits you."

"What the hell's going on Peter?"

He let out a dismissive belch. "What's going on is that those of our chums who went to Timişoara have a hell of a story on their hands while we're sitting twiddling our thumbs waiting for something to happen. Why on earth did you come here Lizzie? You're in the wrong place."

"Why did you?"

"My lords and masters, in their infinite wisdom, decreed that I should remain on guard in the capital, while others more deserving were dispatched to Timişoara to cover the real action."

"What's the latest from Timişoara?"

Pringle took a mighty swig of beer, then pulled a dog-eared spiral notebook from his jacket pocket and read from scribbled notes. "According to the latest dispatch filed a couple of hours ago, a huge crowd has gathered around the Town Hall and Opera House shouting anti-government slogans. The troops are not firing on them and some have even begun fraternizing with the demonstrators. My colleague on the spot says he saw protesters climbing on top of tanks and sticking flags in soldiers' gun barrels. It's enough to make you puke, isn't it?"

"What do you mean?"

"It's cruel being stuck here when great stuff like that is happening just down the road. Right now, I'm barely a one-sentence insert in the story: *'Meanwhile, in Bucharest, correspondent Peter Pringle reports the situation remains calm'.*

"Is this my reward for 20 years of devoted service, for my countless visits to this crappy country? Was it for this I sat through endless interviews with lying bureaucrats, suffered innumerable execrable meals in shitty restaurants and cold nights in squalid, bug-infested hotels?"

"Peter, are you saying the army has lost control of the center of Timişoara?"

"That's what it sounds like, at least for now. How long it lasts remains to be seen. Uncle Nicolae is expected back in Bucharest from Iran at any minute, at which time things could start getting really bloody. He's supposed to be addressing the nation on TV tonight. There's talk he may fire the prime minister, or perhaps offer some economic concessions to the people to calm things down. At least, I'll have something to write when the great man opens his mouth. Hey, barman, bring me another jar of this stuff you laughingly call beer and one for my American friend here."

"No, not for me," I said hastily.

"Rotten sport, Lizzie, leaving a chap to drink alone. You know, I've been reading your stuff in that snotty magazine you write for. I've become quite a faithful fan. You do have a way with words, I have to admit."

"Why thank you Peter. I'm touched. I've been reading you too."

"You use too many adjectives and adverbs though."

"Don't you like adjectives and adverbs? I find them useful at times."

"They're frowned on where I work. Use too many adjectives and your next assignment is writing the daily trading report on the Frankfurt stock exchange—fate worse than death."

"How will you cover the speech tonight? Do you have a translator?"

"Yeah, our local stringer. Little weasel works for the *Securitate* no doubt, but he'll do an OK job translating for me."

"Can I tag along? I won't disturb you. I just need to know what Ceauşescu says."

"Sure. We've got a little office just down the street. Meet me in the lobby at 6:30, we'll walk down there."

"Thanks Peter, I owe you one."

With several hours on my hands, I decided to follow Bărbulescu's advice and take a walk to gauge the mood of the city. The weather was relatively mild, quite different from the bone-chilling cold of my previous visit. I strolled past the National Gallery of Art and the Central Committee Building with its giant neon sign on the roof proclaiming, "*Long Live the Communist*

Party of Romania!" There was little traffic, though I did see several military vehicles speed by. I passed several small knots of people standing together, talking in hushed voices. At the corner of Republicii Boulevard, I could have turned left toward the University, a possible focus of unrest. Instead, I swung right in the direction of Petrescu's apartment, drawn like an iron bar to a magnet. I knew it was dangerous but I couldn't help myself.

As I drew nearer, I found myself praying that by some miracle the place would be unguarded. Wouldn't it be incredible just to walk up the stairs, knock on the door and watch his expression when he opened it? Heart pounding, I rounded the corner and saw two soldiers wearing dark blue uniforms with automatic weapons standing outside his building. Quickly, I turned around, hoping they hadn't spotted me. Stumbling almost blindly, tears leaking from my eyes, I found my way into the Cişmigiu Gardens and sat down on a bench. Suddenly I was weeping uncontrollably. The pain was palpable, a physical ache in my chest. Previously, I had never allowed myself to think in detail about what house arrest really meant. Now, I pictured Stefan pacing the narrow confines of his apartment like a caged tiger, hour after hour, day after day, unable to take a walk in the park or breathe fresh air. My heart broke for him.

I felt a hand on my shoulder and looked up, startled. An elderly man in a Russian-style fur hat was peering at me with concern. He asked me something in Romanian, no doubt inquiring whether I needed help. I shook my head, unable to stop sobbing. He said something else, then seemed to register that I was a foreigner and beat a hasty retreat.

Eventually, the tears died away and I returned to the hotel, physically and psychologically drained. Lying on the bed, I placed my hands lightly on my stomach and closed my eyes seeking calm. Automatically, my mind switched gears. I'd been wondering lately when I might feel the baby move. According to the pregnancy books, that could come anywhere between the 18th and the 24th week—not for another two or three weeks at the earliest. The thought was both scary and exhilarating.

I must have dozed off and was abruptly woken by the telephone ringing.

"Gotta make this quick, Liz," said an excited voice. "Can't talk but for a minute."

I groped for a light and saw it was already five o'clock. I'd been asleep for nearly three hours.

"Oh, Clint," I stuttered, struggling to clear my head. "Where … I mean, what's happening?"

"Liz, did I wake you?"

"It's OK. I'm awake now. What's up?"

"Everything's on hold, waiting for the big man's address tonight. That could be decisive. It's amazing; my phone hasn't stopped ringing these past four or five days. Finally, Romania matters. The whole world is watching."

"What do you think he'll say?"

"If he's smart, he'll talk about making some changes, improving the lives of the people. The situation is on a knife's edge."

"You don't feel it walking around the city. It seems fairly normal to me—quieter than usual if anything."

"None of us outsiders can tell what's bubbling under the surface. But the whole country knows what's been happening. They're all following the news on Radio Free Europe or the BBC. There's got to be enormous anger building up. You don't just shoot hundreds of unarmed civilians in cold blood like that, not even in Romania. I assume you got the statement the White House issued last night."

"No, I've been out of contact."

"It's fairly short but basically President Bush is condemning the killing of innocent civilians and the regime's attempts to cover it up in the strongest terms. You were lucky to get here when you did. The government closed all the borders a couple of hours ago."

"What's happening in Timişoara right now? The last I heard was sometime around noon, when the demonstrators seemed to have taken over the city. It sounded incredible."

"It seems to be true. I've heard reports that the army has actually pulled out of the city center, which can only mean that the government feels it can't rely on the loyalty of some of its units any more. The city is paralyzed by a general strike and the disturbances are spreading to towns and cities throughout Transylvania. We hear there are negotiations going on between opposition leaders and the government but we don't know exactly what about."

"OK Clint, thanks a million. Maybe I'll call again after the speech tonight."

"You can try but I don't guarantee being able to talk to you."

I met Pringle in the hotel lobby and we made the short walk down the street to his office. It turned out to be a tiny, unheated room on the third floor of a half-dilapidated building on Lipscani Street. It was equipped with an ancient black and white TV, a telephone, a printer and a single, word processor that flickered feebly when Pringle switched it on. He gestured to a moth-eaten couch.

"Have a pew. We don't have the latest technology, as you see but it usually works, just about, if there are no power cuts."

"What if there are?"

"I'll pray for a phone line to London and dictate the story. But don't worry. The electricity won't go off during the president's speech, they'll make certain of that. Just sit quietly. You can read the stories off the printer as I transmit them if you like. I'll probably be sending several bulletins while he's still speaking and a proper story when he's done."

The Romanian interpreter, a young, sallow-skinned man, slipped quietly into the room. He shook hands with Pringle and took a seat next to him in front of the TV, ignoring me in the corner. Pringle placed two cassette recorders in front of the TV. Then Ceauşescu's face appeared.

To my admittedly inexpert eye, the supreme leader seemed tired, the lines around his eyes and mouth deeply etched. But he soon picked up steam, gesturing angrily at the camera. The interpreter spoke softly to Pringle, who scribbled notes in shorthand.

After a few minutes, he turned to his word processor and tapped out a single sentence. The printer clattered to life. I read,

"Ceauşescu blames Timişoara unrest on 'hooligans and terrorists'."

It did not appear that the president was in a conciliatory mood. He continued speaking, his voice growing more strident. Pringle's second bulletin a couple of minutes later read, *"Ceauşescu vows no concessions to protesters."*

It was quickly followed by a third: *"Ceauşescu accuses foreign forces of stirring violence, vows to crush unrest."*

As the speech ended with a blaze of patriotic music, Pringle started typing furiously, pausing only briefly to consult his notes. Meanwhile the interpreter was playing back the tape and preparing a full transcript in English. After 10 minutes, Pringle already had a dozen paragraphs on his screen. He read them through and pressed the *'send'* button. I was both fascinated and impressed. I myself was a slow and careful writer who weighed every word and every sentence; Peter had punched out an entire article in less time than it took me to compose a single paragraph. He looked up at me.

"So there you have it dear girl. He basically shits on the whole world. If the Romanian people want any real change in their crappy lives, they're going to have to do it over his dead body. That's the message of tonight."

10 – Bucharest: December 2007

"Welcome to Romania Mom. It's so great to see you."

"Let me look at you Petra. I missed you so much. You look fantastic. Give me another kiss. Did you color your hair?"

"Just a bit. I used henna so it will wear off pretty quickly. Do you like it?"

"It's great. And those clothes. And the makeup. The jewelry. You look all grown up. Your friends on the math team would never recognize you. Let me hug you again. My God, I'm finally here. I can hardly believe this is really Bucharest. All these ads for casinos everywhere, ads even on the floor as you walk through the airport."

"Wait till you see the city. You can see it changing before your eyes. And Stefan is waiting to meet you tonight. He can hardly sit still, poor man."

"Tonight?"

"If you're up for it."

"I don't know. I hardly closed my eyes the whole journey, I was so excited to see you. Maybe it would be better to meet him after I've had a good night's sleep. I'm not sure I want him to see me looking like this."

"Mom, you should if you can. He'll be disappointed. He's already started cooking."

"That was a little presumptuous, without asking me first."

"Don't you want to see him?"

"Of course I do. It's just that … tonight, it's so soon."

"He's invited my two best friends, Mihai and Angela, for dinner so you can meet them too. I really want you to if you can."

"So it wouldn't be just the three of us? That's good. I don't think I'm ready to play happy families with Stefan Petrescu just yet."

"Mom, are you afraid of him?"

"Never mind what I am, Petra. Let me look at you again. Have you lost weight?"

"I don't think so. Here, let me take one of your bags and we'll grab a taxi to your hotel. The traffic is pretty horrendous out there."

"I thought it would be colder here this time of the year."

"It's been a mild winter so far. How was Christmas at home?"

"Very nice. Your brothers send their love and the kids all want to see their Aunt Petra again. How was your holiday?"

"Stefan dragged me to midnight mass. I wasn't sure I wanted to go but it was really awesome. The choir was fantastic. I actually found it quite moving."

"I'm glad your poor father doesn't know. He's probably rolling in his grave."

"It doesn't mean I found God or anything. But you have to be open-minded. Looking back on it, Dad was a bit intolerant. Being religious is a big part of Stefan's life. You just have to accept it."

"Yes, he was devout even back then when I knew him. It's good he's kept his faith. What did you do on Christmas Day?"

"Mostly just hung with my friends Mihai and Angela."

"So tell me about this boyfriend of yours?"

"Mihai? He's great. He's studying composition and he plays in a string quartet. Last week he took me to the opera again. We saw *'The Barber of Seville'*."

"I never imagined you becoming an opera buff. You really have changed. Did you enjoy it?"

"It was pretty long. We left after the second act. It's a drag when you can't understand what's going on and all the sur-titles were in Romanian. My Romanian isn't that good yet."

"How old is this Mihai? I can't wait to meet him."

"You will tonight."

"I hope you're not sleeping with him but if you are, I assume you're taking precautions."

"Mom. Must you? Already? You've only been here five minutes. Anyway we've already been through that on the phone."

"I am your mother, Petra. It's my job to remind you about these things. I'm genetically programmed to do it."

"Well, you don't have to worry. I decided I didn't want to rush that side of things and Mihai agreed. So we're just dating for now. It's all perfectly innocent."

"That's good. I don't recognize anything I'm seeing here. All these car dealerships and advertising placards—it's like a long strip mall. Hey, look there's the Bucharest Arc de Triumph—that's the first thing I actually remember from before. You're right about the city, so much traffic. Who could have imagined so many BMWs and Audis on the streets of Bucharest? In my day, they were reserved for cabinet ministers and top party honchos. Where do they all park?"

"Mostly on the sidewalks. It makes walking around the city a real pain."

"Hey, there's a little Dacia—that's more like what I recall. And over there was the TV studio. There was fighting here back in '89. I rode down this very street on an armored personnel carrier. And this here must be Calea Victoriei Street."

"That's right Mom. Wow, you have an awesome memory."

"This is one place I'll never ever forget. And look, down there was the old Hotel Bucureşti where I heard that dreadful gypsy orchestra with my friend Clint—but what's this glass palace?"

"That's the new Hotel Bucureşti. They rebuilt it from the ground up, like a lot of buildings around here. Now we're coming into Revolution Square."

"Oh my God, so we are. It used to be called something else, Palace Square I believe. What memories! I see they rebuilt the cupola of the library. It was completely destroyed in the fighting. But what's that obelisk thing over there?"

"It's a memorial to the people who died in the revolution. It's called the *Memorial of Rebirth* but most people call it *'The Potato'* because of the oval-shaped metal thingy skewered through the middle of it. It's surrounded by plaques with the names of all the people who died."

"That's the memorial? Stefan's and my name could have been there too. It was a close thing."

"Mom, when are you going to finish writing down your story? I was waiting for the final installment. I want to know what happened to you and Stefan in the revolution. He won't talk to me about it. He says he wants you to tell the story first."

"It's almost done. I brought it with me. I'll give it to you at the hotel. You can start reading as soon as you like. And I guess we'll take a walk around the city and look at some of the places."

"Cool. And around the corner here is your hotel. We're here."

11 – Bucharest: December 1989

I returned to the hotel after Ceauşescu's TV address and started writing an account of what had happened so far to send to Eskew. Just before midnight, the phone rang.

"Hope I didn't wake you," came Pringle's British voice over the line.

"No, I was working."

"I thought you ought to know, word is going around there's

going to be a huge rally tomorrow around noon in *Piața Palatului*, that's Palace Square, right down the street from the hotel, to show support for the government. Ceaușescu will speak and it will be broadcast live on TV and radio."

"Thanks for telling me."

"It's a typically Ceaușescu ploy, an orchestrated pageant to show how much the people still love him, with cheerleaders calling out the chants," Pringle said. "He's done it a thousand times before. They'll be shipping in workers from factories all around the city, no doubt, to show he still has the support of the masses. Only I wonder if it will work this time."

"Why wouldn't it?"

"There's an ugly mood building out there. I was just walking back from the office and I saw several tanks rolling down the streets. It's obvious the authorities don't feel comfortable. They have to be asking themselves, what's to stop what happened in Timișoara happening here? My stringer told me he heard they're calling out every security agent they have, pulling them off their other assignments to flood the city and make sure there's no trouble."

After that, I lay sleeplessly for several hours, my mind churning with muddled thoughts of Stefan and the baby and what the next day might bring. Every few minutes, I leaned over to look at the clock. Time slowed almost to a standstill. The room felt hot and airless but when I kicked off the blanket, I started shivering and had to pull it back again. Outside the window, I occasionally heard the roar of heavy vehicles and muffled shouts. Eventually, near dawn, I fell into a jumpy, feverish sleep, full of incoherent dreams.

I awoke with a new and thrilling idea. Pringle had said security agents were being pulled off their beats to protect the regime. Perhaps that meant they were no longer guarding Stefan's apartment. I grabbed a quick breakfast and hurried out of the hotel, stuffing an extra roll and a piece of cheese into my coat pocket. It was immediately apparent something about the city had changed. On Calea Victoriei, I saw sinister-looking agents on each side of the street, about one every 20 or 30 yards, standing motionless in overcoats and dark glasses. A detachment of soldiers was already patrolling the huge square in front of the former royal palace where the big, pro-government demonstration would take place. Agents with video cameras were taking positions on the roofs of surrounding buildings. Pringle was right; the authorities were taking no chances.

Unlike the previous day, the streets were quickly filling up with people, all moving inexorably toward the city center. Hurrying down Boulevard Republicii, I saw a column of workers heading in the other direction toward the square, many carrying placards and banners over their shoulders. Presumably these were some of the thousands of supporters the government had mobilized for the occasion. They didn't seem particularly fired up, muttering to each other in low voices as they shuffled down the street, refusing to meet the eyes of the people lining the roadway who watched them in silence.

By now, I was half-walking, half-jogging, every nerve end tense with anticipation. Reaching Petrescu's street, I forced myself to slow down to a more natural pace. I couldn't see any guards outside his building but that didn't mean they weren't there. Moving warily, I walked in the front entrance, expecting to be challenged at any moment. A young man hurried out, startling me, but he wasn't wearing a uniform and paid me no attention. I began climbing the stairs, heart pounding, butterflies fluttering in my stomach. There were no lights in the stairwell and I had to feel my way cautiously around the corners, moving slowly until I reached the fourth floor, more out of breath than I should have been. I knocked. No answer. Perhaps the *Securitate* had removed him from the city.

I knocked again, this time more firmly, and called, "Stefan, it's me, Elizabeth," although I doubted he could hear through the thick door. But I did not dare shout too loud for fear of arousing unwelcome attention.

Answer, please, please answer, I muttered to myself as I rapped on the door a third time. There was a faint shuffling sound the other side and the door opened a crack. A pair of vivid blue eyes regarded me suspiciously, widening in amazement.

"Stefan," I hissed. "Open quickly."

In an instant, he'd swung the door open, grabbed me by the arm, jerked me inside, steadied me against him with one hand, slammed the door shut with the other and kissed me hard on the lips. I returned the kiss with equal ardor.

"It's you, it's really you," he gasped as his arms coiled around me, enveloping me in an embrace.

"Stefan, Stefan," I panted in reply, unable to form a coherent sentence.

He released me for a moment to look at my face, whispering, "How did you get here?"—then kissed me again without waiting for an answer. I could feel his ribs through his shirt as he got my coat open; all the weight he had gained in Italy was gone. If anything, he was even thinner than the day we'd first met.

"Stefan, the guards are gone from in front of the building. We have to get out of here before they come back," I said urgently, though my body wanted nothing more than to embrace him forever.

He was instantly alert. "They've gone? Where? Why? How do you know?"

I kissed him gently above the eyes, first the left and then the right. "I don't know why. They just aren't there any more. They may have been called away to help provide security for the big Ceaușescu rally at noon. The city is crawling with agents and soldiers and there are tanks on the streets. The government is expecting trouble."

"I heard about the rally. When did you arrive? What are you doing here? I can't believe it's you, just knocking on my door. It's a dream, a beautiful, wonderful dream."

"It's not a dream Stefan. Everything you said would happen is happening. You were right. You had faith. I was the one who didn't believe."

"Let me hug you again. I want to be sure you're really here."

"We'll have time for that. But Stefan, I need to get to that rally. I have to cover it. Will you come with me?"

"I'll go wherever you go. You don't know how much I prayed for something like this, and now God has answered my prayers."

I placed my hands against his cheeks and drew him to me gently, this time kissing him as softly and lightly as I could. We broke apart before our senses overwhelmed us.

"Come," he said, reaching for a coat and gloves. "Let's go see what the Genius of the Carpathians has to say today."

Back on the street, we joined a surging river of people and were carried along into the heart of the city. At the entrance to the square, uniformed armed men were vetting people, trying to weed out suspicious elements. I flashed my press card and said, "American journalist, let me pass." The soldier looked suspiciously at Petrescu standing just behind me. "He's my interpreter; he has to stay with me," I said, trying to impart as much authority to my voice as I could. Stefan translated; the soldier waved us through.

The large square was full of people, many holding massive banners proclaiming the achievements of communism. Others brandished idealized portraits of the ruling couple, looking at least 30 or 40 years younger than their actual ages. Romanian flags of red, gold and blue with the communist emblem in the center added a splash of color under the blue sky. But the crowd was not too tightly packed and I was able to thread my way toward the front fairly easily, Stefan following just behind. I headed for the phalanx of TV cameras set up on risers in front of the colonnaded Central Committee building, where Ceaușescu would shortly deliver his address from the balcony. The camera crews had small black and white monitors which would allow me to see close-ups of the speakers.

When I reached the scaffolding, I wasn't surprised to see Peter Pringle already in position among a gaggle of other reporters. He reached out to help me climb up and Stefan followed.

"Who's your friend, Lizzie?" Peter asked.

"I hired a translator, his name's Stefan," I said briefly, not wishing to go into detail. It crossed my mind that these two men represented diametrically opposing views about Romania. Peter had argued that Romanians lacked the courage and moral fiber to rise up, while Stefan believed they were just awaiting their opportunity. The next few hours would decide who was right.

We were standing almost directly in front of the balcony. When I turned around and looked behind, I saw a sea of faces stretching all the way back to the wrought iron fence in front of the National Museum of Art. Party organizers in the square kept trying to get some pro-government chanting going but most of the audience seemed sullen and unresponsive, both to them and to the party hacks who took turns trying to warm them up with fiery words from the balcony.

After a few minutes, Nicolae and Elena Ceauşescu appeared, flanked by their most trusted flunkeys. This was the first time I'd seen them in the flesh. The president, wearing a dark overcoat and black woolen cap, stood unsmiling as the local Bucharest party boss introduced him. Then, he stepped forward and took the microphone. His voice seemed hoarse and strained as he began reading slowly from a prepared text, pausing now and again while the front ranks of the crowd applauded ritualistically and chanted, *"Hurrah, hurrah, hurrah!"* Many of those further back remained silent.

"What's he saying?" I whispered to Stefan.

"The usual stuff we've heard a million times before about defending the integrity of the nation against foreigners and traitors," he replied dismissively.

Just then, I heard a noise somewhere behind us, a cracking sound like gunfire—it could have been a firework, or perhaps one of the loudspeakers short-circuiting. Some in the crowd began screaming. Glancing at one of the monitors, I saw a look of confusion pass across Ceauşescu's face. So did millions of ordinary Romanians, watching the speech on TV in their homes. For a few, deadly, indecisive moments, the president stopped speaking, apparently bewildered, almost paralyzed, raising his right hand in an ineffectual effort to quiet the furor. He probably hadn't been interrupted during a speech in 30 years and had no idea how to react. That was the moment, people later agreed, when the country realized the tyrant was nothing but a scared old man, the moment it became clear the emperor had no clothes.

And it was into that decisive moment that Stefan Petrescu stepped. Descending from the riser into the body of the crowd, he shouted a single word, yelled at the top of his lungs: *"Timişoara."* Instantly, others took up the cry. Suddenly a crowd which had been disciplined, if somewhat apathetic, lost its cohesion. People started pushing and shoving; others dropped their pro-government placards and began trampling them into the ground. Anti-government slogans rang out around the square.

The Romanian TV man belatedly aimed his camera at the roof of the building and away from the confused leader so that I could no longer see through the monitor, but the microphones still picked up Ceauşescu's voice vainly trying to re-establish control.

"Comrades, be quiet. Hello. Hello. Don't you hear me? Be quiet! Stay quiet in your places," he called out—but the uproar continued and even intensified.

"Talk to them, talk to them," Elena urged him, her voice also clearly captured by the microphones.

"What are they saying?" I asked Stefan. He translated.

A moment later, I became aware of another disturbance on the perimeter where a group of protesters had suddenly appeared, trying to push their way into the square. Police and soldiers held them at bay and slowly shoved them back, though their chanting remained audible. After a few minutes, the commotion died away sufficiently for Ceauşescu to resume his speech with a quavering voice. But the damage was done. The illusion of a nation united behind its leader was shattered. Suddenly, a good part of the audience no longer wanted to listen to his slogans. Jeers and catcalls rang out periodically. With great fanfare, the president announced some token increases in the minimum wage and social security payments. The front two or three rows applauded but others further back booed and hissed. At one point, Elena herself tried to get a communist chant going from the balcony. It worked for a few seconds and then petered out.

I glanced over at Peter Pringle scribbling in his notebook, a look of ferocious concentration mixed with disbelief spread across his face. After about 20 minutes, the president brought his remarks to an abrupt end and retreated into the building followed by his wife and advisers. As soon as he disappeared, the crowd began to disperse with astonishing speed as if they could not escape quickly enough, leaving piles of broken and discarded banners and placards strewn across the cobblestones. Pringle took off at a canter without saying goodbye, presumably heading for his office to file a story. Stefan returned to the riser and grabbed my hand.

"Come quickly, we have to get out of here."

"Where to?"

"Anywhere. It's dangerous to stay." He pointed toward a detachment of Interior Ministry police in full riot gear who were quickly moving into place. As we exited the square, we were plunged into a seething mass of mostly young people, shouting, chanting, waving fists in the air like fans at a soccer game, and were borne along, coming to a halt in front of the Eminescu bookstore.

Some youths had burst inside and were tossing the collected works of Ceauşescu and other volumes paying homage to the great leader into the street where people were stomping and spitting on them and trying to set them on fire. Watching one young man savagely grinding his heel into an image of Ceauşescu's face, I knew for certain a revolution was underway. I saw it in the faces of the people, previously so guarded and expressionless, now alive with exhilaration, almost drunk on a potent cocktail of defiance, determination, joy, hatred, courage and fear. It had happened with incredible speed. One moment, the city was quiet, the next it had exploded.

Youths ranged along the sidewalk shouting: "Down with the dictator" and "Death to the murderer." One was daubing the walls of a building with anti-government slogans. Riot police appeared, wading into the crowd swinging their clubs. I felt Stefan's hand tugging me in the opposite direction. "Let's get out of here before we get hurt or arrested," he shouted above the tumult.

I allowed him to steer me down a series of side streets, rushing with scores of others to keep ahead of the police. My boots crunched on broken glass from smashed store windows. I thought I heard an explosion in the distance, how far away I couldn't say.

Helicopters whirred overhead.

We emerged just north of University Square on Magheru Street, a major six-lane thoroughfare, where the scene was even more confused. Young people with bullhorns took turns in addressing the crowd which seemed to swell with every moment. That's where I saw the first homemade banner emblazoned with a single word—*"Liberty"*—and then, a couple of minutes later, a Romanian flag with a hole at its center where the communist emblem had been ripped out. As time went on, more and more of these flags appeared. People were yelling, "We are the people, down with the dictator." I heard the wail of sirens approaching and distant gunfire.

Gesturing to Stefan to follow, I waved my press pass, trying to get through to the front of the crowd so I could see what was happening. We eventually broke through only to be faced with a line of armored personnel carriers and fire engines blocking the boulevard. Some of the protesters had gotten down on their knees to signal their unwillingness to fight the troops. Others were talking to the soldiers, trying to persuade them to join the revolution. One old man wearing a large fur cap tried to hug a militiaman. He was an exception—most of the demonstrators were young, some little more than children. The soldier looked embarrassed but accepted the clumsy embrace. Behind them, other demonstrators were trying to erect a makeshift barricade across the street.

Stefan, who had been speaking excitedly to several protesters, turned to me.

"The troops fired on the crowd here just before we arrived and wounded some people, and probably even killed a few," he said. "An ambulance came and took them away. That might have been the sirens we heard."

"Did these people actually see this or is it another rumor?"

"No, this guy here insists he saw it with his own eyes."

"Ask him to describe it exactly." Stefan turned to the young man, waving in my direction. I caught the words "American journalist" several times. The man nodded excitedly and launched into a torrent of Romanian. Others joined in. Stefan gestured to them to stop so he could translate.

"They say there was another big clash a kilometer up the road where soldiers also fired at the crowd. They don't know how many people were hit. Elisabeta, are you sure you should remain here? It's becoming very dangerous. Perhaps there's somewhere safer for you to do your job."

"It seems OK for now. The soldiers aren't firing, despite what these people are saying, and the crowd doesn't seem to want violence either."

"It may seem that way, perhaps, but it will not last. These soldiers are just simple recruits from the regular army but soon they will bring the special units, the anti-terrorist squads, the professional murderers. See down the road; military buses are arriving all the time, bringing more troops. Look at them—look at their guns. They're just waiting for the order to kill. Soon, they will try to drive us off the streets. You shouldn't stay here."

"What about you?"

"Of course, I will stay."

"If you stay, I'm staying."

Even as I spoke, I remembered I was carrying another life within me. But how could I leave at a moment like this? On the other hand, I was a journalist, not a participant.

I turned to Stefan. "OK, let's get back, more into the body of the crowd. I'd like to see what's happening back there anyway."

We retreated in the direction of the university, squeezing our way with difficulty through the mass of people. I spent the next hour and a half interviewing people of all ages, with Stefan faithfully interpreting. The previously taciturn Romanians, who had been afraid even to look a foreigner in the eye, now suddenly couldn't stop talking. They demanded freedom, democracy, a normal life. They wanted food, electricity, heat. Above all, they wanted the Ceauşescus gone and an end to communism.

By now, it was late-afternoon and the December light was fading. Streetlamps were already on, casting an eerie glow. Suddenly there was a commotion somewhere ahead. People started running to escape the unseen danger.

"It's beginning," Stefan said. "You have to get off the street." He pointed at the tower of the Intercontinental Hotel just behind.

"That's the best place. You could watch from there and be safe."

"I won't leave you. I won't," I said passionately. "Not today, not after I just found you again." But he dragged me toward the entrance and I allowed myself to be pulled along. Just then, there was a roar from the crowd and a loud crackling sound.

"Oh my God," I gasped. "The soldiers have opened fire."

People scattered, others hit the ground or scrambled for cover behind cars. In the half-light I saw jets of water engulf the ranks of protesters and smelled the unmistakable odor of tear gas. An armored personnel carrier roared down the street mowing down everything in its path before skidding to a halt. Instantly, a group of people swarmed over it, wresting its doors open, dragging its occupants out into the street, savagely beating them. Looking back, I saw flames erupt from another burning vehicle and heard several more volleys of gunfire. A stray bullet, apparently shot from a rooftop, thudded into the ground a couple of feet away. Stefan was right. This was no place for me and my baby.

"Here, get inside," he shouted, shoving me into the hotel's revolving doors together with a dozen other people trying to escape the bullets.

The lobby was almost as packed as the street. Waving my press pass, I fought my way to the elevator and pressed the button for the penthouse level, thinking to find a vantage point from which to view the battle. I was profoundly shaken by what I'd seen but I knew it was just the beginning.

"What now?" I asked Stefan as we squeezed into the elevator.

"Don't worry, we'll find somewhere safe for you before I return to the street."

"But it's suicide."

"It's not suicide. It's war. The future of my nation is being decided."

"It's not war when only one side has guns. I won't let you go."

"You can't stop me. Nothing can stop me."

We exited the elevator and began walking down a long corridor looking for an open door. Soon, we found one. Inside the large suite, several men were peering out the window. Another was on the phone, speaking rapid German.

"Can I come in?" I asked. "I'm Elizabeth Graham, staff writer for *The Brahmin* magazine."

"Jean-Christian Bertrand, *Le Monde*," said one of the men. "We also have here representatives from the BBC World Service, Radio Free Europe and the London Daily Telegraph. Make yourself at home. This is the best seat in the house. You can see everything that's happening down there. All we need is popcorn."

"I'm going now," Stefan said. I looked at him imploringly, but of course I was powerless to dissuade him.

"Please, love, please be careful. Don't do anything stupid."

"I'll try not to. I'll come back for you in a few hours if I can."

The scene from the 21st floor was surreal. It was like watching pieces of a kaleidoscope form into different patterns, break apart and then come together again in new configurations. I could clearly see tanks and armored personnel carriers advancing on the square ahead of fleeing protesters. By now, the sound of gunfire was almost continuous. Fire engines continued to spray water cannons at the crowd, which would fragment and then, just as quickly reassemble. I saw several bodies lying on the sidewalk.

The other reporters took turns trying to get international lines to update their editors. The radio guys would run down to the street for a few moments, stick their mikes out to get the sound of gunfire or tape a brief interview with a protester and then run back to file quick 30-second reports, one more or less identical to the next. Amazingly, the telephones seemed to be working. I scrabbled for my notebook and started writing, which at least stopped me thinking about what might be happening to Stefan, somewhere down below.

When I'd written a few pages, I asked to use the phone and was eventually put through to Eskew in Cambridge.

"Where are you?" he asked, sounding as if he was in the next room.

"In the Intercontinental Hotel, 21st floor. There's a gun battle raging just below. Are you seeing this on TV?"

"Some of it, but it's hard to understand exactly what's

happening."

"It's chaos—street warfare with guns and tanks on one side and unarmed protesters on the other. It's impossible to say how many people have already died and more are dying every minute."

"Heavens."

"I've written a couple of dozen paragraphs that I can dictate. Of course, whatever I sent you now is certain to be stale by the time the magazine comes out on Monday. I'll try to update you again later but I don't think anything will be decided tonight. This may go on for a while."

"If necessary, we can keep space open for you until Sunday noon, which I believe is around 7 p.m. your time. Don't worry about the politics or the speeches. Our readers can get all that kind of stuff from *The New York Times* or elsewhere. Concentrate on the color; bring it to life. Try to make us feel what it's like to actually be there—the smells, the sounds, the human emotions, as if you were a photographer but your snapshots are in words. Imagine our readers sitting down with the magazine over their breakfast next week. It will be your words they'll be devouring. Give 'em a real taste of revolution with their cornflakes. But avoid clichés and sentimentality. Let the action speak for itself."

It was at moments like this that I realized how inspiring an editor Eskew could be, boosting the egos and confidence of his writers while dispensing sound journalistic wisdom.

"I'll try. Actually, it's terrifying out there."

"I can only imagine. Elizabeth, one more thing: for God's sake stay safe. Don't take foolish risks. Remember, no story is worth the life of a *Brahmin* reporter, not even this one." His voice was quavering; for once he sounded his age.

"I'll try to be careful."

"You must do more than try. I'm the one who sent you to Romania and I feel responsible. When the story is over, I want to hear all your stories over lunch at Jaspers." I could hear him choking up. "I've lost colleagues covering past wars and revolutions so I know what can happen. I had to speak at their funerals. Please, please Elizabeth, don't make me speak at yours."

After dictating my story, there was nothing to do but wait. The battle still waged sporadically below but it was hard to make out what was happening in the dark. As the evening wore on, we continued to hear gun shots, both fairly close and further away. I could not relax, thinking about Stefan, imagining the worst. After a while, one of the reporters said he was going downstairs to try to rustle up some food. He returned with a several packets of nuts and pretzels and some bottles of Romanian cola.

"This is about all they have right now," he said. I realized I'd eaten nothing since breakfast and tore into a packet of peanuts, which only made me thirstier. Then I remembered the roll and cheese in my pocket which I'd forgotten to give to Stefan. I felt a little guilty but told myself I was eating for two.

Two hours later, Stefan returned looking grimy and exhausted. He had ripped up his undershirt to protect his nose and eyes from tear gas. I rushed into his arms, oblivious of the amused glances of my fellow reporters. "Thank God you're safe, what the hell's happening out there?"

"Terrible, terrible things." That made the reporters sit up and take notice and before he knew what was happening, Stefan was holding an impromptu press conference.

"There are still thousands of people on the streets. The soldiers can't control them. They've got some of the main avenues cleared of protesters—they finally dismantled the biggest barrier just down the boulevard from here—but the side streets are mostly still blockaded," he said.

"I saw demonstrators capturing some soldiers and taking away their weapons, so the revolution is no longer completely unarmed. But that will only lead to more confusion and bloodshed. You can't tell who is shooting at whom."

He shuddered. "I saw one guy in a black leather jacket—I suppose he was *Securitate*—arrest a young man, put him against a wall and execute him with his pistol in cold blood, just shot him in the head. There are also snipers on rooftops, picking people off like it was target practice. I don't know how many people have been killed and wounded but certainly dozens, if not hundreds—and it's still going on." He put his head in his arms, trembling violently, as the reporters scribbled in their spiral notebooks.

"Can you tell us who you are sir?" one asked.

"My name is Stefan Petrescu. I am a poet. Until this morning, I was held under house arrest in my apartment as an enemy of the people."

"Wait, let me set up my mike," said the man from Radio Free Europe. "I'd like you to tell the whole thing, everything you saw. When we're done in English, I also want to record you in Romanian. We have hundreds of thousands of listeners in your country. They need to hear your voice."

"I'd be honored," Stefan said.

When the reporters ran out of questions in English, he switched to his own language. Even though he spoke slowly in carefully measured tones without raising his voice, I could feel the fervor, the passion in his words. I realized it was for this moment he had returned, for this he had been willing to sacrifice our love. When his interviews were finally over, I pulled him to the side of the room and hugged him fiercely.

"What did you tell them?" I asked.

"I said now is our moment to fight for freedom and I urged people to come to Bucharest tomorrow—from wherever they are—to rally for freedom—because the fate of our nation is in the balance."

It suddenly occurred to me that in the hours we had been together that day, I hadn't yet had a chance to tell him I was pregnant. Then I realized that if I did, there was no way he would ever allow me to leave this room while there was any hint of danger outside. Better he didn't know. Pregnant or not, I had a job to do. I'd save the revelation for a better moment.

"Is there any chance of getting back to the Athénée Palace?" I asked. "That's where all my stuff is. We could shower, maybe grab a couple of hours sleep."

"No Elisabeta, it's much too dangerous." His answer confirmed my decision to keep quiet about the baby, although I wasn't about to question his judgment about the situation on the streets.

"So we'll have to stay here the rest of the night. Is that OK?" I asked the French reporter.

"Of course. My floor is your floor. Stay as long as you want."

We were both exhausted but it was impossible to sleep while the battle still raged below. Eventually, around three in the morning, the avenue emptied. Shortly after, in a bizarre attempt at normalcy, municipal cleaning crews moved in to try to clear up the debris and paint over the anti-government slogans daubed on the walls.

"I think it's done for tonight, but it's far from over," Stefan said. "The dictator is still in his palace. Tomorrow will be even more important than today."

I found a place on the carpet in the corner and lay down, beckoning Stefan to join me. We snuggled together, matching our breathing. Within seconds, we were asleep.

12 – Bucharest: December 2007

Petra knocked on the hotel door just as Liz was emerging from the shower. "Did you have a good sleep Mom?" she asked.

"How can a person stay up all night on a plane, be absolutely exhausted and still not be able to get to sleep?" Liz asked. "And when I did finally drop off, a car alarm went off, really loudly, just outside the window."

"That happens all the time here, almost every night," Petra said. "You have to get used to it—that and the construction work that goes on at odd times."

"You're sure we have to do this dinner tonight?"

"Stefan is cooking up a storm. Mihai and Angela are coming. You don't have to stay too late. Look Mom, you'll have to see him some time. You might as well get it over with."

Liz sighed. "I suppose you're right. Help me on with this blouse." As she held up the dark red, silk garment, Petra looked at her mother's scars, two jagged, crisscross lines on her back, just beneath her left shoulder, now faded but still clearly visible.

She'd seen them a thousand times before. She even remembered as a little girl asking what they were. Liz told her they were from an accident she'd had before Petra was born. Almost against her will, Petra found herself tracing the shape on her mother's soft skin with her index finger.

"I never really thought about your injuries till now," she said.

"Petra, we don't have time for this now. Stop tickling me and zip me up. I need to make myself half-way presentable for this grand occasion you've talked me into."

"You're more than presentable, Mom. I wish I could be glamorous like you." Petra also wished she could have her mother's generous body, but she didn't say so.

"I don't feel very glamorous. Actually, I can't remember the last time I did."

"You are. You're all the things I'm not—totally elegant and sophisticated. That's the way you've always been."

Liz smiled, flattered. "Well, if you say so it must be true. But some of those things, you'll find, come with age, along with a lot of other, less desirable side effects. Anyway, your boyfriend evidently finds you attractive."

"He says I'm cute, like a puppy is cute." Petra gave her mother's scar a light kiss and zipped up the blouse. "It must have been so painful. I can't imagine what it was like for you," she said.

"You mean the injuries themselves? Yes, they were painful, although I'm sure Stefan had it a lot worse. His injuries were more severe and he was stuck in a Romanian hospital while I got the best American care money could buy."

"I meant reliving it—writing it down for me. That must have been painful."

"So now you're my shrink? Yes, it's been difficult but also—what's the right word in psychobabble? ... Cathartic! I didn't want to do this. You forced me into it. But now that it's done, I suppose I'm glad. By the way I brought you a little gift."

"What?"

"While I was writing down the story, I dug up my old notes to refresh my memory. Things get confusing after all these years, especially that final day. It was such a blur. Anyway, I brought you my reporter's notebook—the one I had in my pocket when I was taken to the hospital. One of the doctors who operated kept it for me. It's over there in that plastic folder on the desk. I want you to have it."

Petra opened the folder to find a small spiral notebook, the kind that fits in a breast pocket, a bit bent and mauled around the edges but still quite legible inside. On the cover was written, *"Elizabeth Graham, Bucharest: December 22, 1989."*

She opened it at random and read, *"Dacia St. Body of young man, shirt ripped open exposing his torso, lies half on sidewalk, half in street. Pool of blood leaks from his head."* She could see Liz had filled entire pages with similar terse observations, short interviews and quotes, obviously scrawled in haste. Sometimes, she'd pressed down so hard her pen had almost gone through the paper. Some of the pages were smudged with grime, perhaps also with blood and tears.

"Wow, Mom, this is amazing," Petra said, deeply moved, her voice suddenly choking up. There was something about the notebook that made her mother's ordeal much more real to her than it had ever been before. "I'll always treasure it. And one day, maybe, I'll give it to my daughter."

"I hope you do," Liz said in a brisk voice. "But don't read it now; you can look at it all you want later. We have to get going. Hand me that pashmina there, won't you please honey? I bought it especially for this trip. What do you think?"

With an effort, Petra closed the notebook and replaced it in the plastic folder. "You look totally, totally awesome Mom. Let's go knock them dead."

They stepped out of the hotel into the cold night air.

"Careful where you step. The sidewalks are uneven and there's dog crap everywhere," Petra said, linking arms with her mother. They walked along side streets for a little and turned into a busy main road. "This is Regina Elisabeta Boulevard. Stefan told me he thinks of you every time he sets foot on it."

"Heavens. I remember this street but it had a different name then."

"I love that name he calls you—Elisabeta. It's way romantic

like something in a novel by Tolstoy or Victor Hugo, much better than Liz. Mom, do you ever think about him the same way?"

Liz paused, searching for the right words. "Petra, I don't know what adolescent fantasies you've been cooking up about Stefan and me or what expectations you have, but please forget them. I know you read that sonnet he wrote me and it probably set your imagination working overtime. When I looked at it again, it had me weepy too. But you have to realize, there's a big difference between romantic words and reality."

"What do you mean?"

"We're not about to fall into each other's arms. Yes, we had a brief affair and yes, at the time it was intense—but that was a lifetime ago. So much water has flowed under the bridge since then. Neither of us is a spring chicken any more. We have much more of our lives behind us than ahead. I don't know who he is any more; he doesn't know me. He has his life here in Romania and I have mine in the States. What could we possible have in common?"

"You do have at least one thing in common," Petra replied heatedly. "Me. That's not going to change, no matter how hard you fight it."

"That's true, which is precisely why I agreed to come tonight. I intend to be friendly and polite. I'd like to have a civilized relationship and I'm sure he thinks the same about me. That's all one can reasonably expect." Even as she spoke the words, Liz wondered if she believed them.

They passed the Cişmigiu Gardens where Christmas lights were twinkling. The pond had been converted into an ice skating rink, crowded with people streaking in circles to the sound of pop music blasted from giant speakers.

"Gosh, this is different from the way I remember. Can we take a look?" Liz asked. They wandered in the crowd, between vendors selling popcorn and cotton candy, past the adventure playground where parents watched their children climbing on bars and slipping down slides. One tiny kid carried a stick of cotton candy larger than his head. To Liz, the wonder of the scene was that it was so normal. It could have been any park in any city.

"Mom, it's time to go," Petra said. "We can come back here tomorrow if you're so fascinated. It's just a garden."

"Not just any garden," Liz replied. "This one has special memories." But she allowed herself to be steered away.

As they turned into Stefan's street, she gave a gasp. "He still lives in the same apartment? I always imagined he moved somewhere nicer. It was awfully small and seedy as I recall."

"It's small—just two bedrooms—but no way is it seedy," said Petra, calling for the elevator. "I guess he renovated it. Wait till you see the art—really cool stuff."

They arrived at the fourth floor and Petra opened the front door with her key.

"It's us, we're here," she announced.

"Make yourselves at home. I'll be out in a minute," came Stefan's voice from the kitchen. Liz gave a start. Hearing him was …uncanny. Suddenly, her heart was racing, she was sweating. It was the same musical voice, that accent spiced with just a touch of the strange and exotic.

"Can I help?" Petra called.

"No, I'm almost done. I just can't leave the stove right now."

Liz wondered if she should go into the kitchen to greet him. She felt foolish standing there, smelling the delicious aromas, waiting for him to emerge. She busied herself looking at some of the paintings—mostly brightly colored landscapes in post-Impressionist style. The bell rang and Petra opened the door, ushering in Angela and Mihai, who arrived carrying his violin case.

"I wanted to impress your mother," he whispered. "I thought I play something for us all later."

Even Angela had toned down her appearance in honor of the occasion. Her hair was back to dark brown and none of her tattoos were showing. Petra made the introductions. Mihai surprised everyone by kissing Liz's hand instead of shaking it, sending Angela into a fit of giggles.

"She's not Queen Elizabeth," she sputtered. "Are you?"

"Not as far as I'm aware," Liz said. "But it was a lovely gesture anyway." She wanted to make Mihai feel better. The poor boy was blushing to the roots of his hair.

Then, Petrescu emerged from the kitchen wearing a chef's white hat, carrying a spatula in one hand, his apron spattered with tomato sauce.

"Ah, there you all are," he said. "Mihai, Angela and …" he looked at Liz and his voice faltered "…and Elisabeta."

Liz took one look at him and didn't know whether to laugh or cry. This could not possibly be the Stefan Petrescu she had known, this comic creature with the bushy mustache wearing a ridiculous hat over that theatrical eye patch. He looked like a cross between Long John Silver without the parrot and Julia Child. He'd gained a lot of weight too, although a second glance revealed that much of it seemed to be muscle. Gone was the skinny, half-emaciated body she remembered. This version of Stefan Petrescu had evidently put in many hours in the gym. Then he removed the hat, revealing his spiky gray hair, and she could see it was really the same man, though the years had done their work and all the pain had left its mark.

"Stefan," she said in a wobbly voice, meeting his one good eye, which still smoldered with the intensity she recalled. "How good to see you."

"And you too Elisabeta. You look …" He paused for a second searching for the right word. "…You look ravishing."

He held out his hand; she took it and, just for a fraction of a second, the world stopped turning. Even though she'd been mentally preparing herself for this moment for weeks, the visceral effect of his touch, the strength of his grip which seemed to radiate warmth from his fingers into hers, came as a profound shock. It was all she could do to stop herself falling into his arms. Instead, she found herself looking for somewhere to sit down and sinking gratefully into a chair behind her.

My God, she thought in awe. *The electricity, the connection, it's still there. I wonder if he feels it too?* One look at his face told her that he did.

Neither of them spoke much during the meal, leaving it to the young contingent to carry the conversation. Liz wasn't aware of consciously avoiding his gaze. It was just that every time she sneaked a peek at him, she found him looking at her as well. Suddenly Angela started giggling.

"What's the matter dear?" Liz asked in a tone she usually reserved for uppity interns at the magazine. "Did someone say something funny? Perhaps you'd like to share it with the rest of us."

"It's you two," she said. "The way you keep gawking at each other when you think nobody's looking. I've never seen old people behave like that before. And the rest of us are all sitting here pretending to ignore it."

Annoyed to be so easily discovered, Liz gave her a frosty look.

"First of all, we aren't old. Fifty five is the new 30. Hadn't you heard?" she asked sarcastically. "And second, young lady, are you always this direct with someone you only met an hour ago?"

That made everyone at the table laugh. "Oh Mom," Petra said. "You don't know the half of it." And she launched into an account of their Thanksgiving dinner.

"You know, I do miss old Constantin sometimes," Angela said plaintively, setting them all laughing even harder. "You can make fun of him but I haven't yet found anyone to equal him."

"Yes, we all miss him, especially his scintillating conversation," Petra said.

After they had eaten and Mihai had played a Bach prelude to general acclaim, Liz said she had to go. "It's the jet lag kicking in. I haven't slept for 48 hours. If I stay here any longer, I'll just collapse head first into my dessert dish."

"I'll call you a taxi," Stefan said. "Petra, do you want to go spend the night with your mother?"

"No, that's fine honey," Liz said quickly. "You stay here with your friends. Call me tomorrow; we'll take a walk around the town. There are some places I want to see."

The truth was, Liz felt dizzy and discombobulated and it wasn't just from lack of sleep. One little touch of Stefan's hand had knocked the world off kilter. She badly needed time alone to regain her bearings, absorb what had happened and figure out her next move.

But in the taxi and later, lying in her bed, all she could do was ask herself over and over, *Could this really be happening?* and *How is it possible?*

13 – Bucharest: December 2007

Petra lay in bed that night, flicking through her mother's notebook. This is what she read:

— Republicii Blvd, 3pm. Young girl with big smile ties armband with colors of Romanian flag around soldier's sleeve. Cristina Cobuz, 31, hotel cleaner: "Today is our day, the people's day. All I want for the future is a normal life—my son doesn't even know what a banana tastes like."

— Palace Sq. Incredible view from balcony: Huge crowd, many clutching red or white carnations, waving fingers in air showing V for victory sign, shouting, "We're not leaving, we're not leaving." Wild rumors about whereabouts of Ceauşescus.

— Woman with white fur cap embraces soldier. He's holding bunch of white carnations in one hand and gun with red carnation sticking out of barrel in the other.

— Interview with steel worker, Ovidiu, 45, (refused to give full name): "They should shoot the bastard after what he did to the country. But maybe now things will be better for all of us."

— Magheru St. Group of soldiers sit atop tank with flowers sticking out of their guns. One smells white carnation.

— Helmeted soldier lies dead on the ground, tricolor armband around one arm. Women and one soldier stand over body. His knapsack lies beside him. Not clear who killed him. Lots of shooting from rooftops. Nobody knows who is firing.

— Daniel Mitrica, engineer (36): "This is happiest day of my life. Prayed for moment like this. May it all end well." Asked about Ceauşescu, said, "May he and his monster wife rot in hell."

— Man with a Romanian flag draped around his neck gives box of bread and pastries to group of soldiers lying on their stom-

achs. More firing coming from above.

— Soldier arrests another man in uniform who walks ahead of him, arms held out wide, coat opened. Many different uniforms in evidence, must ask Stefan which is which.

— Dacia St. Body of young man, shirt ripped open exposing his torso, lies half on sidewalk, half in street. Pool of blood leaks from his head. .

— 4:45 pm. APC drives through cloud of smoke, Romanian flag with the center ripped out flapping behind. Getting quite dark and scary now.

— Cosmina, 24, student (refused to give full name): "I'm afraid this is not over yet. Regime had many forces, they're not about to give up. Also we keep hearing about terrorists in the city. Pray to God to save us."

— Young man in shabby suit, hair greasy and disarrayed, stands by door with submachine gun slung over his shoulder. Rumors flying about terrorists moving through secret tunnels built by regime. Feeling of euphoria changed to near panic on streets.

—Magheru Blvd. Dark now. Student points to rooftop, where firing has been coming from, showing direction to soldier. Wild shooting from all directions. Going to be a bloody night.

That was the last note.

14 – Bucharest: December 1989

I awoke, still in Stefan's arms. At least four other reporters had spent the night on the floor, as well as two in the bed and one on the sofa. I looked at my watch, saw it was just past six and thought with trepidation of the day ahead. We'd been asleep less than three hours. My bladder was full and when I staggered into the bathroom on stiff legs, I felt dizzy and faint from hunger. Returning to the room, I peered out the window and saw that the dark street below was still almost deserted.

"Stefan, Stefan, wake up," I hissed, nudging him.

"Who's there? What's happening?"

"I'm going to try to get back to the Athénée Palace."

"Why?" He shook his head, trying to clear away the cobwebs.

"It seems fairly safe now," I said. "I have to eat something before I collapse from hunger and I need a shower and change of clothes. I feel absolutely gross. I must stink to high heaven."

"OK, I'll come with you. God forbid that the star reporter Elizabeth Graham should cover a revolution stinking to high heaven."

We emerged cautiously into the square and began walking. I gave a start when I saw a bus trundling toward us, thinking it might be carrying troops. But, incredibly, it seemed to be pursuing its normal route as if nothing out of the ordinary had happened.

It soon became evident there was no way we could reach the Athénée Palace. The hotel was adjacent to Palace Square, the heart of the communist power base, where Ceauşescu had held his disastrous rally the previous day. Now the whole area was cordoned off, protected by a ring of tanks and military vehicles.

"We'll go to my place. I might have a little bit of food lying around and you can wash up if you don't mind freezing cold water," Stefan said.

"Are you sure it's safe? They might come looking for you," I asked. After his call to arms on the radio the previous day, I feared his very life would be at risk if the regime survived.

Stefan laughed. "Not today they won't. They've got a lot bigger problems to worry about than me right now."

Back in the apartment, he found half a loaf of stale bread which he cut into thick slices and tossed into a frying pan with a lump of lard. I devoured my share as if it was a gourmet meal in a five star restaurant.

"Wash up quickly. We need to get back out there," Stefan said. But it hardly seemed worth it to shower without clean clothes to change into.

"You know what, if I stink, I stink," I said.

Stefan came close and sniffed me, inhaling deeply. "You smell absolutely wonderful to me." He nuzzled my neck. Automatically, my arms encircled him and then we were kissing again. Seconds later, we both pulled away.

"Once this is over, I'm going to make love to you for days and weeks without end," Stefan said.

"Is that a threat?"

"It's a solemn promise."

"I'll hold you to it."

We grabbed our coats and Stefan also took a small, transistor radio which he stuffed into his pocket. "This might be useful to find out what's happening as the day goes on," he said. I rummaged in my bag and found a brand new reporter's notebook. I wrote my name and the date on the cover.

We'd only been in the apartment for about an hour but during that time the scene on the streets had been totally transformed. Descending, we found Republicii Avenue fast filling with people. Helmeted soldiers in olive green overcoats stood across the road several rows deep, trying to bar access to the city center, but the crowd kept growing. Talking to people, Stefan found many had come from the suburbs or from outlying towns and villages, outraged by the bloodshed which they'd heard about on foreign radio stations or from friends. Many had heard his interview on Radio Free Europe. These were not the overwhelmingly young student demonstrators of the previous day. They were farmers and factory hands, nurses and school teachers, truck drivers and mechanics, army veterans and housewives—an entire cross-section of society. Many waved flags with their middles ripped out. A helicopter appeared overhead, dropping leaflets on the crowd, ordering people off the streets, warning them it was not safe. The crowd ignored them.

I saw a couple tanks and a truck filled with reinforcements rumble down the avenue to buttress the troops, who stood with submachine guns lowered. It was a crucial moment. One soldier firing his weapon could have triggered a massacre or a stampede. Miraculously, they all held their fire. The soldiers didn't want to fight. I could see it on their scared, confused faces. Nothing had prepared them for this. Most were just frightened teenagers—poorly trained and badly equipped draftees doing their national service. Faced with such an enormous throng of fellow citizens urging them to join the revolution, they no longer had the discipline or the will to resist. A couple of women started handing out carnations. The soldiers hesitated for a second and then accepted them.

Suddenly, pushed from behind, the crowd surged forward propelling the front ranks of demonstrators almost into the arms of the troops, who stood indecisively for a few seconds before allowing themselves to be overwhelmed. Within second, they had been swallowed up in the throng. It was like watching a massive wave engulfing a sand castle. As tension gave way to relief and then to euphoria, a chant went up, *"The Army is With Us, The Army is With Us."*

Strangers were kissing and hugging one another. I saw a soldier with a carnation stuck in his gun barrel embracing a young woman; both were crying unashamedly. For a few moments, I was on the verge of tears myself, my mouth dry from pent-up anxiety, my hands shaking as I tried to scribble notes. But then I thought of Eskew, his red editorial pen hovering, ready to strike at the slightest hint of cliché or sentimentality, and my moment of weakness passed.

I became aware Stefan was tugging my hand, pointing ahead where a dozen protesters, one waving an enormous flag, had climbed up on a tank. More people pulled themselves aboard until 20 or 30 of them were sitting on the turret and gun barrel, swarming all over the hull, the hatches and engine compartment. As it slowly wheeled around, the crowd began chanting, *"To the square, to the square,"* and gushed forward once again, this time heading for the Communist Party headquarters where the Ceauşescus still lurked.

I turned to Stefan, to find him clutching his radio to his ear, trying to hear above the general hubbub. "What's happening?" I asked.

"Milea's committed suicide."

"Who?"

"Vasile Milea, the defense minister, the man in charge of all the armed forces."

"He killed himself?"

"That's what they're saying on the radio. They say he was a

traitor and he shot himself just a couple of hours ago. Maybe someone helped him."

Within seconds, word had spread from mouth to mouth. People speculated Ceauşescu had ordered the minister executed after he refused an order to kill as many people as necessary to crush the uprising. The news enraged the crowd which began to move forward with renewed purpose, sweeping us along with them. As we approached Palace Square, I remembered the crescent of tanks I'd seen early that morning guarding the perimeter. These were presumably manned by the troops Ceauşescu trusted the most to defend him and I began to worry anew about what might happen when the protesters came into contact with them. But we arrived to find the tanks and APCs in full retreat and people pouring unimpeded into the square to face a government that was suddenly unprotected.

By 11:30, there must have been at least twice as many chanting, fist waving people crammed into the square as on the previous day. Anxious to reach the TV risers so I could see what was happening, I began pushing forward, Stefan following close behind. But it was slow going and we were still stuck in the middle of the plaza when I first heard and then saw a helicopter swoop down, hover for a few seconds and carefully land on the roof of the Central Committee building.

The crowd reacted to the sight with howls of anger and chants of *"Murderer, murderer."* Five minutes later, there was a stir and a figure in a black overcoat and hat approached the front of the balcony. After a second, it became clear it was Ceauşescu himself, who apparently still believed he retained the love and loyalty of the people, despite all evidence to the contrary. As he began speaking, the boos, hisses and catcalls reached a tremendous crescendo. I heard Stefan shouting *"Liberty, liberty,"* over and over.

The supreme leader, a small, insubstantial figure from where I was standing, tried to appeal to the crowd but it was useless and his aides soon ushered him inside. Even as he disappeared, protesters were storming the building, bursting through the front doors, amazed to find them unbarred and undefended. A couple of minutes later, the helicopter that had landed on the roof barely a half hour before struggled slowly aloft, hovered for a few seconds and disappeared to the north.

"That's them, they're running away," Stefan shouted. Others in the crowd reached the same conclusion and a mighty cheer went up.

"How do you know?" I asked.

"If they'd have waited another five minutes, they would have been captured and we'd have heard it by now."

Even as we spoke, he was pressing forward toward the building. The first revolutionaries had already appeared on the balcony. One began addressing the crowd, which continued chanting, *"Romania, Romania, Liberty, Liberty."* Unbelievably it seemed the entire regime along with all its organs of repression had collapsed like a house of cards.

"Come, I want to get into the building," Stefan yelled.

"Where do you think they'll go, the Ceauşescus?" I asked.

He shrugged. "Maybe they think there are still elements of the armed forces around the country that support them and they'll try to mount a resistance. There are so many people who owe their entire existence to Ceauşescu. If he goes, they go too." His words provided a needed dose of reality. The story was not over yet.

"Maybe they'll try to flee abroad," I speculated.

"Who would have them?"

"North Korea, Iran maybe."

"I hope not. We need to put the devil on trial and hold him accountable," Stefan said grimly.

We reached the massive front doors of the building and entered to find a chaotic scene. Party functionaries and men in uniform wandered around as if shell-shocked, unable to grasp the sudden disintegration of the world as they had always known it. A horde of young men and women, some with submachine guns hanging around their shoulders, rampaged joyously through the lobby, ripping portraits of the ruling couple from the walls, bursting into offices, rummaging through drawers and files, tossing papers on the floor and out the windows. Other held urgent conversations in corners, trying to figure out how to reassert order. Stefan stood near the entrance, his mouth agape, as if he wanted to remember the moment forever. A heavy, thickset man saw him and grabbed his arm.

"Stefan Petrescu?" he asked.

Stefan nodded and the two of them hugged, kissing each other on both cheeks. The man began speaking in Romanian, gesturing to Stefan to come upstairs with him. I gave him a questioning look.

"He's an old friend, a fellow writer. He wants me to go to the balcony and address the crowd. He thinks my voice should be heard now," Stefan said. "Should I do it? It feels strange."

"This is your moment, Stefan," I told him. "This is what you came back here to do."

He nodded and followed the man upstairs. I trailed a few steps behind. We passed through a sumptuously furnished room and suddenly we were in the open air, looking down on an ocean of faces below. Someone else was addressing the crowd, shouting over and over, *"He's gone, the devil has gone, Dracula is gone!"*

Stefan's friend tapped him on the shoulder, gesturing for him to wind up his remarks. The man, flushed, almost drunk with excitement, reluctantly relinquished the microphone and Stefan stepped forward. When he introduced himself, the crowd gave a rousing cheer and then settled back to listen, punctuating his remarks with frequent applause. Unlike the previous speaker, Stefan spoke calmly, rarely raising his voice. He had that rare ability to command attention almost effortlessly. Watching him, my heart burst with pride. After about 10 minutes, he thanked the people for listening and handed back the microphone. Once again, chants of *"Liberty, liberty, liberty"* swelled up from the square.

As we stepped back into the room, a bevy of people surrounded Stefan, slapping him on the back, shaking hands, kissing and hugging him.

"What did you say?" I asked, as soon as I could get his notice.

"I just said it was important for everyone to stay in the square and protect the revolution. The Ceaușescus might be gone but that doesn't mean they're finished. If people want real freedom and democracy and if we wish to reclaim our heritage and rightful place in the family of nations, we must demand these things now and never agree to anything less."

Another young man approached, speaking in urgent tones. He grabbed Stefan by the sleeve, tugging him back toward the stairway.

"He wants me to go to the TV station to repeat my speech there," he told me. "A convoy is setting off right now. He said the whole nation needs to hear what I have to say."

"Right, let's go," I said. I had never felt such exhilaration. Not only was an entire people throwing off the shackles of tyranny and claiming their freedom, but my lover was a key actor and I, as a reporter, had a front seat to witness the drama. The future was opening up before us. Surely now, there could be no bar to us being together, especially after I got the chance to tell Stefan about our child.

As we left the building and returned to the square, a mighty roar arose from the crowd. Everyone was looking up at the roof where a group of soldiers and civilians appeared beneath the giant neon slogan— *"Long Live the Communist Party of Romania!"*— that had loomed over the capital for so many years. As I watched, the men armed with crowbars began prying away the letters of the word *"Communist."* It teetered for a moment and then crashed to the ground.

"Come, come, there's no time," someone yelled at Stefan. He took my hand and we made our way to the perimeter where an armored personnel carrier already swarming with people, stood waiting. Someone lifted me on to the front mudguard and Stefan grabbed a place beside me. Then we were off, edging slowly through packed streets, cheered on by delirious throngs of people. It occurred to me that though I would never know what it felt like to have a ticker tape parade in my honor down Wall Street, this came close. Our truck became hopelessly jammed in the mass of celebrating people so I got off and started interviewing them, looking for anyone who could speak some English, scribbling furiously in my notebook. Then, a way cleared for the APC to start moving again and I climbed back aboard.

Eventually, we reached the TV headquarters where everyone jumped down and ran inside the building. I followed more slowly, pushing through an excited knot of people all speaking and gesticulating at the same time. I couldn't understand what they were saying so I stepped aside to observe. For the first time, I was feeling a little left out. The others were truly living this event; I remained an observer. After a minute, Stefan came to join me.

"What's going on?" I asked.

"The guys who run the TV studios don't want to let us inside. They're all Ceauşescu's creatures, of course, otherwise they would never have been allowed to work here. They can't accept that he's gone. They keep saying they were expecting him here any minute to address the nation. My friends are trying to convince them they must allow us access to the studio because we are the new Romania. If they don't agree, they'll have to be removed by force. I hope it doesn't come to that."

After a few noisy minutes, the TV officials were persuaded to give way. Stefan and I headed for the control room to watch the historic broadcast. Cameras began whirring and a face appeared on the screen and began speaking.

"It's Ion Caramitru, a famous actor," Stefan whispered. "He's telling how we arrived here on tanks and how we represent thousands of ordinary Romanians who have risen up for freedom."

After years of nothing but official party propaganda, the abrupt appearance of this disheveled figure without warning on their TV screens must have come as quite a shock to viewers around the country. That was just the start.

Next to speak was Mircea Dinescu, like Stefan, a dissident poet. He began with a simple, direct statement, "The dictator has fled." The effect was electrifying. This was the first time most people outside the capital would have heard this.

As more people took their turn in speaking, it all became a little much. Still suffering from lack of food and sleep and faced with an endless stream of words I couldn't follow, I found myself in a weary daze. But I jerked abruptly awake when Stefan's face appeared on the monitor. Seen in black and white, he seemed both absurdly young and immensely ancient. It was as if everything he had experienced was carved into his rough, unshaven face. The dark circles under his eyes only accentuated their intensity. Despite his torn jeans and stained sweatshirt, he carried himself with instinctive authority. As he spoke, I remembered the first time I'd seen those eyes in the photograph Eskew had handed me in an overheated Boston office. It seemed as if half a lifetime had passed since that day; in fact it was less than a year.

After Stefan finished speaking, I asked, "What now?"

"Back to the square. There are meetings going on inside the Central Committee to form a new government. They want me to take part."

"Are you going to join the government?" This was a new and unwelcome thought. I didn't want Stefan involved in Romanian politics. I wanted him for myself.

"There are some who are suggesting it. I shall refuse. I'm not a politician, I'm a poet and that's all I want to be. But of course it's important we launch the new Romania on the right path. Getting rid of the dictator was the first step."

His words reassured me. I asked, "How will we get back to Palace Square?"

"On foot since I can't commandeer a tank. It's quite a long walk but we can do it."

We stepped out the gates of the compound surrounding the TV studios and walked 150 yards down the street. Suddenly, a burst of gunfire erupted. Instantly, instinctively, I hit the deck and rolled behind a tree.

"Who's shooting?" I yelled. A bullet zinged over my head, alarmingly close. Another hit a cobblestone a couple of yards away.

"We have to try to get back in the building," Stefan shouted, diving to the ground beside me.

Bent double to present a smaller target, I started edging back the way we'd come, but the shooting only intensified and now it was being answered by soldiers guarding the TV station. I fell back to the ground, pressing myself into the concrete, not daring to raise my head. We were caught in the crossfire, unable to move in either direction. I felt shockingly exposed, defenseless and very scared.

Stefan crawled slowly toward me. "Try to get behind that car," he said, pointing at a parked vehicle some 20 yards away. "Wait for a break in the fighting and then run like hell."

"Too dangerous," I panted, terrified of moving, although what he said made sense. The shooting was now continuous; it was coming from all direction, wild and undisciplined, and getting heavier. It wasn't aimed specifically at us. We just happened to be in the wrong place at the wrong time. The thought flashed through my mind that if I and my unborn child were killed, no-one would ever know I'd been pregnant.

"We can't stay here. We'll be picked off if we do," Stefan said. "Come Elisabeta, don't give up. Just wait till I give the word. We'll be OK, I promise." A few moments later, the firing slackened and he said, "Now!" Springing to his feet, he pulled me upright and started sprinting toward the car, dragging me along behind him, never relaxing his grip. As we reached its shelter, he dived like a running back heading for the end zone, while I did an awkward flop, turning on my side as I landed, afraid of hurting the fetus. He turned and grasped me in his arms.

"Thank God, that was a little too close for comfort," he said. Ironically, now that we'd reached relative safety, the firing died away.

"What the hell's going on?" I asked.

"I guess it's *Securitate* agents or remnants loyal to the regime." He reached inside his jacket pocket and pulled out his transistor, fiddling with the tuning until he found a station. As he listened, his face became grimmer and grimmer.

"What are they saying?" I wanted to know.

"Wait. I'll tell you in a second." Two minutes later, he switched it off and turned to me. "We've got to get to safety. This is no place for you."

"What did they say?"

"All kinds of terrible things are happening. I don't know how much of it is true. They said there are terrorists trained by the regime, wandering around the city killing people in cold blood. They're moving from place to place through secret tunnels that Ceauşescu built under the city. There are also reports of militia units preparing to launch a counter coup. They said an armed column is on its way here to take back the TV station. They could arrive at any moment."

As he spoke, I heard renewed sporadic firing a few blocks away and flinched. It was cold sitting on the ground and my hands beneath my gloves were trembling.

I stood. "Then let's get the hell out of here."

We walked a few yards and were confronted with the sight of a dead soldier, lying in the gutter, half his head blown off. His helmet lay beside him, unscathed. Why on earth had he taken it off? He had a tricolor tied around one sleeve; he'd been supporting the revolution. I was shocked at how dark the puddle of blood around him had turned, more black than red.

"Come, there's nothing we can do for him," Stefan said, trying to pull me away. But I seemed rooted to the spot. This boy was someone's son. I pulled out my notebook, determined to remember the moment in its full horror and to bring it to my readers back home. It was the only first of many bodies I saw that day.

Over the next two hours, as we moved cautiously from block to block, I discovered what a dreadful thing it was when a city became a war zone. The images I saw and described in my notebook merged into a tapestry of terror. The worst of it was, nobody could figure out exactly what was happening. Most of the shooting seemed to be coming from invisible gunmen hiding on rooftops. A quiet street corner one moment could explode into mayhem the next. Some of the fighters wore uniforms of various shades, others merged into the population. Terrified citizens huddling in doorways, appealed to soldiers for help, pointing out the source of the most recent fire. Bodies lay where they had fallen; it was too dangerous to recover them. The soldiers were just as scared as everyone else. I saw several shooting wildly in the general direction of where they imagined their unseen enemy might be, emptying their magazines in orgies of useless fire, riddling the fronts of buildings with bullet holes, hitting nobody.

I had no idea gunfire at close range could be so loud. My ears were ringing. I couldn't make sense of what was happening—it seemed so arbitrary, so senseless. Occasionally, in the distance, I heard deeper booms and occasionally saw flashes of artillery or tank fire. An acrid cloud of smoke gathered over the streets.

As darkness fell, the city fell into anarchy. Bands of youths wandered around smashing windows and looting. Others carrying loudspeakers or bull horns exhorted the crowd to stand their ground against the shadowy army of terrorists said to be roaming the streets. I saw police and soldiers searching people at random, demanding identification, taking several into custody. Scariest were the civilians with pistols visible beneath their leather jackets who had emerged as self-appointed vigilantes. I was certain that most had been working for the regime just a few hours earlier, and many might surreptitiously still be doing so. Stefan kept listening to his radio which reported fierce fighting in various parts of thc city. Some of the worst seemed to be in Palace Square itself where armed men loyal to the regime were said to be rampaging through the National Gallery vandalizing priceless paintings. Across the plaza, the graceful cupola of the university library had been set ablaze by tank fire.

By this time, we were on Enescu Street, walking past the small white church at the corner of Calea Victoriei. I allowed myself a sigh of relief. My hotel was just around the corner. In another minute, we'd be safe. That's when I felt a sudden stinging sensation and looking down saw blood pouring from a wound just above my knee. I seemed to hear the shot only a split second later.

"I've been hit," I screamed, although for the moment I felt no pain. A second bullet grazed my neck and then Stefan was diving on top of me, pushing me to the ground, covering my body with his own. I felt a bullet thudding into him, I couldn't say where, and looking up, glimpsed a gunman with a telescopic sight on a roof just across the street preparing to fire again. Another bullet tore into Stefan; I heard him groan and felt his warm blood on my face. His body twitched alarmingly, like a fish out of water. "Stefan, Stefan," I sobbed, not certain he could still hear me. Christ, we were both going to die. Strangely, there wasn't enough time to be scared, even though I knew I wanted so much to live, to bring new life into the world. "My baby, my baby," I gasped. With an immense effort, I pushed Stefan's body off me and tried to get to my feet, intending to pull him out of the line of fire if I could. But two more bullets ripped into my shoulder from behind, spinning me around, and I fell back to the ground, staring upwards. The last thing I saw was a man silhouetted against the white church, standing over us with a rifle butt raised, about to bring it down on Stefan's head.

15 – Bucharest: December 1989

The following was broadcast on December 26, 1989 by Bucharest radio:

On Dec. 25, 1989, the trial of Nicolae Ceauşescu and Elena Ceauşescu was held before an extraordinary military tribunal. The charges were:

1. Genocide. More than 60,000 victims.

2. Undermining of the state power through organization of armed actions against the people and the state power.

3. Destruction of public property through destruction and damaging of buildings and numerous explosions in cities, etc.

4. The undermining of the national economy.

5. The attempt to flee the country by taking advantage of more than $1 billion deposited in foreign banks.

For these crimes against the Romanian people and Romania, the culprits Nicolae Ceauşescu and Elena Ceauşescu were condemned to death and the confiscation of their wealth. The sentence was definitive and has been carried out.

16 – Bucharest: December 2007

"This is the place," Liz said pointing to the little alley that ran by the side of the church. "After the last bullet hit me, I think I wound up right about this spot where we're standing now. It looks different with all the cars parked and the advertising hoardings and this store selling lingerie and the hairdresser here, but I still remember this little church so well. For a long time, it was in my nightmares. Funny, you can still see bullet holes in the walls of the buildings."

It was her third day in Bucharest and she'd finally steeled herself to return to this spot.

Petra shivered. She'd walked down this street countless times, looked in the fancy store windows, and never noticed the pockmarked buildings or imagined her mother lying here in a pool of blood. She'd even passed this church one Saturday when a wedding was going on and lingered for a few minutes with the photographer outside the front door, listening to the singing inside, waiting for the bride to emerge.

"So what happened next, after you were hit?" she eventually asked.

"What they told me later was that some soldiers saw what was happening, chased away the attackers and called for an ambulance. Luckily, it arrived pretty quickly, which was a miracle in itself with so many dead and wounded all over the city. I was unconscious through all of this. I have a fuzzy memory of waking up briefly when they brought me into the emergency room and again after the first operation, but most of what happened to me in the next couple of days is a complete blank because I was heavily sedated. I do remember them driving me to the airport but I slept through the flight itself. I didn't even know where they were taking me and I was in no condition to ask."

"Did they ever find out who did it?"

Liz shrugged. "Could have been anyone. We were lucky. If those soldiers hadn't arrived when they did, we'd both have bled to death. When the doctors discovered I was an American journalist, they called the U.S. embassy. My friend Clint arranged for me to be flown out to a U.S. military hospital in Germany as soon as I could be moved and that's where I had the second operation. When I woke up from that, Tom was standing next to the bed. The first words I said were, 'My baby, my baby.' Tom said, 'The baby's fine. Everything is going to be just fine.' And in a way, I suppose it was."

"What about Stefan?"

"You should ask him about his experiences. I can't imagine what he went through. He was in a lot worse shape than me. I remember at least two bullets hitting him and then there was the guy who whacked him with his rifle butt, which was the last thing I remember seeing. I guess, thinking back on it, that was the blow that cost him his eye. Luckily, he was already unconscious by then, so he probably has no memory of that moment—but it was a horrible, dreadful memory for me. I kept seeing it in my dreams for years and years."

She stopped speaking to pull out a tissue and dab her eyes. Petra didn't know what to say. She'd never seen her mother so vulnerable before. Usually elegant and self-assured, she suddenly seemed small and frail. Petra thought about hugging her but that seemed contrived.

After a few seconds, Liz continued: "Of course, I asked how Stefan was as soon as I could—I think I was already in Germany by then—and they told me he was seriously injured but was expected to live. That was a huge relief. I really thought he was dead. But I don't know what happened to him in the hospital here. I think he must have suffered terribly."

Petra said, "He told me he caught a nasty infection in the hospital and almost died. It took him ages to get over it."

"Poor Stefan. It's a miracle he's alive, and no thanks to me. That's one reason reliving this experience has been so difficult. I feel very guilty. At the vital moment, he was willing to lay down his life for me—and how did I repay him? I took care of myself and my baby and left him to fend for himself. At the time, it seemed like the only thing to do. I had to put you first. But now..."

"But you didn't just forget about him."

"No, I never forgot him. He always stayed in my heart."

"So why didn't you write to him to find out what happened?"

"I did. I wrote to him several times as soon as I felt well enough but he never replied, or at least I never received his replies. I thought he was angry with me for abandoning him. He didn't know I was pregnant. I'd never gotten around to telling him. Tom made me promise not to contact him but I tried a few times anyway. I remember once—it must have been shortly after you were born—I tried calling him on the phone. I wanted to tell him he had a daughter and that I'd named her Petra. But he never answered. I called every day for about a week and then I gave up. Then, a year or two later, I heard from Clint that he'd gotten married and I just tried to put the whole thing behind me."

"He says he was the one who wrote to you over and over and didn't hear back," Petra said. "So which version is true?"

"I think maybe they both are, honey. I believe Tom may have been intercepting our letters. He wanted to keep me for himself, and you too, once you were born. Listen, it's getting cold out here and this place is giving me the creeps. Let's go back to the hotel. We can finish the story there."

Back in the hotel coffee shop, Liz reached into her wallet and pulled out a small, blood-stained business card. "They found this in my pocket when I arrived in Germany," she said, handing it to Petra. One side said, *"Prof. Tudor Bucur, chief of surgery."* On the other, someone had written, *"Christmas Greetings from Bucharest, 1989."*

"How weird. This was the guy that operated on you?" Petra asked.

"I wrote to thank him and for a few years we exchanged Christmas cards. Then I heard he died. Pity, I'd have liked to have been able to thank him in person." She took a sip from her cappuccino.

"So what happened after you got to Germany?"

"They operated on me again. About a week later, I was well enough to fly back to the States and I moved back in with Tom. I needed somewhere to recover—a safe place to mend myself and prepare for the birth. In the state I was in, I couldn't imagine bringing a baby into the world alone. And Tom swore he'd change. He'd already quit drinking and he'd abandoned his dreadful novel. He said all he wanted was to be a good husband and father. And for the most part he was."

"Are you angry at him?"

"Tom?"

"For stealing your letters to Stefan."

"What's the point? He probably felt he was acting in all our best interests."

"But what about Stefan, the so-called love of your life? I still don't understand why you two didn't try to get back together. Didn't you miss him?"

"Petra, you have to understand, I'd been traumatized by the whole experience. By the time I'd recovered from my wounds, I was already heavily pregnant and I had to focus all my energy on that. There was no way I was going back to Romania. I couldn't face it. The place was too unstable, too dangerous and unpredictable. Food was still in short supply; people lived from hand to mouth. The hospitals were filthy. This was no place for you to be born. Then, the pregnancy turned difficult. I was stuck in bed most of the final six weeks and you were born a little premature. After the birth, I felt very depressed. Maybe it was post partum, maybe it was losing Stefan, I don't know."

"Couldn't you have brought him to the States?"

"If he'd responded to my letters, maybe I could. But I never received an answer. I know what you're going to say—that if I'd have been really determined, I would have found a way. But I was so tired and scared and freaked out. I was barely functioning as your mother. That experience of almost being killed—of seeing my own death happening before my eyes—it broke something in me. I kept having flashbacks. Almost every night, I saw that guy with his weapon about to crush Stefan's skull and finish me off. I couldn't sleep without pills. Sometimes, I'd burst out crying for no reason. I think in retrospect I may have been suffering from Post Traumatic Stress Disorder although I didn't realize it at the time. All I knew was, I'd had enough passion and danger to last a lifetime. I wanted to stay where it was safe, a refuge where I could just curl into a ball and let other people take care of everything."

"Poor you," Petra said, genuinely sad for her mother. "I had no idea you suffered so much and for so long."

"Then, a few months after the revolution, shortly after you were born, there was another round of student demonstrations in Bucharest. People were already disappointed with the revolution—they wanted real democracy. The new government was mainly ex-communists who made a few cosmetic changes but blocked real political and economic reforms. When people started demanding true democracy and meaningful changes, the government brought in a bunch of coal miners—thugs really—to crush the protests, which they did by rampaging through the city, killing dozens of people. I was completely disillusioned. It was almost unbearable to think that the glorious revolution that had almost taken our lives was nothing but a sham. After that, I wanted nothing more to do with Romania."

"So Mom, what are you going to do now?"

"What do you mean?"

"You and Stefan—what are you going to do about him?"

"What makes you think I have to do anything about him?"

"Mom, you two still love each other. It's obvious. Why shouldn't you be happy after all these years? What's stopping you now? And don't give me all that stuff about how you each have your own lives that you can't possibly disrupt. You're both free, you can do whatever you like."

Liz was silent.

"Mom?"

"Petra, it's not so simple. It's not like teenagers falling in love. Stefan and I have a history and it's full of grief. We had a few, giddy wonderful days followed by half a lifetime of pain. Yes, right now I feel like a giddy young girl in love again—but I'm not a young girl, I'm a middle-aged widow, and the truth is, I hardly know this man. The short time we were together does not form the basis for a healthy relationship, especially not at our age. I need to be sensible."

"Bullshit."

"Watch your language young lady."

"I don't buy a single word you said."

"There's more. I told you how I betrayed him, how I let him down. That's something that would always be there between us. Sooner or later, it would be bound to come up."

"Mom, he doesn't care about it. It's ancient history."

"Maybe for you, not for us. Anyway, that's not the point."

"Then what is?"

Liz didn't answer.

"Mom?"

In a tiny voice, hardly more than a whisper, Liz said, "Don't you see Petra? I need to forgive myself."

17 – Bucharest: December 2007

It was almost midnight on December 31 and the residents of Bucharest were on the streets in their thousands celebrating the New Year. Salespeople were hawking light sticks and pointy wizard hats. In front of the Athenaeum concert hall, rock groups had been belting out music for hours to a steadily growing crowd, their efforts projected on giant screens. Parents hoisted young children on their shoulders, ready for the big moment. Green lasers punctured the darkness, throwing dancing beams of light on the National Gallery, the university library and just a little further down the street the former Central Committee Building of the Communist Party from where Ceaușescu had addressed the crowd 18 years ago. What would the dictator have thought if he could have been here to witness this scene?

Petra and Mihai stood arm-in-arm watching a pop diva dressed in a white jumpsuit prance around on the stage. Next to them were Liz and Stefan, not touching. Suddenly, Liz felt a tap on her shoulder. Turning around, she saw pointy little mouse face, smiling broadly at her.

"Pringle," she cried in delight. "Peter, what the hell are you doing here?"

"I might ask you the same question, Lizzie Graham. They sent me back here for one final assignment—old hack's last hurrah."

"I thought you would have retired by now."

"Nearly, nearly dear girl. This is my last trip here. My little house on the Costa Del Sol beckons. Sun, sea, sand and terminal boredom. Perhaps I'll write my memoirs. What about you?"

"Doing well, Peter, doing well. Thanks for the sweet card you sent all those years ago and the flowers. I always knew you were an old softie."

He reddened. "It was nothing old girl, least I could do. I thought about you a lot over the years. Should have kept an eye on you during the revolution."

"Nonsense. You had your job to do, just like I did."

"Mom, won't you introduce us?" Petra said, tugging at Liz's sleeve.

"Of course, how rude. Peter, I want you to meet my daughter Petra and her friend Mihai. And this is Stefan Petrescu, a Romanian friend of mine. You may have read his poetry."

Peter gave her a meaningful look. "Ah, yes, jolly fine to meet you all. Your daughter is lovely Lizzie, just like her Mum. But duty calls, it's almost midnight. What if we met for a drink tomorrow, say six o'clock? In the English bar at the Athénée Palace for old times sake?"

"Love to," Liz said.

"Righty ho." And just like that, he was gone, swallowed up in the vast crowd.

By now, people were shaking up their cheap champagne bottles ready to pop them at the stroke of midnight. The band on the stage began its final number; the giant screen started its countdown, the crowd cheered and began chanting the numbers. *"Four, three, two, one —Happy New Year!"* Fireworks exploded above them, confetti rained down, thousands of cameras flashed, people embraced their loved ones. Mihai and Petra were kissing enthusiastically. Drops of sickly champagne fell on their coats, their necks, their faces. Liz and Stefan looked at each other; she leaned forward to peck him on either cheek but he forestalled her, enveloping her in a bear hug, pressing his lips against hers until she was forced to respond. It felt different kissing him because of the mustache. But a second later, it felt the same and the years rolled back. After a second he pulled away, leaving her gasping a little. Then they both hugged Petra and Mihai.

Later, as they walked back to his apartment, he asked the question she had been asking herself ever since she arrived.

"So Liz, soon you'll be returning home to America and Petra will follow in June or July. I can't let you go without asking you about the future, about our future. I need to know, do we have one?"

"I don't know, Stefan. I've been thinking about it nonstop since I arrived."

"Do you still love me?"

"You know I do. But it's not so easy. We both have our lives. I'm not about to leave the United States and I know you won't leave Romania."

"What makes you so sure?"

She looked at him in the half-light of a street lamp. "What do you mean?"

"I was waiting for the right time to tell you. I guess this is it. I have a job offer to teach poetry beginning next fall at a small school in Manchester, New Hampshire—St. Anselm's College. I believe it's not so far from where you live."

Liz felt completely taken aback. "It's not far away at all. But why? Are you doing this for me?"

"I'm doing it for us, Elisabeta. For us. We deserve a chance to be happy. True, we aren't so young any more, but we aren't so old either. We can hope to live for another 30 years at least, God willing, and I'd like to spend them with you. Please Elisabeta, tell me you will."

Liz choked back a tear. "It's a beautiful offer but are you sure you mean it after the way I abandoned you? Be honest Stefan. I know you love me but deep down, in your gut, in your soul, aren't you still angry for what I did?"

"Nonsense. I told you once before how I let go of my anger many, many years ago. You did what you did for reasons you felt were right at the time. And looking at the way our daughter turned out, who can blame you? Elisabeta, she may never see me as her true father but I love her as a father. She's the only daughter I'll ever have. And one day, perhaps you and I could be the grandparents of her children."

"So you want me because you'd like to be a grandfather?"

"Stop twisting my words, Elisabeta. You know that's not what I mean. How simple can I make this? I love you. I've always loved you from that first day when you walked into my apartment and kissed me. I know we can't go back to that time or recapture that feeling, but we can move forward together—we can grow old together…"

"Oh thanks very much," Liz interjected.

"Or we can grow old apart. Those are the choices. Think about it. Is that what you want—to grow old alone?"

They reached the apartment building and began climbing the stairs. "By the way, where's Petra now?" Liz asked.

"I think she's going to spend the rest of the night with her friends. She won't be back to bother us." He unlocked the door, switched on the light and they went inside.

"Stefan, did you and Petra plan this little scene together?" Liz asked sharply.

He reddened. "I needed some time alone with you. Petra knows that. She's smart. It's not a little scene. I just needed you to stop running away from me and listen."

"OK, I'm listening."

"Wait." He went over to the CD player and switched it on. It was already cued to a specific track. The strains of Chopin's Ballade filled the room. He switched the light down low.

"Dance with me, Elisabeta."

"Isn't this a little corny even for you?"

"Was it corny in 1989? Stop thinking, stop agonizing for five minutes and let's just dance. Listen to the music and listen to your heart."

He opened his arms. She hesitated … and then she came to him and it was like coming home, the same city, the same music and for a moment Liz could almost imagine they were the same two people who had met a few short moments before and were even now falling in love.

"I was always a lousy dancer," she murmured as they began drifting slowly around the room.

"Will you please just shut up?"

He kissed her and she felt that familiar response. Her body knew what it wanted. Why couldn't her mind cooperate? Why was she still afraid? But as the music began to invade her head, she felt herself relax. *"Could this truly be? Do you feel it too?"* She heard the words in her head, as clearly as she'd heard them 18 years before. *"Is this real to you? As it is to me?"*

It could not be denied. This was her Romance Language, the truest language she had known. She had to speak. "Oh Stefan, I do love you. Of course I do, although I hate your eye patch."

"I'll get rid of it."

"I've never felt this way with anyone else," she continued as if he had not interrupted. "I know I never will. I'm just terrified. What if it doesn't work out? What if we start to get on each other's nerves. I let you down once. What if I did it again? How could you forgive me? How could I forgive myself?"

She was aware of tears trickling from her eyes, gently falling down her cheeks, but made no effort to wipe them away.

He didn't answer for a moment as they continued dancing. Then he murmured, "Elisabeta, people who truly love each other have to forgive—each other and also themselves. They have to have faith and trust one another. They have to take a chance on one another. They have no choice. Why not let go of the anger, the guilt, let go of all the burdens we carry from the past and just keep the love? Nothing else matters. Won't you give us a second chance?."

The music grew stormy, the theme enveloped in a rumbling swirl of base notes. But she heard it still, shining through, like a ray of sunlight penetrating a gap in the clouds. *"Is this real to you? As it is to me?"*

It was real. The music had a truth that could not be denied.

Liz had run out of arguments, run out of excuses, run out of words.

All except one.
It was time to answer.

Author's Note:

The idea for *Romance Language* came to me when I had the opportunity to spend nine months in Romania teaching journalism and promoting the values of a free, democratic media as a Knight International Press Fellow in 2007. I'd like to thank the International Committee for Journalists and the Knight Foundation for the opportunity and the Center for Independent Journalism for hosting me in Bucharest.

Many Romanians generously shared their memories of the Communist era and the revolution. Unfortunately, I can't list them but I extend heartfelt thanks to all.

We enjoyed matchless hospitality, valuable insight and true friendship from Justyna Pawlak, the gracious and talented Reuters Bureau Chief in Bucharest.

Thanks to John P. Travis at Portals Press for his faith in the story.

A very big thank you goes to my students in Bucharest who gave me an entrée into the city's student life and culture. Our weekly classes and frequent one-on-one sessions helped me understand their concerns and passions. We also discussed their relationships with their parents' generation, their views about the revolution and their hopes for the country's future. As is often the case, the teacher probably learned more than his students. We also forged lasting friendships which I value greatly.

My superb Romanian language teacher, Leila Tobin, struggled valiantly to overcome my linguistic inadequacies. My vain struggles with irregular verbs and the subjunctive mood, which Romanians insist on using so much of the time, in no way reflects on her talents.

I want to thank my colleague David Storey for sharing memories of reporting in Bucharest during the Communist era. David did not inspire the character of Peter Pringle but his accounts of the toppling dessert cart and the visit to the tractor factory did wind up in the book.

For a time, it seemed as if everything that happened to me in Bucharest went straight into the book. I was bitten by a dog and a couple of weeks later so was Petra. My wife and I visited Sinaia and hiked up to the Franz Josef Rock. Petra and Mihai followed in our footsteps. Liz and Stefan end up getting shot right outside our apartment building on Strada Enescu in front of the "White Church." You can indeed still see bullet pockmarks on the surrounding buildings.

Although all of the characters in this book with the exception of the Ceauşescus are fictional, I tried to make my account of the revolution as accurate as possible. Any mistakes are mine alone.

Finally, my deepest thanks as usual go to my wife, Shulamit. I wanted to write a book that took seriously the idea of true love. I know it exists with absolute certainty because I felt it the first moment I laid eyes on her and I continue to do so every single day.

Books by Alan Elsner:

Gates of Injustice: The Crisis in America's Prisons
Guarded by Angels
The Nazi Hunter
Romance Language

Journalist and novelist Alan Elsner has a distinguished 30 year-career with Reuters News Service during which he served in Jerusalem, London, Stockholm and Washington DC covering many major U.S. and international stories. His career has been marked by a passion for justice and truth, unquestioned integrity, and a willingness to confront the powerful, the complacent and the evasive.

Elsner's first book on the U.S. prison system was hailed by Sen. Edward Kennedy as "a wake-up call for federal, state, and local governments across America." His second, a memoir of his father's experiences surviving World War II has been described as a major addition to Holocaust literature.

Publishers Weekly called Elsner's first novel, *The Nazi Hunter*, a "gripping debut" while *Kirkus Reviews* noted its "intriguing protagonist, terrifying historical lessons and well-orchestrated, pulse-pounding conclusion."

In 2007, Elsner was a Knight International Journalism Fellow in Bucharest, Romania, where he researched *Romance Language*.

He lives with his wife Shulamit in Rockville, Maryland. For more information go to www.alanelsner.com. You can Email the author at gatesofinjustice@aol.com.

Praise for *The Nazi Hunter*

"*The Nazi Hunter* grips the reader from the start. I seriously hope that this is not the last readers will hear of Marek "Mark" Cain and his job as Deputy Director for the Office of Special Investigations. "

— Tracy Farnsworth, *RoundTableReviews.com*

"An experienced journalist with two nonfiction books behind him, Elsner now makes his thriller debut, focusing his intense beam on a young lawyer who hunts Nazis for the feds in Washington, DC ... engagingly written and attentive to the work of authentic Nazi hunters, Elsner's novel chimes with the bells and whistles of a thriller while tracing the honest emotions of its appealingly sincere characters."

— Barbara Conaty, *LibraryJournal.com*

"*The Nazi Hunter* is a brilliant novel that mixes imagination ... and gut-wrenching facts ... the plot is tautly woven with unexpected masterful twists, the pacing impeccable, although it gives readers little time to breathe. Historical accuracy (by way of eyewitness accounts to actual atrocities) provides poignancy that will bring tears to your eyes and anger to your heart. *The Nazi Hunter* is a must read."

— Karri Watson, *CurledUp.com*

"Elsner possesses a command of Holocaust history, and the plot twists accelerate nicely. He plays, too, with the ways that religious obligation might hamper a protagonist—it's hard to imagine Rambo, for instance, sequestering himself in mid-crisis because it's Shabbat and he can't drive or turn on a light. An intriguing protagonist, terrifying historical lessons and a well-orchestrated, [and] pulse-pounding conclusion ..."

— *Kirkus Reviews*

Praise for *Gates of Injustice*

"Alan Elsner's powerful book demonstrates that our $40 billion corrections system for both adults and juveniles is badly broken. Our jails and prisons and penitentiaries are failing us at enormous cost in money and in danger to society. Elsner makes an overwhelming case for reform, and his many sensible proposals deserve to be implemented. This book should be a wake-up call for federal, state, and local governments across America."

— Senator Edward M. Kennedy

"The book gives a chilling insight into the human cost of America's massive resort to incarceration in the past few decades, which sees the U.S. today with around a quarter of the world's prison population. It charts the negative impact on both inmates and society of what is essentially a wasteful and inhumane system. The author offers a series of practical proposals for reform, which are long overdue. This is an important book for anyone interested in human rights and penal policy."

— Irene Khan, Secretary General,
Amnesty International

"Engaging, crisply-written, filled with powerful vignettes, Alan Elsner's picture of life behind bars in the United States is a searing look at the crisis in America's prisons."

— Jamie Fellner, U.S. Director, Human Rights Watch

"Even the most skeptical reader will be fascinated by the gripping stories of prisoners and their families. Alan Elsner has written an enormously compelling book. His lucid and informative analysis provides a framework for understanding why the crisis has occurred and what can be done to end it. This book should be read by everyone who cares about America's future."

— Jean Maclean Snyder, MacArthur Justice Center,
University of Chicago Law School

Romance Language can be purchased at:www.portalspress.com or from Amazon.com and other booksellers..